Praise fo

"I'll read anything by Susan McBride."

—#1 *New York Times* bestselling author
Charlaine Harris

"Written with touching insight into family relationships and what we call home, *Little Black Dress* is a lovely and entertaining journey into the magical side of things. I bet you'll never look at your closet the same way again."

—Sarah Addison Allen, bestselling author of
The Peach Keeper

"*Little Black Dress* is a delightful, emotional, and thoroughly engaging exploration of the connections that bind women together and the magic that's created when mothers, daughters, and sisters learn to open their eyes and hearts to their truest desires."

—Marilyn Brant, author of *Friday Mornings at Nine*

"With a deft hand and a sensitive heart, Susan McBride spins a magical tale. A bittersweet, Gothic past melds perfectly with a tender and revelatory present. Part mystery, part love story. Emotionally satisfying, *Little Black Dress* is an enchanting escape into a magical and wonderful world. A delight to read."

—M. J. Rose, internationally bestselling author of
The Book of Lost Fragrances

"*Little Black Dress* is a luminous story filled with magic and hope. I loved this tender, touching, and enchanting saga about the unique bond of mothers, daughters, and sisters."

—Ellen Meister, author of *The Other Life*

"*Little Black Dress* is big on heart, secrets, and magic. This enchanting novel is a bookshelf essential."

—Karin Gillespie, author of the
Bottom Dollar Girl series and coauthor of
The Sweet Potato Queen's First Big-Ass Novel

"Susan McBride's *Little Black Dress* sparkles with magic! It's part love story, part mystery, part family saga, all wrapped together in the wonder of an amazing little dress that will leave you crying and cheering. I loved this book!"

—Judy Merrill Larsen, author of *All the Numbers*

"I'm madly in love with this full-of-surprises story about secrets, family ties—and one magical little black dress. One of my favorite novels of the year."

—Melissa Senate, author of
The Love Goddess' Cooking School

"With sparkle and wit, Susan McBride crafts both a family saga of painful secrets and a modern story of a woman who thinks she's got it all under control—until everything she thought she knew blows apart. *Little Black Dress* is a beguiling story of fate, love, and magic."   —Kristina Riggle, author of *Keepsake*

The Truth
About Love
and Lightning

The Truth About Love and Lightning

Susan McBride

WILLIAM MORROW

An Imprint of HarperCollins*Publishers*

P.S.™ is a registered trademark of HarperCollins Publishers.

THE TRUTH ABOUT LOVE AND LIGHTNING. Copyright © 2013 by Susan McBride. Excerpt from IN THE PINK copyright © 2012 by Susan McBride. All rights reserved. Printed in the United States of America. No part of this book may be used or reproduced in any manner whatsoever without written permission except in the case of brief quotations embodied in critical articles and reviews. For information address HarperCollins Publishers, 10 East 53rd Street, New York, NY 10022.

HarperCollins books may be purchased for educational, business, or sales promotional use. For information please write: Special Markets Department, HarperCollins Publishers, 10 East 53rd Street, New York, NY 10022.

FIRST EDITION

Designed by Betty Lew

Library of Congress Cataloging-in-Publication Data has been applied for.

ISBN 978-0-06-202728-3

13 14 15 16 17   OV/RRD   10 9 8 7 6 5 4 3 2 1

To the newest love of my life,

Emily Alice,

who has proven without a doubt

that lightning can strike twice

and miracles do exist

ACKNOWLEDGMENTS

I found out I was pregnant as I worked on this book, which made the story all the more poignant to write. It also made me a wee bit slower on the take, and I sincerely thank my wonderful editor, Lucia Macro, for her patience while I finished. A big thanks as well to my agents, Andrea Cirillo and Christina Hogrebe, who have been unfailingly supportive and encouraging every step of the way. To the rest of the fabulous folks at JRA: My hat's off to you. Know how grateful I am for your hard work every day. My heartfelt appreciation goes to Stephanie Kim, Mary Sasso, and the amazing crew at William Morrow. I could not ask for a better publishing family! And last but not least, big hugs to my friends and family and to my incredible readers, who have tirelessly cheered me on. Love you all!

Annika Brink could not tell a lie.

From as far back as Gretchen could remember, her mother had been unable to utter anything but the cold, unvarnished truth—or, at least, the truth according to Annika—and, as Gretchen learned quickly enough as a child, often the truth set no one free and was downright painful besides.

As when the twins were born when Gretchen was five. "They are not right," Annika had insisted, her pale hair wild and hands on her hips, such a ferocious frown on her lips that it looked as though she might want to take them back to the county hospital posthaste.

Which had Gretchen wondering if one could return babies the same way one returned a glass bottle drained of soda to the grocer's for a nickel.

"Do you not see what I see?" Annika had nagged her very tolerant husband.

"They look fine to me," Gretchen's father had replied, and he'd bent over the double-wide crib to first rub Bennie's belly and then Trudy's. "They've each got ten fingers and ten toes, a perfect button nose, and ears like tiny seashells."

"Then you are as blind as they are," Annika had bluntly stated. "Look at their eyes! They're such a milky blue, and neither so much as blinks when I pass my hand before them. Do you think it's my fault, for painting while I was pregnant?" she had asked, madly pacing. "Was it the fumes from the oils or the turpentine? As an artist, I can't imagine a more horrible curse than to lose one's sight!"

"Oh, I can think of plenty," Gretchen's father had coolly replied, his knuckles turning white as he gripped the crib's railing. "Would you cast out a calf because it couldn't see, when its milk will be no different than a cow with sight?"

"Please!" Annika had loudly and dismissively snorted. "I know you believe animals are like people because you spend more time with beasts than humans," she'd told him, "but these are our daughters, not barnyard creatures!"

For a long moment, Gretchen had shut out their voices. She'd heard them argue enough before about her father's job as a farm veterinarian, how it kept them in Walnut Ridge when Annika found so much about small-town life uncultured and unfit.

Instead, Gretchen had crept toward the bars of the crib and peered through as if staring at a pair of sleeping monkeys at the zoo. If there was something wrong with her new sisters, she couldn't see it from where she stood.

"C'mon, Anni, enough." Her father had expelled a weary sigh. "Nothing's your fault. Nothing's anyone's fault. Sometimes things just happen, and no one's to blame. If it's not life or death, we'll get through it."

"They will never have normal lives."

"Normal is overrated," he'd declared, shaking his head. It was a minute before he seemed to realize Gretchen was there beside him, her upturned face full of worry. "Better to be different, don't you think, sweet pea?" he had said, his voice suddenly lighter as he ruffled her bright yellow curls. "That's how you make your mark. Not by being the same as everyone else."

But Gretchen had not agreed. Her mother's words had her frightened.

"What will happen to them?" she'd asked and had slipped a small hand through the crib rails to poke tiny Trudy. She was no bigger than a pot roast, although pot roasts didn't drool in their sleep. "We'll keep them, won't we?"

"Of course we'll keep them," Daddy had told her, squatting down at her side. "They're your sisters, and we love them. Everything will be fine."

Annika had groaned. "How can you tell her that in all good conscience? Because you can't possibly know. You've never been blind. Neither of us can be sure of what will become of them."

"They have us to protect them," her daddy had said with a nod. "That's all that children need."

"But what happens when we die? Who will they have then?" her mother had cried. "We have no family anywhere near."

"Me," Gretchen had said quietly as her fingers reached for Trudy's dimpled elbow. "They'll have me. I won't let anything happen to them, Mommy. I promise."

And Gretchen had meant it.

The twins were eventually diagnosed as legally blind, their sight limited to discerning shadows and shapes, darkness and light. But there was nothing positive about their situation in

Annika's eyes. When they went into town to visit the shops on Main Street, Annika would push Trudy and Bennie up the sidewalk in the double stroller and Gretchen would walk a few steps behind, peering into windows and listening to her mother bluntly answer those who asked, "How are your darling babies?"

"They are as blind as bats," she'd tell them, sounding as if it were the kiss of death. "I hope we can keep them with us and won't be forced to send them to an institution."

Gretchen usually tried to remain silent and not challenge anything Annika said, but with each passing year, she had found it harder and harder not to chip in her two cents. "Bennie can hear the postman coming way before I can see him," she had finally dared to rebut, "and Trudy knows every spice in the rack by scent alone."

"Is that so?" Annika had said, her pale eyes narrowed.

"It is," Gretchen had replied and had managed not to flinch, even though she knew it wasn't precisely the truth, merely a candy-coated lie. Bennie *could* hear things before anyone else, and Trudy *could* identify countless items by their smell alone.

Her sisters were special, Gretchen knew, regardless of what their mother believed, and she was determined to prove that they had no limitations.

So as the twins had grown, Gretchen had been their shepherd, watching over her sheep. She took them by their hands when they were old enough to walk, teaching them where every stick of furniture sat in the house, where every tree grew outside, where every step or gate or wall existed. Even more important, she reminded them over and over again that they were no less for not having eyeballs that worked like everyone else's.

"Maybe your gifts are in your other senses," she would tell them, and Bennie and Trudy would smile their precious smiles as if such a thing seemed perfectly reasonable.

When Gretchen was in the fifth grade, she learned that the school librarian, Miss Childs, had grown up with a blind mother and knew Braille well enough to instruct Bennie and Trudy. Miss Childs also took the liberty of ordering them Braille textbooks and such. Soon Gretchen's father asked the librarian outright if she'd become the girls' private tutor. She did such a good job with the twins that Annika ceased uttering the word *institution,* and Gretchen's father seemed happier just having the very agreeable Miss Childs around.

By the time Gretchen was in high school, Bennie and Trudy had blossomed into capable young ladies, able to do all the things that Gretchen did around the house: dress themselves, tie bows in their hair, make their beds, clean their rooms, sweep the porch, and even climb the lowest branches of the maple tree out front. Thanks to Miss Childs, both girls were reading well beyond their grade level. Indeed, Gretchen's father had become so fond of their tutor that he'd left to drive her home one day and had never returned.

I'm sorry, Anni—had read the note he'd left behind—*but I can't handle so much truth anymore. Sometimes ignorance is truly bliss, and what I need is more bliss in my life.*

Her mother had cried on Gretchen's shoulder, asking her, "Am I so horrible to be around? Am I that unlovable?"

Instead of being honest, Gretchen had told Annika what

she knew her mother had wanted to hear, words cribbed from *Wanton Wild Love,* the romance novel she was in the midst of reading, tucked upstairs beneath her pillow. "Miss Childs was nothing but a temptress, Mother, a seductress out to lure away what belonged to another."

"Do you truly think so?"

"I do," she said, even though Miss Childs looked nothing like the half-naked woman with flowing red hair on the book's torrid cover. In her prim sweater sets and too-long skirts, with her plain brown hair and bespectacled eyes, Miss Childs had appeared the very stereotype of what she was: a school librarian. Still, Gretchen's lie seemed to make Annika feel better, so what was the harm?

It would not be the first nor the last time she fibbed to her mother.

The year her father left, during the summer before her senior year in high school, when Gretchen lost her virginity to a questionable young man and wound up pregnant, she lied to her mother again. Only that particular lie was different. That lie was a lot like her belly: it just kept growing and growing until it created a life all its own.

The Twister

And the stars of heaven fell unto the earth,
even as a fig tree casteth her untimely figs,
when she is shaken of a mighty wind.

—REVELATIONS 6:13

ONE

April 2010

Bam bam bam!

Loose shutters banged against the house, pounding the clapboards like angry fists as the wind kicked up and howled around the eaves, drawing Gretchen Brink to the half-opened window above the kitchen sink.

A minute earlier, the sky had been a pristine blue, the April sun showering warmth upon the walnut farm while a gentle breeze ruffled the leaves of the just-bloomed peonies below the sill. Out of nowhere, fierce gusts forced their way through the window screen, batting at Gretchen's hair and stirring up the scent of rain and the rumble of thunder. Beyond her pale reflection in the glass, the sky turned black as pitch and a startling crack rent the air. A great *boom* followed as a bolt of lightning hit, causing her to see stars and jarring the floor beneath her feet.

"Good heavens," she said as goose bumps leaped across her flesh.

As quickly, the air turned an eerie shade that seemed a cross between gray and yellow. Some might call it green, but Gretchen could only describe it as menacing. Thunder crashed, rattling the glass. She jumped away as a downpour began to pelt the panes, blurring her line of sight, but not before she watched a gnarled branch ripped from a full-grown maple and hurled across the lawn as if made of feathers.

"Someone's angry," she said, rubbing the gooseflesh on her arms and wondering what had nature so riled up that it wrested branches from trees and tossed about everything that wasn't fastened down.

"Gretchen! We must get to the cellar this instant," the elder of her twin sisters, Bennie, declared as she came up from behind, hands outstretched as she felt her way into the room, the creaking floor announcing her every step. Bennie stopped before a high-backed chair and tightly grasped it, tilting her head toward the ceiling though her milky eyes stayed downcast. "Can't you hear it?" Her round face grew grim. "It's close, and it's coming straight at us."

"What's coming toward us? I can't hear anything above the wind," Gretchen said and tensed just the same, because what *she* could hear didn't matter. Bennie might have been blind since birth, but she had ears like a bat. She could sense impending disaster more accurately than a meteorologist's Doppler radar.

"A twister," Bennie said quite plainly, and her chin began to quiver. "It's dropped right out of the sky very near, and it's on its way. We're dead in its path."

"Where's Trudy?" Gretchen asked, trying hard not to panic.

She knew good and well that tornadoes didn't mess around, not when they plowed through tiny Missouri towns, and Walnut Ridge was about as tiny as they came. A twister's only job was to make a mess of all it touched. They had been lucky these thirty-nine years since her Abby was born, the bumpiest weather seeming to miraculously bypass the farm, but maybe their luck had run out.

"Trudy!" Gretchen began to shout, heading for the dining room as the thunder and shrieking winds shook the house. "Trude, where are you?"

"I'm here," the younger twin called back, appearing beneath the curve of the arch separating dining room from kitchen.

Trudy looked the mirror image of Bennie: round head fringed with faded brown stuck atop a thin neck and slight frame, with slender arms and legs far stronger than they appeared. She was forever clad in cotton smocks with ample pockets to carry odds and ends, like tissues, bits of string, and treats for her cat, Matilda. In fact, at that very moment, she clutched Matilda to her breasts, not about to let her go, despite how the hairless feline wiggled and squirmed.

"It's bad, isn't it?" Trudy said, scurrying toward Gretchen as another boom of thunder shook the tiny farmhouse. "I can smell the change in the air. It reeks of anguish and unfinished business."

"Bennie says a twister's headed straight for us, and she's never been wrong."

"No, she's never wrong," Trudy grimly agreed.

And Trudy's nose had never been wrong either.

Matilda mewed, her pale skin stretching over her skeletal body as she climbed toward Trudy's shoulder. Gretchen took her sister's arm and hurried her through the kitchen and to the stairs, descending behind Bennie, whose heavy clogs clip-clopped down the steps.

"It's so dad-gummed dusty, like I'm breathing in the musty scent of every soul who's ever lived here," Trudy remarked and sneezed, losing a startled Matilda from her shoulder in the process. The tiny feet padded lickety-split into the cellar and out of sight.

"It's a hundred-year-old basement, Trude," Bennie said, her voice made hollow by the stone walls surrounding them. "It's practically made of dust."

At the top of the stairs, Gretchen shut and latched the door for good measure before she trailed the twins belowground, to where the dirt floors and rock walls were lit only by a single sixty-watt bulb. She found the flashlight she kept at the base of the steps, switching it on just as the electricity flickered and went out.

Though she paused in the darkness as she swung the beam of the flashlight to guide her, her sisters didn't hesitate in the least. They had no need for light to lead them. They knew every inch of the old house tactilely. They hadn't grown up inside its walls, but they'd been living within them for nearly as long as Gretchen. She'd moved them in with her four decades ago when she was barely eighteen and they were just thirteen, once she'd inherited the place from Lily and Cooper Winston, a year after she'd given birth to Abby. "Sam would want his daughter to grow up here, nowhere else," Lily had insisted, and Gretchen had not disagreed. Just as the home had been a cozy nest for Sam Winston and two generations of his family before him, it had quickly become Abby's and Gretchen's home-sweet-home as well.

Dear Sam, God rest his soul.

The place still rightly belonged to him as far as Gretchen was concerned, but she'd stopped feeling guilty for being there. She loved it as deeply as anyone could, and every inch of it was a constant reminder of him and how his selflessness had saved her.

She told herself that caring for the farm as much as she did was repayment enough for her betrayal, even if she wasn't entirely convinced.

"It's at the fence line already," Bennie said, interrupting Gretchen's thoughts.

"And it's getting closer."

The three of them settled into a tiny room with rounded walls where a trio of metal folding chairs awaited them.

Bennie reached for Trudy's hand and clutched it. "Oh my, it's barreling up the front drive. Can you feel it shake the ground?"

"Oh my, oh my, oh my," Trudy echoed.

Gretchen didn't feel the ground move so much as she felt Matilda padding back and forth between her ankles. The noise of the wind was less fierce underground and still she heard a high-pitched keening, angry and insistent.

As she settled into the tight circle with her sisters, a loud pop rent the air, and then a crash that made the small house shudder. Gretchen dropped the flashlight from her hands, and it clattered somewhere near her feet.

Matilda hissed as if telling her, "Watch where you put that thing!"

"Please, Lord, protect us," Trudy whispered, and Gretchen reached for her sisters' hands, grabbing on when she connected; all of them were trembling.

Please don't let us die down here, and I swear I'll never tell another lie. Gretchen squeezed her eyes closed and prayed, though she didn't entirely mean it.

TWO

"It's not possible. It can't be."

Despite what appeared to be the cold, hard facts, Abigail Brink simply refused to believe that she was pregnant.

Even the queasiness that gripped her sporadically from dawn to dusk, the bloated belly, the pressing need to frequently relieve herself, and the two missed periods weren't enough to completely convince her. These were all things caused by stress and she certainly had that in spades. The small art gallery in Chicago's Lincoln Park where she'd directed sales for the past eight years had been gradually cutting back on staff and was forever on the precipice of closing, thanks to newly budget-conscious customers and shrinking commissions. She couldn't afford to lose her job, not when she would have to pay the rent solo since Nate had moved out.

Abby felt quite a lot like a walking cliché: on the brink of forty, careening toward a midlife crisis, and barely holding it together. So she couldn't be pregnant, not now of all times. Having a baby didn't fit into her plans, and it made no sense besides.

"It just can't be," she kept telling herself, because she'd heard statistics on women her age conceiving naturally and the numbers bordered on anemic. Still, somewhere in the back of her head there was a tiny seed of hope it might be true.

To stop herself from second-guessing, she went by the drugstore on her way home from work, buying a new toothbrush, a bar of soap, and a box of First Response. Not even bothering to take off her coat, she'd shut herself into the bathroom and locked the door, despite being the only one there. Since their argument weeks before, Nate had moved across town and was camping out on the couch of his brother, Myron.

Gulping down water in between, she somehow managed to pee on all three plastic sticks within an hour, and she stared at each for a full ten minutes until every blank oval had sported twin pink lines.

Pregnant. Pregnant. Pregnant.

Though the package insert illustrated that she was clearly knocked up, a tiny warning indicated that women aged forty and up might show false positives because of something called "pituitary hCG." Abby had months to go before she gave up thirty-nine for good, but it was enough to fan the seeds of doubt.

She showed up bright and early at her doctor's office the following morning, waiting to have blood drawn, all the while trying to convince herself that she had something else, like mono, Epstein-Barr, or anemia. Surely those things could throw over-the-counter pregnancy results off-kilter, and any one of those diagnoses made more sense, considering how she'd been regularly missing meals and rest.

And still, she couldn't concentrate on work or sleep that night, pondering what the blood tests would reveal. She stayed awake, gazing at the ceiling, wondering how this could be happening to her at such an inopportune time.

When Dr. Epps had phoned the next afternoon with her lab results, Abby couldn't help asking, "What's the verdict?" all the while gnawing on a coarse bit of skin near her thumbnail. "Please tell me all I need are iron pills or a vacation."

"Well, I'd hardly advise any patient against a vacation, but that won't change the facts. Everything's perfectly normal, but"—there, Dr. Epps had hesitated.

"But what?" Abby had asked, biting the inside of her cheek and tasting blood.

"Congratulations, Abigail. You're absolutely, one hundred percent pregnant."

"You're sure?"

"Sure as shootin'," the doctor had chirped. "We should set up an ultrasound so we can figure out better how far along you are, although your hormone level's consistent with seven or eight weeks. We also need to get you on prenatal vitamins. Should I turn you over to Nancy to make the appointment?"

"Um, no, not just yet," Abby had mumbled. "I'll have to call back, okay?"

At which point she'd dropped the phone to the floor and stood with her mouth open, eyes wide, and knees wobbling, certain she was having an anxiety attack. When she'd recovered enough to cross the kitchen, she'd grabbed the calendar from the refrigerator door, counting backward, trying to figure things out.

Had she and Nathan even had sex those two months past? They'd been growing increasingly distant since New Year's, and it was both their faults. Though, really, all it took was once, right? One night without a condom when a single sperm got lucky enough to do the deed. If only they hadn't argued, she thought; if only they hadn't been living such separate lives. How Abby wished things were different, how desperately she wanted to call Nate straightaway and say, "Babe! You're not going to believe this!" But she couldn't.

She had to quit staring at the calendar when her eyes began to blur. She was too tired to pinpoint dates, exhausted by long days at the gallery and late evenings squirreled away in the spare bedroom with her easel and paints, deliberately avoiding the things that were missing from their relationship. And if she'd been hiding out, Nate had been no better, burying himself in his laptop, endlessly working on new apps and often disappearing at odd hours for meetings at coffeehouses, clearly more committed to his goals than to Abby.

Her last attempt to put them on the right path had failed miserably. "We need to do something about our situation." She had confronted him two weeks before, after gathering up the courage to instigate the kind of conversation she knew Nate dreaded most. "We can't go on this way. It's not healthy."

"If it ain't broke," he had countered. And though he'd grinned a nervous grin, Abby had read the panic in his eyes.

Any stabs at discussing their living arrangements always made Nathan so jumpy. She could mention something as simple as needing new silverware, and he took it as a prelude to a lengthy discourse on the M word. Maybe it was her small-town roots or being raised without her father, but Abby had a traditional streak that went beyond the need to share a bed and an apartment. She'd always assumed that living together would eventually lead to marriage, but as she found herself wanting to nest more and more, she'd sadly realized that Nate wasn't quite so willing and able.

"I feel like I'm floundering," she'd told him, and not for the first time. "Don't you want to move forward instead of running in place?" she couldn't help asking him. "Don't you want to make this permanent before it's too late?"

"When is it too late? There's nothing wrong with taking the proper time to figure things out," he had replied, as if reminding her that six years together didn't ensure that they were meant to be. "My parents were married twenty years before they divorced," he'd added, his routine argument in such a case. "There are never guarantees that how you're feeling today will be precisely what you're feeling tomorrow."

Okay, sure, Abby understood that his folks' splitting up had traumatized him, but she'd never known how much until she'd experienced his resistance to lifelong commitment. Unless it was just a convenient excuse for him. Either way, his argument was getting old, as was she. If you truly loved someone, she believed, being with them forever should feel right, destined even.

"There aren't guarantees for anything," she'd remarked, another tidbit she'd thrown at him over and over. "My mom didn't even have a chance to marry my dad before he went overseas, and I know she always regretted not asking him to stay."

Gretchen Brink had never married, had never even been in love with anyone else but Sam Winston, so far as Abby was aware. Not that her mother had said as much outright, but it was clear in the way she behaved, in her tone of voice and the softening of her eyes whenever she mentioned Sam's name. Abby didn't want to end up like that, alone and always wondering what could have been. She and Nate had to seize the day. No one could see into the future. They could both live another fifty years or fall off the El platform onto the tracks and get run over tomorrow.

Because, when it came down to it, Abby truly loved Nathan March. If Nate's passion was equally intense, then expressing his commitment to her—say, in the form of an engagement— seemed perfectly reasonable.

"Love is all you need," she had insisted because she believed it.

Nate had merely sniffed. "That's a Beatles song, not reality."

But Abigail had always believed that songs, like art, often revealed universal truths, and the fact that love made the world go round was one of them. What she wanted was an unshakable commitment to a future together, not a roommate who paid for pizza and kissed her and told her she was sexy (however nice all those things might be). It took everything she had to finally put her foot down and give him an ultimatum.

"If you're not sure in this moment that you want to be with me forever, then I think you should move out until you make up your mind."

"You want me to go?" At first, Nate had seemed truly stunned. Then he'd burst out laughing. "You're joking, right? You're kicking me to the curb because I don't share your fairy-tale view of marriage?"

"I'm not kicking you anywhere, Nathan. I'm merely suggesting that you leave until you decide whether I'm 'the One' or not," Abby had explained in the clearest way possible.

He had arched a furry eyebrow. "*The One?* Do you know how archaic that sounds?"

"Maybe to you, but not to me." The more he seemed to mock her, the angrier she'd become. How could he be so dense, as if after six years together he had no clue about her desires? When it came to marriage, he seemed to have a complete mental block. "If you don't know for certain and you think there's someone better for you out there, I can't have you around. I turn forty this year. I don't have time to waste, and I need to know I'm as important to you as you are to me. Right now, I have my doubts."

"C'mon, Abs, this isn't funny." He had stared at her until his smile died, finally grasping the idea that she wasn't joking around. "You're really serious?"

"Totally."

"Wow." His Adam's apple had bobbed, his wide forehead pleating. "You know I love you or I wouldn't be here. I would have left ages ago. But I stay because I wake up in the morning and want to be with you that day. Isn't that enough?" Heat had flushed his cheeks. "Do you want me to drop down on bended knee and propose? Should I promise you forever because it's what you want to hear?"

"No"—she had shaken her head as tears stung her eyes—"not if you don't really mean it."

He'd pinched his lips together, looking pained, and his hazel eyes had darkened, wounded. "I'll do whatever you want," he finally told her, grudgingly. "It's your call, and maybe you're right. Maybe we both need some space to think."

"Yes, space to think," she'd agreed, though it tore her in two just to say it.

And, just like that, Nate had stuffed his gym bag with underwear, T-shirts, socks, toothbrush, and toothpaste. He had held her hand for a moment before he'd walked out the door, mumbling something about crashing with Myron until she came to her senses. His head low, he'd dragged his heels down the hallway as though, any second, she would call him back and tell him she didn't mean it, that having a ring on her finger didn't matter.

But it did. It really did.

So Abby had shut and bolted the door behind him, thinking that any minute she would hear his key in the lock, that he'd come back and blubber that she was most assuredly the One and he couldn't live without her.

Five minutes passed, then twenty more, until an hour had gone by and Abigail had ascertained that he wasn't returning. At least not right away. She had messed up her bed and now she had to lie in it.

That fight seemed so long ago, especially since her call from Dr. Epps. Two weeks apart from Nate felt like years; fourteen long days in which they had spoken only a few times when he'd phoned to say he needed to drop by to pick up a gadget or more underwear. Abby had been careful not be anywhere around when he did. That would have only confused her all the more.

Despite the fact that she considered herself an independent

woman, she felt unsettled and weak without him, as if she'd re-moved an internal organ required to properly function. Then to hear that she was having a baby. Nate's baby.

It was almost too much to take.

Abby knew she couldn't stay in the apartment alone, not while she was so aware of the new life taking root inside her, the tiny seed of a baby that was partly Nate's too. If she was going to get through this, if she was going to figure things out, it wouldn't be here. She couldn't tell Nate. She refused to have him beholden to her because of her pregnancy. If he came back—if they decided to make a go of it again—it had to be because of love and love alone.

She couldn't explain to her friends in Chicago, because they were Nate's friends, too. They would spill the beans to him, and she wasn't ready for that yet.

The only place where she could take refuge was home. She craved a chance to pause and draw in a deep breath. Lots of deep breaths. Becoming a mother changed everything, and she was sure her own mom would understand better than most. When Gretchen had given birth to Abby, she had done it alone, and Abby needed reminding that such a fate wasn't the end of the world.

Besides, she felt inexplicably drawn to the farmhouse where she'd been raised. She yearned to soak in its calm and sleep in her old bed in the room that had once been her father's—the father she'd thought about so often as a child, the one she'd wished so hard would return every time she'd blown out a candle on a birthday cake. Though she'd never met the man, he still loomed large in her life. Samuel Henry Winston, son of a walnut farmer, grandson of a rainmaker, and "the best friend I ever had," according to her mother.

Abby had only his photograph, one Gretchen had given her ages ago, of a teenager in overalls with a long face, dark hair, and piercing eyes. "He was like no one else, attuned to nature in ways most folks aren't," her mom had said. "When Sam wept, the clouds would open wide and cry with him," Gretchen would explain while Abby ate up every word like she was listening to a favorite bedtime story. "And when he smiled one of his rare smiles, the sun beamed so brightly it was blinding."

"Do you figure he can see me?" Abby would frequently ask, and her mother had replied with an ebullient nod. "I have a feeling he's watching you always and that he's much nearer than you think. If he could find his way back, he would, I'm sure of it."

Just as Abby needed to find her way back now.

Perhaps the baby was a sign that she'd gotten off track, that she'd lived her life according to Nate for so long that she'd pushed aside what was most important. Her mom and her aunts. The farm. The family. Her dad.

"We're going home," she said and put a hand on her belly. Exhaling softly, she picked up her cell phone, hesitating but a second before she dialed Walnut Ridge. Her mother's phone rang and rang and rang without an answer, which worried her a little. Someone was always around the house, if not Gretchen then Aunt Bennie or Aunt Trudy.

She hung up and tried again, only to get a rapid busy signal.

Maybe they were having trouble with the lines. Could be a squirrel had chewed through them again. That had happened on more than one occasion, and it took the devil to get the service truck out to the old farm for repairs.

Well, no matter, she told herself, ending the call. She'd call the office and tell Alan she was taking some sick days. Then she'd pack a bag and catch a cab to the train station. Her mom had told her over and over again, "If ever you need me, I'm here for you, any day, rain or shine."

And, at the moment, Abby needed her something fierce.

THREE

Time stood still as Gretchen listened to the freight-train-like charge of wind and the barrage of hail pelting the house with a relentless *rat-a-tat-tat*.

"It's right on top of us," Bennie said, gripping her sister's hand so tightly that the blood ceased to flow to Gretchen's fingers.

Matilda scrabbled over her feet to get to Trudy's lap, and Gretchen found herself holding her breath until she finally had to gasp, sucking in dusty air that tickled her throat and left her coughing.

As suddenly as it had arrived, the barrage of noise receded, as if someone had shut off a giant switch, and then the room grew deathly still, the only noise their anxious breaths and Trudy's voice, repeating in a hushed whisper, "We're okay, we're okay, we're okay."

When only silence followed, Gretchen dared to open her eyes to see an impatient Matilda pacing. "Is it gone?" she asked.

Bennie loosened her death grip and tipped her head from side to side. "Yes, it's gone," she said and smiled with relief. "We made it."

So far as we know, Gretchen mused. At least, the house hadn't fallen down around their ears. Still, she was afraid to see what was upstairs and even more frightened of what lay outside.

"Let me go up alone to check," Gretchen said and released her sisters' hands before rising from the folding chair. She turned the flashlight toward the stairs and headed up. Though the ceiling bulb remained dark, she didn't worry about leaving Trudy and Bennie in the gloom. They were perfectly capable without the light and, besides, they wouldn't go anywhere until she gave the all clear.

She could barely breathe as she unlocked the door at the top of the stairs and opened it, part of her fearing there would be nothing beyond but rubble. Instead, she peered into the kitchen, where everything was as they'd left it.

"We're good!" she called down to her sisters. *We lucked out,* she told herself as she heard the scuffle of their footsteps on the steps behind her, Bennie appearing first and then Trudy, just as they'd emerged from Annika's womb.

"It's so gray in here," the elder twin said, touching her way toward the kitchen sink. "The electricity must be off, eh?" she asked, perceiving the subtle change of dark and light.

"You're right," Gretchen confirmed and tried the kitchen switch, thumbing it on and off to no avail.

"Well, it's a good thing we have a gas stove," Trudy cheerily remarked, easing her way across the room toward the pantry. "I'll put a kettle on and make us all a cup of tea. Chamomile, I think, to calm our nerves. My heart's still racing."

Gretchen wandered through the dining room, the front hall, and the parlor, making sure all was safe. Thankfully, framed embroidery and mirrors still hung on the walls, the

windows appeared intact—albeit muddied by wet leaves—
and the ceiling sported no new stains, merely cracks in the
plaster that had been there for an eternity.

"The house seems to have held together," she called out
as she walked toward the kitchen, Matilda nearly tripping
her as the cat howled and ran past her, heading for the back
door.

"I hope the shutters stayed on," Trudy said, fingers reaching into cupboards that held the china cups that had once been
their mother's, while Bennie filled the kettle at the sink. "If
anything's broken, we'll have to call Walter."

She said it so eagerly that Bennie teased, "You're sweet on
the handyman, are you, Trude?"

"Go on, you!" Trudy said, giggling.

"Well, I don't figure we'll need Walter for the shutters anyway," Bennie announced as she shut off the faucet and moved
the kettle to a burner. "I didn't hear them do anything but
bang, and Gretchen wouldn't have let us up if any windows
were broken, would you, sweet?"

"Not a chance," she told her sister, "but I haven't checked
the upstairs so you girls stay down here until I do."

"You won't find anything wrong with the house but bumps
and bruises," Bennie said matter-of-factly as she fingered the
knobs on the gas stove and got the proper burner lit with a
pop and a hiss. "I believe we've survived intact despite Mother
Nature's reminder of who's in charge."

"Strange," Trudy said and stopped setting cups on saucers
to lean toward the half-opened window above the sink, her
nose wrinkling like a bunny's. "I caught a strong whiff of lem-

ongrass just now. I haven't breathed that scent since . . . well, a long time ago. You know who that reminds me of, Gretch—"

"Yes, I know," she said, cutting Trudy off, because her sister had often remarked that Sam Winston smelled of "truth and lemongrass." The funny thing was, Gretchen had been thinking of Sam, too. She couldn't help it, not with the way the storm had kicked up and blown through.

"Perhaps it's an omen," Trudy added.

"I hope it's a good one," Gretchen replied, her mouth dry.

"Me, too."

But as Gretchen walked toward the window that faced the front drive, she didn't feel very hopeful. Though the house appeared to have withstood the twister's winds without damage, the rest of the property had not. Branches littered the lawn and the gravel drive; leaves had been stripped from standing trees. Farther off in the distance, she discerned black power lines and telephone cables that should have crisscrossed the sky but no longer stretched from pole to pole. Instead, they sagged like old clothesline. Despite the sun's attempt to peek between scudding gray clouds, the aftermath was hardly heartwarming. It looked an awful lot like a battlefield.

Gretchen set aside the flashlight and went straight to the old Bakelite phone. Picking up the receiver, she put it to her ear and listened for a dial tone. "Hello?" she said, tapping on the reset buttons. "Hello?" she tried again, putting a finger in the rotary dial and giving it a spin.

She heard nothing.

"The phone's dead," she announced.

"Nuts." Bennie sighed and felt her way along the counter,

pausing at the stove and waiting for the teakettle to whistle. "Though I don't feel much compelled to call into town at the moment, it's not very reassuring that I couldn't reach anyone beyond the fence if I wanted to."

"You never did get that cell phone Abby gave you working, Gretch, did you?" Trudy asked.

"I couldn't get a signal." Gretchen sighed. Nothing wireless seemed to function on the farm, and they'd tried plenty of times to get connected. But they'd given up the idea of laptops or cells once they realized it was futile. One frustrated wireless technician had suggested there was something magnetic in the air interfering with the signals, and Gretchen could only imagine what that was, maybe the spirits that Abby had always blamed for anything odd that happened on the farm while she was growing up. Like when the doorbell rang but there was no one there, or when the lights mysteriously turned on and off, as though communicating in an otherworldly Morse code.

"I'm sure they'll be out to repair things in no time. We'll be fine," she reassured her sisters, a false promise to be sure as they were five miles outside town and often the last in line to get attention. "If you two will stay put, I'll venture out and see what else needs fixing."

That said, Gretchen headed toward the back door, located her knee-high rubber boots, and plopped down on the bench to remove her sneakers and pull the boots on.

Matilda pushed past her legs as Gretchen opened the mudroom door and stepped out onto the rear porch. She let the screen door slap closed behind them.

As she ventured onto the lawn, the first thing that struck

her was the scent of the earth, damp and loamy, and the starchy smell of a freshly scrubbed sky. She heard the *drip-drip* of water, sluicing off the roof and tree branches, errant sprinkles splashing her cheeks like teardrops. Birds began to twitter from above, emerging from their hiding places to inspect the world poststorm.

Ignoring the twigs and limbs strewn about, Gretchen focused on the old farmhouse, walking steadily around it, taking in the whitewashed clapboards above the stone foundation. Two loose shutters hung cockeyed on their hinges, but otherwise she didn't spot anything dangerously amiss. The soles of her thick rubber boots crunched on ground that felt uneven, like a carpet of nettles.

As she rounded the corner, a voice called out from the kitchen window, "Gretch? Everything okay out there?"

"It's a bit of a mess but nothing too bad so far," she replied as the sash creaked wider and Trudy's face appeared behind the screen.

"Bennie wondered if a tree fell in front," Trudy said. "She felt the ground shudder so she thinks it might be a big one. You should check that out," she suggested before the sash came down so the window was open only a crack.

If Bennie thinks a tree fell, then a tree fell, Gretchen mulled as she went around the front to find all the wicker tossed into a heap on the porch. She started up the steps, compelled to right everything, but Matilda appeared out of nowhere, weaving around her ankles. The cat's hairless tail was raised like a flagpole and anxiously twitched.

Matilda howled, and Gretchen bent to scratch the cat's

wrinkled head. "I know, girl," she said, "Everything's a smidge topsy-turvy, but it'll be okay."

Then Matilda did something she'd never done before: she opened her mouth and bit Gretchen's hand. Not hard enough to break the skin, but enough to leave fresh tooth marks.

"Hey!" Gretchen stood and rubbed the spot on her palm.

"Mew!" Matilda mournfully cried, her ghostly form pacing back and forth. "Mew!"

The cat appeared possessed, her blue eyes staring up with such purpose that Gretchen instinctively took a step after her as Matilda sprang off the porch and raced toward the walnut grove. Only Gretchen had promised Trudy she'd see about the fallen tree, and that she would do first.

"Sorry, girl," she called to Matilda's fleeing backside, and she headed toward the graveled drive, finding more branches down and more debris scattered across the lawn. Well ahead, she made out gaps in the line of fence where some of the rail-road ties had been knocked down.

"Damn," she let slip, pausing with hands on her hips, figuring at least Trudy would be pleased that she'd definitely need a hand from Walter to pick things up and put them back together again.

Gretchen kept walking, boots slogging through the muddied gravel, the high humidity making her feel like a damp dishrag. She'd barely gone half a mile toward the dirt road when she saw something that provoked an involuntary groan.

Oh, no.

Dead ahead lay a mammoth shape, like a dinosaur collapsed on its side. A pit formed in her belly, a terrible sadness. For

Gretchen knew it wasn't a napping T. rex but the hundred-year-old oak that had stood sentry at the entry point to the Winston farm forever. Her chest ached to see it. It was akin to a death in the family.

The oak had been ripped from the ground, its roots protruding at the base, the ground gaping beside it. Boughs that had once touched the sky now seemed sprung from the earth, extending over fifty feet and blocking the mouth of the drive entirely so that no car could get through. Gretchen certainly couldn't get her truck out. With the phone lines down and no ingress to the farm, the tornado had done a bang-up job of cutting them off from the rest of the world. Somehow, she felt as if it had done that on purpose.

"It'll take Sheriff Tilby and his boys a week to cut that up and haul the pieces away," she said aloud, and Matilda suddenly reappeared beside her, meowing her concern.

Gretchen drew in a deep breath and let it out, willing the worry out of her chest. She reminded herself that if that was the worst of it, they'd gotten off easy. She knew folks who'd endured twisters dismantling barns, homes, and silos, killing animals and family alike. Compared to that, a fallen oak was nothing.

"C'mon, cat, let's get on in," she said and turned to head back toward the house.

Only Matilda had other ideas. The bony feline dashed in front of her, tripping up Gretchen and nipping at the toes of her rain boots. Gretchen shooed her off, but she persisted, howling in such a guttural way, like a spirit possessed. It made Gretchen's hair stand on end.

"Okay, Lassie, what's up? Has Timmy fallen in the well?" she asked the cat, and Matilda ceased howling, shooting Gretchen a soul-searing stare before she took off, again running toward the walnut grove.

Rather than ignore the frantic feline, Gretchen went after her, noticing along the way how the grass had been flattened; no, not just flattened, but swirled as in crop circles, the blades bent so that they seemed a different green entirely from the rest of the grass on either side. It was as though the tornado had created a path toward the grove, after barreling into the oak in front, curving away from the house and past the weathered barn.

At least the twister couldn't do much real damage in the grove, Gretchen realized, since the trees had been barren since before Abby was born. They had stopped producing fruit shortly after the grim-looking pastor from the Presbyterian Church had shown up on the Winstons' front porch to tell them Sam had disappeared from the humanitarian aid camp in Africa and was presumed dead. The fellow had given them a plastic bag with a few of Sam's personal effects: his bound passport, the black comb he forever carried in his back pocket, a battered Hemingway novel, and a photograph of Gretchen so manhandled the color had nearly washed away.

Gretchen had been with Lily and Cooper Winston on that fateful afternoon, her belly ripened just enough to get the town's gossips squawking. She realized Sam's parents suspected their son might be the baby's father, considering the longtime friendship between Gretchen and Sam. But once Gretchen witnessed the devastation on their faces as they were informed that Sam was missing and likely dead, she couldn't help the words that had spilled out of her mouth.

"Sam isn't gone, not entirely," she'd told them, pushing herself out of the rocking chair and standing before them, cradling her tiny bump. "He's left part of himself behind. I wanted him to be the one who told you, but since he can't, I'll speak for him now."

"Did he know about the baby before he left?" the usually stoic Lily had asked through her tears.

"Yes, he knew," Gretchen said, relieved that at least that part wasn't a fib.

The way they had smiled despite their devastation, embracing her so tightly she thought they might never let go, had thoroughly convinced Gretchen that telling them the baby was Sam's was hardly a terrible lie, not when it made their suffering less difficult to bear. If she had to do it again, she knew that she would.

"Matilda, where'd you go?" she called out, having lost sight of the cat, her boots crunching over ground that grew increasingly pebbled. She recalled the *ping* of hail hitting the house, but she didn't spy frozen balls of ice when she glanced down at the trampled path ahead. What felt like rocks beneath her feet weren't nettles either. Instead, the earth was riddled with walnuts, many still in their green husks, blending in against tall spring grass.

Lord Almighty. Gretchen's eyes went wide as she scanned the floor of the grove. There were hundreds of walnuts carpeting the soil, perhaps thousands.

But how on earth could that be?

The hair rose on her arms, and her heartbeat ramped up to an unnatural speed.

Where had they come from? Not from the barren trees. Besides, it wasn't even the proper season. She found herself looking up, wondering if they had rained down from the sky. Was it some kind of sign?

Gretchen tipped back her head, watching as steel-gray clouds began to evaporate like mist, leaving the gentlest blue in their wake. Sunlight sluiced through boughs above and caused the rain-damp leaves to glisten. She closed her eyes for a moment as its warmth washed over her face.

It was almost enough to convince her that the storm had never passed through the farm at all. She could have savored the calm had Matilda not materialized before her, howling like a banshee and circling something crumpled beneath a walnut tree.

"Mew, mew, mew!"

"Okay, okay," Gretchen told the cat, striding toward the mysterious object. Was it sheets blown from a clothesline? Or a scarecrow tossed from a nearby cornfield? Or was it a trick of her eye, like the time she'd glimpsed an injured squirrel on the drive only to rush outside to discover it was merely leaves and shadow?

"Uhhhh."

As she approached, she heard a sound that was neither a bird's cry nor Matilda's noisy meows. It was a moan, low and guttural, and she quickly grasped that its source was very human and very real.

Gretchen ran forward, ducking beneath twisted branches, her mind racing with each fevered step.

Oh God, oh God, oh God.

Soon enough, she glimpsed pale flesh, and her heart caught in her throat at the sight of the man lying prostrate upon the ground beneath the boughs of a gnarled walnut, its trunk split at the crotch. His arms spread and legs extended, he was bearded and barefoot, looking for all the world like a modern-day Jesus.

"Mew, mew!"

"Hush!" Gretchen brushed Matilda aside and sank onto her knees, daring to touch the weathered face, so drawn it seemed gray. The skin felt clammy but not cold. Soft puffs of air emanated from pale lips. Leaves and twigs tangled his long gray hair and a beard that reached his collarbone. Dirt stained a torn white button-down shirt. Even his jeans had a rip across one thigh, and his feet were exposed as if the twister had shredded both his socks and his shoes. At first, she thought his hands and feet were burned. Had he been struck by lightning?

"Are you all right?" she asked, crawling around him, noting that his reddened palms and soles were thick with scars, but she spied no blood or protruding bones. "Can you hear me?"

The worst of his injuries appeared to be an angry-looking bruise centered on his brow. A swollen mix of green and purple, it mimicked the color of the sky before the storm.

"Are you awake?" Gretchen tried again, kneeling over him. This time, he moaned, head slightly turning. "Do you know how you got here?"

His eyelids fluttered, opening just wide enough that she could discern his unfocused pupils within irises as silver-gray as an old buffalo nickel.

"Am I alive?" he murmured, so quietly she barely heard him.

"Yes," she said, and a shiver sliced through her as their gazes met, just for an instant. If she hadn't known better, she could have sworn those eyes were Sam Winston's. But it couldn't be him. It wasn't possible. This stranger looked older than the almost sixty years Sam would have been, and besides, Sam Winston had died long ago. "Who are you?" she asked, a tremble in her voice.

"Don't know," he whispered back and winced.

"It's okay." She squeezed his shoulder gently. "Do you think you can get up?"

"Help me?"

Gretchen held on to him as best she could, offering support as he slowly staggered to his feet. As lanky as he was, his dead weight felt like a bag of bricks as he leaned hard against her, making their progress from the grove a Herculean effort.

"Careful," she told him as his bare feet slipped over the walnuts strewn in their path. It seemed an eternity had passed before they reached the farmhouse, both of them out of breath. "We're nearly there."

Up the back steps they went, Gretchen's legs wobbling and arms aching. The man swayed unsteadily, seemingly ready to collapse at any minute. She braced herself before releasing him long enough to pull open the screen and kick wide the mud-room door.

Overhead, the porch light flickered like a firefly, which made no sense at all, considering they had no power.

The man sucked in a painful breath, and Gretchen shouted into the house: "Bennie! Trudy! Help! Hurry!"

"What the devil's going on?" the elder twin asked, grabbing for the door and keeping it open as Gretchen half dragged the man into the house. "Is someone with you?"

"A man . . . he's injured," was all Gretchen could say between huffs and puffs as she urged the stumbling fellow through the kitchen and dining room, into the parlor. Along their path, lamps stuttered and came on again, and Gretchen couldn't help but wonder if the fierce lightning had left behind some kind of residual charge.

"Does he need a doctor?" Bennie asked, doing a good job of following in their footsteps. "Though we can't call out with the phone dead—"

"And we can't drive him anywhere either, not with the oak blocking our way out," Gretchen told her as she struggled beneath the man's weight, drawing him toward the claw-foot sofa.

"No doctor," the man managed to say, shuffling alongside her. "Just need . . . lie down."

"Okay," Gretchen agreed, knowing that unless she walked the five miles into town for help, they were pretty well stuck out on the farm anyway. "Here you go," she said and, as gently as possible, let him down on the couch.

He crumpled like a rag doll upon the worn linen cushions, and she gently lifted his legs and settled a pillow beneath his head. She rested her palm against his grizzled cheek as his head fell slack, his eyes closed.

"Sir, are you still with us?" she asked. "Can you speak?"

He didn't answer. Didn't even moan. He'd slipped hard and fast into unconsciousness.

"What's going on? Who's with you, Gretch?" Trudy wondered aloud, coming up behind her sisters.

"She found a man," Bennie said.

"Out on the farm?"

"In the walnut grove," Gretchen told them both, watching the slight rise and fall of his chest. "He was lucid and he's breathing, just banged up a bit."

"What if he's got internal injuries?" Trudy wrung her hands. "We could be doing him more harm than good by keeping him here."

"But we have no choice," Gretchen insisted and took a deep breath. What did they expect her to do, perform surgery with a steak knife and suture with knitting needles? They had little more in the house than a basic first aid kit. "Look," she said and rose from her crouch, facing her sisters, "I won't let him out of my sight tonight, okay? And when the phone's back on, we can call for the doctor. We can't haul him anywhere until the tree's been cleared. So we've got no choice but to stay put. We'll have to do the best we can and hope that it's enough."

Trudy nodded. "You're right, of course, Gretch. I didn't think."

"Well, at least the power's back on." Bennie squinted milky eyes, looking around them. "It's brighter than it was before. Did they fix the line already?"

The lights were indeed on, but Gretchen had no explanation for it. The house had been dim before she'd brought the man inside. "I can't honestly say that anything's fixed."

Trudy touched her twin's arm. "How can you worry about

the lights when there's a mystery right in our midst? Don't you wonder who he is and where he came from?"

Bennie nodded, tilting her wide face toward Gretchen. "Indeed, I do. Where did you say you found him?"

Gretchen wiped grubby hands on her jeans, ignoring how her fingers trembled. "He was lying in the walnut grove looking as though the tornado had flattened him," she explained, having no earthly explanation for how he'd gotten there. "Matilda led me to him. She threw quite a fit until I followed her. He was at the end of a path of trampled grass and walnuts."

"Walnuts?" Trudy repeated. "From our trees?" Her eyebrows knitted together above the wide bridge of her nose, sporting the same puzzled expression as Bennie. "That's impossible. The grove hasn't produced in years, not since the day the old pastor told you Sam wasn't coming home."

"I haven't a clue where they came from," Gretchen said and held on to the nearest chair as she bent to tug off her muddied boots. "It's like the sky spit them out instead of hail."

"Ah, that's the second time the heavens have rained walnuts on this farm," Bennie muttered and reached for Trudy's hand, giving it a squeeze. "Who did you say this man was again?"

"I didn't say, because I don't know," Gretchen answered, tucking her boots aside, very glad the twins couldn't read her face. Because they would have seen quite clearly that she wasn't telling them the truth, not the whole truth anyway. There was something about the man that seemed far too familiar, beyond the color of his eyes, beyond the strange coincidence of the walnut rain. "I asked who he was but he couldn't remember. I'm sure it's because of the bump on his head. Let's let him sleep, and when he awakens, we can ask him all the questions we want."

But her sisters weren't done giving her the third degree.

"Is he old or young?" Trudy asked, taking a step closer to the sofa and hovering, as though she could see the stranger lying on the divan.

"More old than young, but mostly filthy," Gretchen said, pushing ashy strands of hair from her face.

"Tall or short?" Bennie asked next.

Gretchen sighed, impatient to get to the kitchen. "He's taller than I am."

"He smells of loss and deep sorrow," Trudy declared as she squared her chin. "Like he's been wandering for years and years."

"He smells of something, all right," Gretchen agreed, though she would describe it more as mud and sweat.

Gretchen left them for a minute to fetch a clean dish towel, which she dampened with warm water. Then she returned to the parlor, settling on bended knees beside the couch. For an instant, she merely studied the angular shape of the face, the width of his brow, the set of his chin. Even half smothered by hair entangled with dirt and grass—despite the damage inflicted by the years—there was definitely something there, something that reminded her of Sam.

"Let's clean you up a bit," she said quietly and gingerly brushed a matted lock of gray from his brow before she touched the moist cloth to his cheeks. His soot-dark eyelashes twitched, and she wondered if he could feel her presence, even in his unconscious state, wishing she could voice aloud what she couldn't stop thinking.

Samuel Winston, is it you beneath the dirt and changes wrought by forty years? Could you have returned after all this time? Did you not really die in Africa? Did it merely scar your hands and feet, weather your skin, and turn you into an old man before your time?

Yes, it was far-fetched, desperate even. But what if this man truly was Sam? What if he'd been dropped back into her life after all this time—after the big lie she'd told since she'd last seen him? What if he'd come back to the house that was rightfully his, to the farm his parents had left to her and Abby, believing she was Sam's one true love and Abby his only child?

What if he woke up, remembered all, and exposed her whopper of a fib?

Stop it, Gretchen told herself and expelled a held breath. She'd been shaken by the storm, unsettled by the felled oak and inexplicable shower of walnuts. Those were muddling her mind, causing her to leap to an improbable conclusion.

"The walnuts," Trudy said, as if sensing the direction Gretchen's thoughts had taken. "Don't you figure they must mean something? Didn't they always say that he could control the sky?"

"And make the rain," Bennie chimed in.

"It has been rather quiet since he left for Africa."

"Like the farm has been holding its breath—"

"Stop it," Gretchen said aloud, concerned that her sisters had begun to wonder about the very same things that needled her. "Those stories about Sam, they're just tales that grew taller after he disappeared. Just small-town gossip because Sam's grandfather was a shaman. Sam Winston was a man like any other man," she remarked, although that in itself was a lie. Sam had been like no one she'd ever known, a fact she hadn't truly appreciated until he'd vanished from her life forever.

"But, Gretchen—"

"I mean it, Bennie," she cut off the older twin. "Not another word."

Even as she pooh-poohed their suspicions, she felt the strangest pull, a physical tug that wouldn't let her go. Like a part of her had been awakened from the deepest sleep and now twisted and turned within her breast, pressing at her from the inside out. Regardless of what common sense insisted, a tiny hope grew within her, tingling through her limbs, the nerves catching fire, causing the tiny hairs on her arms to stand on end.

It was as though she'd seen a ghost, and the sort that was not wispy and translucent, but instead was solid to the touch and smelled like a real man.

"Was there a car or truck near him?" Bennie asked, clearly unable to resist asking questions altogether. But at least this one was reasonable. "I didn't hear the crash of metal, but there was so much other noise besides."

"I didn't see a car dumped anywhere," Gretchen admitted. "He has no shoes and his feet look scarred, but they're hardly filthy enough to have walked a long ways. Who knows how he got here," she said and stood between the twins, gazing down at the man.

"Only one thing makes sense," Trudy said in her ever-quiet way. "He rode in on the twister."

"You know, Trude," Gretchen whispered, "I do believe that he did."

It was as if the sky had opened up and dropped him right into her lap.

FOUR

An entire day slipped by as Abby alternately drew in her sketchbook and stared out the window of the Amtrak train, seeing but barely noticing the passing countryside. Her mind raced faster than the *clickety clack* of the wheels on the track, leaping ahead, imagining what it would be like months from then when her belly swelled to the size of a watermelon and she gave birth to a squealing infant.

She squeezed her eyes shut, clutching the sketchbook against her thrumming chest as she envisioned cradling the child in her arms. Would it be a boy or girl? Would it look like her or Nate, or a combination of the two of them?

She could hardly breathe, wondering suddenly: What if Nate really didn't come back? Would she be alone through it all? Could she have their baby without him? Was she strong enough for that?

That she couldn't answer any of those questions caused her head and heart to ache.

By the time they pulled into the Washington, Missouri, station, dusk had firmly entrenched itself over the landscape. The sun had vanished below the distant tree line, and deep plums and pinks streaked across the horizon like the blur of watercolors smeared across a sheet of rag paper.

A kindly older man who'd sat across the aisle from her throughout the trip—who'd given her a pack of peanut butter crackers—picked up her suitcase from the train and plunked it down on the platform. Abby thanked him profusely before she slung her purse across her chest and picked up her bag to haul it around the building.

The noise of crickets lightly floated on the air, a sound she hadn't heard in ages. Not that they didn't have crickets in Chicago; but those crickets played solos. Here, they played symphonies. Once she'd called a cab to fetch her, she sat on her suitcase and listened until the yellow car pulled up. She gave it a wave and stood.

It was another fifteen miles down the rural route to Walnut Ridge and the Winston farm on its outskirts. As near as she was to home, she still couldn't reach her mother. Every time she dialed, she got the same rapid busy signal, which had her on the verge of panic. "I can't seem to get through to my family," she said aloud, frustrated.

"Don't know if you heard, but a storm passed through Walnut Ridge earlier," the driver told her as they hurried along the one-lane road, although Abby didn't see any sign that a storm had been anywhere near Washington. As if reading her mind, he went on, "It was very localized, they say. Didn't get a drop over this way, though we could've sorely used the rain."

"Sometimes these things are hit or miss."

"This one sure was."

In the car's headlamps, the asphalt looked gray and dry, the surface cracked. Even in the quick sweep of light, she could tell the brush on either side was brown with dust.

The driver was right. The earth needed a good drenching.

Abby leaned her brow against the glass, tensing more with each passing mile, knowing things were different now and would never be the same.

Though she'd been home four months ago for the Christmas holiday, she viewed the shadowed landscape with a changed eye. She had grown up in these parts, had a primal affection for the region—for the barns and silos, the clapboard houses and rows of crops seaming the dirt, the vast spaces between a farm and its neighbors—and yet she missed Chicago something fierce.

She missed Nathan.

She had left him behind without so much as a word about where she was going or when she'd return. Even if coming home was something she had to do for herself, she knew it wasn't fair to have done it like this. She was keeping a secret from Nate, and it felt nearly as awful as lying. And Abby hated lies more than anything else.

"So you haven't talked to anyone at home?" the driver asked, obviously making small talk, as she'd already told him she couldn't get through to the farm.

"No," she said. "Their phone doesn't seem to be working."

"Weatherman on the radio said there might've been a funnel cloud a few miles outside Walnut Ridge proper," the driver remarked without taking his eyes from the road. "Something popped onto the radar from out of nowhere and disappeared in a matter of minutes."

A funnel cloud? Okay, that was more than a spot thunderstorm. Why hadn't he mentioned it before?

"Was there damage? Was anyone hurt?" Abby asked and leaned forward, the shoulder belt tugging against her. Instinctively, her arms enfolded her belly as she fretted about her mom and aunts. Without a telephone, they were cut off from the outside world. She knew they didn't even keep a laptop at the farmhouse, since Gretchen insisted they couldn't get online even if they tried. "The house must not want it here," her mom had said, but Abby hadn't wondered if it was more like Gretchen didn't want it. It was better that way, according to her mother. *I'm not going to live and die by gadgets, Abs. I want to talk to the people I love face-to-face, and I want them to listen.*

And so the computers remained entrenched at the Winston Walnuts storefront in downtown Walnut Ridge. Not that they had any walnuts to sell these days. But they did a decent business in carved bowls, serving pieces, jewelry, and other decorative items made from the wood. In fact, every now and then, Gretchen would ask Abby to consider coming back and building more of a gallery to feature local artists of all stripes, not just those who made pretty things from chunks of wood.

The idea of returning to her small town hadn't appealed to Abby with her life and Nate's in Chicago. So she hadn't even dwelled on the idea except in passing, not until the past few weeks.

"Sometimes it's hard to get a read on things in these rural areas," the cabbie was saying, interrupting her thoughts. "Especially with power and phone lines knocked out." His dark eyes met hers in the rearview mirror. "So just 'cause you haven't heard from your kin doesn't mean much. I'm sure your family's fine."

"I hope you're right," Abby said, settling back against the vinyl seat, hardly reassured. She recalled her mom describing a twister that had hit the farm before she was born, right after her dad had died in Africa. Gretchen had spoken of walnuts falling like hail, lightning setting the sky afire, and winds swirling through the grove of trees until every branch was stripped bare. Whatever damage it caused must have been fierce, as those trees had never produced another crop. And though they'd tried to replant, nothing grew in the soil. It was as though the farm itself had given up the day that Sam Winston was lost to them.

Abby could only hope that twisters were like lightning and didn't strike the same place twice. She couldn't imagine what she'd do if anything happened to her mom or her aunts. Nate might be her one true love, but they were her heart and soul.

The cab bumped along for another dozen miles as the last vestiges of deep purple were swallowed by navy blue and night swooped in for real. Abby's stomach tightened the nearer they got to the farm, and she found herself following the crooked line of the railroad tie fence that encompassed the property, biting her lip when she noticed more than a few lengths missing.

"No wonder you can't get a call through," the driver said, ducking his head to gaze up through the windshield.

Abby had to roll down her window and stick her face out to see what he was looking at. The moonlight blackened the tangle of utility lines dangling from the sky.

"Wow," she breathed.

But that wasn't what really spooked her.

As the cab veered off the rural route onto the unpaved

drive that led to the farmhouse, Abby spotted the broken tree limbs strewn about, like large bones from an enormous skeleton, arms detached, fingers clawing at air.

"Whoa!" the driver said, hitting the brakes and jerking Abby forward. He switched on the high beams as he stopped, wet gravel popping beneath the tires. "Jesus, Mary, and Joseph!"

Abby pressed her palms flat against the front seat, holding steady, her heart pounding. "What is it?"

"I can't go any farther, miss, I'm sorry."

"What? Why?" she said at first, before she unfastened her seat belt and peered through the plastic partition, seeing quickly enough what the problem was. Something gray and enormous lay in their path, blocking the drive.

Abby's brain took a second to process what it was, and then she found herself choking up. "The old oak," she uttered, the words emerging as a sob.

"That's some tree," the driver said. "Must be a good nine foot around."

It had towered over the front lawn since Abby could remember, shading the grass, providing a haven for so many birds that whenever she'd stood below it, it had seemed the whole tree was alive with chatter.

"Guess this is it," the man said, the interior light switching on as he pushed open the door. "I've got bad knees, I'm sad to say. I couldn't haul your bag all that way for you even if I tried."

"It's okay."

He got out and rounded the car, popping the trunk to remove Abby's suitcase.

She emerged from the backseat, her legs unsteady from sitting on the train all day, her heart breaking at the sight of the fallen oak. She was too far still to see the house, but she could feel it there, waiting.

"You want me to stay here? You can call from your cell when you reach the door," the driver said as he came up behind her and set her suitcase down on its wheels.

No, I can't, she wanted to tell him. Her cell wouldn't work on the farm. It never did.

Instead, she said simply, "I'm good, thanks." Then she dug into her purse for the fare plus a tip. Even on the off chance that no one was home, she knew where Gretchen hid the key. "Don't fret about me. I'm right where I want to be."

He pocketed the cash but seemed hesitant to leave. Pushing back his plaid cap, he scratched his thinning scalp and said, "You sure I can't hang around a few minutes? If no one's there or the place is damaged, I can take you into town. It's just another five miles up the road."

"Someone's home," Abby said, because she knew her family was there. She felt it in her gut. Where would they be besides? "You can go, truly," she told him and smiled, wondering if she was giving off pregnancy vibes. She was too tired to glow, but perhaps he could sense the tiny life inside her. It would explain why he was acting like an overprotective dad.

"Take care, miss." He tipped his hat to her and left.

She grabbed her suitcase by the handle and dragged it aside while the man got back into the cab, red brake lights sparking as he backed up until he could turn around.

Tires skittered on gravel before he rolled away, quickly swallowed up by the night.

Abby drew in a deep breath, full of cool air and worry, then she began to make her way around the fallen oak, her suitcase bumping over soggy earth and damp grass.

From the fence to the farmhouse wasn't much more than half a mile, but it seemed to take forever to traverse. There were so many twigs and broken branches to weave around. Abby's suitcase fell over twice before she pushed the handle down and carried it, panting as she walked and wishing she hadn't brought so much with her. But she couldn't leave behind her sketchbooks or her beloved college art history text—heavy though it was—and the weather was so changeable in April that she'd stuffed in plenty of sweaters and jeans and even her boots, just in case. If she could have fit her latest canvas into her luggage—an Impressionistic oil of a tiny raindrop rippling a puddle—she would have packed it as well. Then she reminded herself that she wasn't going to be gone forever, perhaps a week at most. If she'd wrapped up her paintings to bring with her, it would have felt like she had given up. And she hadn't, not yet. She'd even left a note for Nate in the kitchen in case he should turn up while she was away. *Went home for a few days*, she'd written. *Need to sort things out*. She didn't know if Nate would see it; wasn't sure that, even if he did, he'd care where she'd gone. Between her broken heart and the baby hormones, Abby had cried as she'd filled her suitcase and finally closed the zipper.

You made the right decision, coming back, she told herself as she shifted the suitcase into her opposite hand, pausing to catch her breath. As she glanced ahead, she realized she'd gone far enough down the drive to see the house through the trees. But instead of discerning the dark shadow of the roofline against the night sky, she saw something else entirely. She asked herself, *How can that be?*

Light spilled through the falling night, emanating from the windows along the porch, the whitewashed railing gleaming like teeth, grinning at her arrival.

Maybe her mom had invested in a generator, although she heard no telltale hum.

Nothing else would explain the house having power when the lines were down.

But then, strange things had seemed to happen at the farm ever since she was a kid. Odd things that no one could explain, not with any kind of commonsense answers. Like the day Abby had found her mother crying in the kitchen. She'd broken a bowl, one with alphabet soup letters running around the rim. "It belonged to Sam," Gretchen had told her and sobbed as though the world had come to an end. "Another piece of him I've shattered," she'd said, sighing as if the weight of the world rested on her shoulders, or perhaps on the condition of the alphabet soup bowl.

Only seven, Abby hadn't understood what she meant, but she'd felt Gretchen's sadness, like a part of her was broken, too. "We can fix it," she'd told her mom. "We can glue it back together like my piggy bank." But Gretchen had shaken her head, tears skidding down her cheeks. "No one can fix it, Abs, not even you." Which, of course, had made Abby start bawling as well, feeling a bit like the unfixable bowl was her fault, even though it was her mother who'd dropped it.

As if their combined sobs weren't noise enough, a crack of lightning and a rumble of thunder had shaken the walls before the sky had turned entirely black. The rain had begun to fall in earnest as Abby had raced out of the house and up the gravel drive, eager to chase the sadness right out of her soul. The drizzle fell upon her like tears, wetting her face and shirt. But when she got to the fence line and took a step beyond it onto the rural road flush with wildflowers and weeds, she realized the rain had stopped. Well, it hadn't stopped exactly. It just wasn't raining anywhere beyond the property line. Not a drop. When Abby had turned around, she saw the sky above the house was gray as gunmetal—but everywhere else, the sky was blue.

Could breaking Sam's bowl have caused his spirit to cry upon the farmhouse? Her mother insisted that he was and always would be there, looking out for them. "Sometimes, when you're sad and it rains, it means he's right beside you, and he's feeling just as sad, too," Gretchen had told her.

Abby had rushed back through the rain and inside to tell her mother what she'd seen and what she believed it meant. Gretchen was, by then, mopping up her tears and picking up broken bits of porcelain, clearly in no mood to entertain a child's vivid imagination. "We live in tornado alley, Abs," her mom had said, shrugging off any theory of rain-making spirits. "Weird weather is the only kind we get."

But Abby had known there was more to it than that. She had always believed that some kind of spirit—a ghost or restless soul—lurked around the walnut grove, something that had to do with her father and the past, something that no one else could understand.

Even now as a grown-up, Abby sensed a presence, and it filled her with peace.

"It's good to be back," she said aloud and released a slow breath, gazing at the farmhouse, the knot in her shoulders loosening, warmth flowing through her despite a chill in the air. This was her home—it had belonged to Sam's family, to the grandparents who had loved and cuddled her as an infant, though she'd been too young to remember anything but the idea of them. With every step forward she took, Abby couldn't help but feel embraced by invisible arms. Her heart thumped with each footstep, as if to say *I belong, I belong, I belong.*

From within the cloudless sky, the rising moon illuminated a path bright enough that she could avoid storm-tossed limbs and divots in the grass. Somewhere above, a whippoorwill sang its melancholy song, pausing between each verse as if hoping others would join in. Abby was tempted to coo, "Whippoorwill, whippoorwill," so the poor bird wouldn't feel so alone. But she was too anxious to reach the porch and hurried her gait, picking up her suitcase and marching toward the steps.

When she finally made it to the front door and settled her suitcase on the welcome mat, her entire body sagged, thoroughly exhausted. If this wasn't the longest day of her life, it certainly ranked right up there. She'd been dying to talk to her mother, to tell her about Nate and, more important, about the baby. Not being able to reach Gretchen had made her feel starved in a way that had nothing to do with hunger. To know that her mom was on the other side of the door caused her fingers to tremble as she reached for the knocker and banged it solidly against the wood.

Abby didn't realize she was holding her breath until she heard the turn of the knob and the creak of hinges. She exhaled a noisy "oh" as the door was drawn inward. She read the concern on her mother's face as soon as it peered out: all worry lines and narrowed eyes, messy bits of pale hair on her cheeks, loosened from her ever-present ponytail.

"Abigail!" Gretchen said, eyes wide with shock. "How did you get here? You didn't walk all the way from the station?"

"Not all the way, no," Abby said as her mom stared at her. "I had a car drive me to the property line." A nervous smile twitched upon her lips. "The driver was reluctant to leave me here." She turned her head to see the jumble of wicker furniture at the end of the porch. "You sure got whacked by the storm, huh? Did you know the old oak fell and blocked the drive?" Despite her best efforts, she felt the tears coming. "I never thought I'd live to see the day that monster came down."

"Baby, what's wrong?" Gretchen pulled the door wide and reached out, cupping her chin.

"Who's there?" a soft voice asked, and Abby saw her aunts scurry into the foyer, clutching each other's arms. "Abigail, is that you?"

"Yes, it's me," she said, brushing at her tears.

Certainly, Aunt Bennie had recognized her voice the instant she'd first spoken, and Trudy had doubtless breathed in the scent of her once the door had opened. Abby wondered what strange things she smelled like now that she was pregnant. Talcum powder and pickles?

"I've been trying and trying to call, but your phone's dead," she explained, glancing above her at the porch light. A moth flitted about its weak glow. "I figured your power was out, too, but I was wrong."

"Oh, yes, that," her mother said, waving a hand in the air, not offering any sort of explanation. Instead, Gretchen peered around Abby's head. "Where's Nate?" she asked.

"Isn't he with you?" Trudy inquired, hands toying with whatever she'd buried in the pockets of her smock. "Surely he didn't let you come alone?"

"Sweetheart, what's got you choked up? You don't sound right," Bennie said, picking up on the tremor in Abby's voice.

The three women huddled in the doorway had such concern on their faces that the dam broke wide in Abby's chest. "Nate moved out two weeks ago," she confessed, and her shoulders began to shake. She took in a great gulp of air before blurting out, "And I just found out that I'm pregnant."

"*What?*" her mother and aunts said at once.

"It's true. I'm going to be a mother." Abby gripped the handle of her suitcase, somehow getting the words out. "I took three at-home tests and saw the doctor, and I've been a basket case ever since. So can I come in? Because I'm afraid if I stand here much longer, my knees are going to give."

FIVE

Good Lord, Abby's having a baby?

How could that be?

Not that Gretchen didn't know how babies were made. Of course she did. But Abby and Nate had always been so careful about such things, and she remembered Abigail remarking that she wasn't even sure she ever wanted to have children, which had broken Gretchen's heart to hear.

"I don't know if I'm equipped to be a mother, and I'm too old besides," Abby had declared this past Christmas, though Gretchen had told her that was utter hogwash. The girl wasn't yet forty, and plenty of women had babies at that age and beyond. As for feeling equipped to be a parent—ha!—no one ever was. It wasn't as though you were magically handed all the tools to get it right once the baby emerged. When it happened, you figured it out, day by day, just like everything else. Children were a lesson to which "live and learn" perfectly applied. The most important thing was to love them wholeheartedly. If you did that, the rest would fall into place.

"She's having a baby," Trudy breathed, and a slender hand clasped at her gingham-smocked breast. "Did you hear that, sister?"

"You bet I did," Bennie said, reaching for her twin's arm as the two of them turned downright giddy. "You'll have to start knitting the child a hat and booties."

"We can bring Abby's bassinet down from the attic," Trudy suggested.

"And dig the baby quilt out of mothballs!"

Gretchen ignored the buzz of her sisters' voices, her own head suddenly filled with a noisy hum all its own. "Are you positive?" she asked. "There's no question?"

"None." Abby bit her lip, looking for all the world like the sky had fallen.

"Oh, my," Gretchen said, barely able to breathe. She had one hand at her throat and the other settled on her own abdomen.

A tiny thrill wiggled through her at the knowledge that her flesh and blood would beget a new life, that fragments of herself—and even honest-to-a-fault Annika—would trickle down to another generation. Abby seemed far less certain, wearing a shell-shocked expression, as though the concept of carrying a child at this stage of her life was too enormous to grasp. Gretchen had no doubts her sensible daughter was already pondering how exactly she'd nurture a tiny being inside herself, watching her skin stretch and her belly expand, all the while understanding that giving birth meant someone else would depend on you wholly for years and years and years to come. Everything changed the moment you brought a baby into the world. *Everything.*

My God. Abs was pregnant!

As tickled as Gretchen was, she figured it would take a few days before it had sunk in with her as well. It seemed only yesterday that she'd found herself in the same pickle, although she'd been barely seventeen, with a furious mother and the baby's father out of the picture.

"What about Nate?" she asked abruptly, wondering how he could have walked out on Abby under these circumstances. Unless he didn't want children and that was what had caused their split. "How does he feel about this? Is he unhappy? Doesn't he want to be a dad?"

"I couldn't say," Abby told her quietly, "considering he doesn't know."

"He doesn't know?" Gretchen's voice rose, though she fought to keep the disappointment from her tone. She had so little right to judge anyone else.

"Nate's in the dark?" Trudy and Bennie echoed, and their happy chatter ceased. They, too, stood stock-still, awaiting Abby's response.

"I couldn't bring myself to tell him." Abby sucked in her cheeks. "The timing's rotten."

"Oh, Abs, there's no such thing as good timing when it comes to babies," Gretchen said, not intending to chastise. But she'd chatted with Nathan March on the phone and been around him enough holidays these past six years to be certain he loved Abigail as much as he possibly could. He certainly wasn't perfect—he worked too much, didn't share in chores, had all the same bad habits inherent in nearly every straight man on the planet—but she couldn't imagine he'd walk out on Abby when she needed him most. If she had one criticism of Nate, it would be that he wasn't serious enough; but she would never have said that he wasn't devoted.

"Mom?"

"What?"

Abby shuffled her shoes, which looked rather wet. "Are you going to make me stand out here all night?"

"For Pete's sake, let her in," Bennie directed.

"We'll make her a cup of tea," Trudy chirped.

"Oh, sweetie, forgive me"—Gretchen sighed and took Abby's hand, drawing her daughter inside the house—"but we've been shaken up quite a bit today already. My brain's still catching up."

"There's a lot of that going around," Abby murmured.

As soon as the girl was inside, Bennie and Trudy swarmed her, enveloping Abby's slender body in a group hug. "So have you left Chicago for good? Will you stay here till the wee one's born?" they asked, fussing as they touched her hair and her face so they could "see" her better.

"Leave the poor child alone. She's only just arrived." Gretchen hauled the heavy suitcase toward the stairwell, then went back to soundly close the door. "Come, come," she said and shepherded them all into the kitchen, where a copper-tiled ceiling reflected the lamplight and lent the room a burnished glow. "We've just eaten supper," she explained to Abby. "Peanut butter sandwiches and soup."

Even though the power had miraculously come back on hours ago when she'd brought the man who fell from the sky indoors, Gretchen had been half afraid to open the fridge, thinking the lights might go out again and all the food would spoil. But she would gladly take the chance for Abby's sake.

"Do you want something?" she asked and went over to pull

on the big chrome handle. "I could whip up another sandwich or make some toast?"

"Not just yet," Abby replied, dumping her oversize bag onto the oak table with a thud. The humidity had set her dark hair into rumpled waves around her face, and her pale skin was makeup free, her lips without gloss. She looked less like a self-confident Chicago art gallery director and more like a teenager, awkward and unsure of herself.

"How about a glass of milk?" Gretchen offered.

Abby shrugged. "I mean, I guess I should get something in my stomach soon since I'm feeding two now, but not yet. I need to decompress first."

"Don't take this the wrong way"—Gretchen couldn't resist brushing an unruly strand of brown from her daughter's cheek—"but you seem scared to death."

Abby choked up. "I guess I am."

"Sweetheart, it's okay." She sighed and pulled Abby against her, enfolding the girl in her arms and holding on tightly. "It's going to be all right."

The muffled voice croaked against her breasts, "Is it? Is it really?"

So Gretchen replied the only way she could, with words she wished her own mother had uttered to her all those years ago when she'd been just as petrified. "Yes," she said, stroking Abby's hair. "Yes, everything will work out. It always does in the end. We're here for you, whatever you need. Please, believe that."

Making promises like those wasn't lying, not really. Of course, she couldn't see the future, but Gretchen wasn't about to tell Abby anything else. She figured it was far better than the accusatory *What in God's name have you done?* that Annika had shrieked at her when Gretchen had been forced to confess about that summer night when she'd been so unbelievably reckless. As long as she lived, she would never forget the mortified look on her mother's face, the disappointment in her voice. "And I thought you were such a smart girl. I thought you'd be going to college, that you'd make something of yourself outside of Walnut Ridge. How disappointing this is." Annika had all but spat the words. "If you had asked for a condom, I would have marched you down to the drugstore to purchase some. But since it's too late for that, we must deal with the consequences of your actions. So tell me, who is the father?" she had demanded, hands on her hips, using the tone that Daddy used to call "Mommy's mean voice."

Who *was* Abby's father?

That was the all-important question in those days. Forty years ago, unmarried girls who got pregnant were little more than tainted goods. It didn't seem to matter that someone of the opposite sex was equally at fault. Regardless of how it had happened, once the word got out, you were never looked upon the same again. If Gretchen had told the truth, it would have been far worse. So it had seemed better—safer—to answer as she had. She told her mother exactly what she'd told Cooper and Lily Winston.

"It's Sam's," she'd lied, sure it was the right thing to do. His was the only name that came to mind, and hadn't he very clearly told her he'd do anything for her? But now she wondered if lying about something so big, even with the best of intentions, had finally come back to haunt her.

And it could very well have, if the man in the parlor was who she thought he might be. If he was really and truly Sam Winston.

"Mom?" Abby drew away from her embrace, sniffling as she brushed tears from her cheeks. "Is everything all right with *you*?"

Despite the fact that a man with Sam's eyes was passed out on the parlor sofa, the phone was dead, the front drive was blocked, and the power was on despite the snapped lines, Gretchen gave her daughter a smile meant to reassure. "We survived a twister pretty much unscathed, and you're back home with us, Abs. I'd say we're doing great."

"That depends on how you define great," Bennie harrumphed. "Tell your daughter what the cat dragged in. She's going to find out soon enough."

"What the cat dragged in?" Abby echoed, and her brow furrowed as she looked at her mother. "You mean Matilda brought something inside? Like a mouse or a rabbit?"

"Oh, far bigger than a rabbit," Bennie remarked in her know-it-all way, and Gretchen wished she had a dish towel in hand to swat her.

"Please, let's not go there," she muttered, keeping an arm firmly around Abby's waist.

"Why not tell her?" Trudy urged, shoving thin hands into her smock pockets and rocking back on her heels. "Tell her what the tornado dropped into the grove along with all the walnuts. It'll take her mind off things."

"Walnuts in the grove? But that's impossible, isn't it?" Abby's tired eyes squinted. "What's going on?"

"Later," Gretchen insisted, ignoring the determined set of her sisters' faces and focusing solely on Abby. "Let's get you and your suitcase up to your old room before we do anything else." With that, she steered her daughter through the dining room, toward the stairs, impatient to get her settled. Abby clearly looked exhausted. "I can fill you in after you've gotten some rest."

"Why not now?" Abby dug in her heels at the base of the steps. "What are you hiding? Is someone else here?"

"Mmmm." As if on cue, a low moan crept through the stillness, and Abby's focus shifted toward the parlor.

"Someone else *is* in the house," she said and wrested her arm from Gretchen's grasp.

"Abs!"

When Gretchen caught up with her, Abby stood on the threadbare rug in the center of the parlor, directly in front of the claw-foot sofa, her arms stiffly at her sides.

"I don't understand," she said. "Who is this? What happened to him?"

A solitary lamp burned, casting Abby's profile in shadow as she watched the man who lay so still, his eyes closed, limbs twitching, an occasional groan escaping chapped lips. Though a quilt covered his body, his face was fully visible above it. Gretchen had wiped the worst of the dirt from his skin and hair, then had taken careful scissors to his overgrown beard, trimming it to his jawline. He looked more human now, less gray than pink. The knot on his brow had already calmed from an angry purple to a rather dull red.

"Is he okay?" Abby whispered. "Was he hit by the oak when it fell?"

"He was hit by something," Gretchen said, leaning close to her daughter. "He spoke a little when I brought him in but not enough to tell me anything."

And he hadn't opened his eyes since he'd collapsed. He felt warm to the touch but not feverish. Gretchen didn't think he was truly delirious, merely in a deep sleep, thanks to the trauma his body had suffered.

"He seems familiar somehow." Abby cocked her head, looking at him. "Is he from around here?"

Gretchen hesitated before answering as carefully as possible. "When I asked, he couldn't remember his name. He needs to sleep and heal."

"So the tornado picked him up and dropped him onto the farm, is that it?" Abby tugged on the fringed hem of her sweater. "And it touched nothing else? Not the house or the barn?"

"That's pretty much it," Gretchen replied, though Abby hardly looked satisfied by her answer. "Okay, here's what I know," she began, before falling into storytelling mode as she'd done so many times when Abby was a child. She described the ferocious storm that had come out of nowhere, the winds that had battered the house, banging shutters against clapboard and sending the women to the cellar, and finally the twister that had felled the mighty oak and showered the farm with debris.

As she spoke, Abby bent nearer and nearer the fellow, examining him far too closely for Gretchen's comfort.

"C'mon, Abs." She touched her daughter's arm, willing her

to move away. "He needs to rest. There's nothing we can do for him at the moment."

But Abby wasn't listening.

"Doesn't this recent storm remind you of another storm you told me about a dozen times before? Of rain and wind and lightning, and walnuts dropping from the clouds in scores?" her daughter said, straightening up and tucking dark hair behind her ears.

"It certainly does," Bennie muttered and began feeling her way to the foot of the couch. Her chin tipped toward Abby, though her gaze drifted up toward the ceiling. "As I see it, there's a simple connection, one soul who could stir things up like that."

"Yes, yes, and who could cause the scent of lemongrass to carry on the wind," Trudy chimed in.

"For Pete's sake," Gretchen said, hating that her sisters were feeding Abby's fertile imagination. "Please, don't do this." She knew how much Abby had always yearned to have her father back, but she didn't want her child to believe what wasn't real; no matter that Gretchen had been wondering the same thing herself. "We know nothing about this man, not who he is or where he came from."

"But do you think it could be him?" Abby crouched beside the divan much as Gretchen had earlier. She couldn't seem to take her eyes off the injured man. "Does any part of you believe that he's come back?"

Gretchen squirmed, wiping damp palms on the thighs of her jeans, relieved when neither Bennie nor Trudy responded. Surely neither wanted to encourage Abby any more than they already had.

"You're tired, Abs," Gretchen said and took her daughter's hand, rubbing gently. "You're upset about Nate and the baby. You're seeing what you want to see. That's perfectly natural."

"You can't tell me you're not curious." Abby stared at her mother, her brow furrowed. "It's his long face and the bump on the bridge of his nose. Those high cheekbones, too. And what about his mouth? That same thin line from the photograph," Abby went on, her eyes too bright, her cheeks too pink. "Lots of things can change, but bone structure doesn't lie."

She sounded like Annika, seeking the truth in cheekbones. Gretchen glanced at her sisters for help, knowing they could sense her need even if they couldn't see it. But neither uttered a word.

He's not your father, she wanted to say to her child, but couldn't bring herself to do it for so many reasons.

"You used to tell me he'd come home someday," Abby went on, eyes filling with tears. "So why can't this be real? Maybe he was on his way when the storm hit and got caught up in it. Or what if he made the rain? What if the twister was his way back? You used to say that was his gift. So what if that gift brought him home?" Her slender hand reached for Gretchen, grabbing hold of her sleeve. "You're the one who made me believe all those things in the first place. Were they all lies or was any of it true?"

Any words caught fast in Gretchen's throat. How exactly was she supposed to respond to that? Tell her vulnerable child that those stories were gross exaggerations?

"My sweet Abigail," she said, deciding to take the path of

reason. She grasped Abby's arms, holding on tightly. "If this man is Sam, why didn't he contact us sooner? Why would he wait until now when he's had forty years to do it?"

"I don't know." The girl sighed, drawing away and shaking her head. "Whatever kept him away must've been something powerful, something beyond his control. Still, he must have heard me every time I wished for this. All those candles on every birthday cake."

Wishes aren't magic, Gretchen wanted to remind her, but she couldn't bring herself to do it. Because she had shared with Abby what Lily Winston had shared with her: larger-than-life tales of Sam's lineage, of the men who'd come before him and the mysticism surrounding them. But if that magic were real—if it were true—was it strong enough to bring someone back from the dead, or wherever it was Sam had gone?

"We know nothing about this man, only that he needs our help," she insisted, trying to calm Abby down, finding herself the voice of reason simply by default. "Sometimes even strangers can look like those we love and miss."

"He must have an ID, a driver's license, something," Abby said and looked ready to pick the man's pockets.

But Gretchen caught her arm. "Baby, there's nothing there," she told her. "We already checked."

Abby backed off, heading over to a nearby wing chair. With a heavy sigh, she slumped into its arms, tilting her head against its high back. "Please don't look at me like I've lost my mind," she said, gazing up at her mother. "Because I haven't, I promise."

"I don't think that at all," Gretchen said.

"Goodness knows, you're no crazier than the rest of us," Trudy remarked and wandered over to the chair, standing beside it, showing her support for Abby.

"Maybe we're due for a miracle," Bennie added, not about to be left out of things.

Oh, boy.

Gretchen crossed her arms tightly, cursing the timing that had brought the injured man to the farm and Abby home on the same day. She was afraid of what such a deep-seated longing could do to Abby when she was already in such a churned-up state. The girl was fearful that she'd lost Nate, frightened about having a baby, and now she'd begun to convince herself that her long-lost daddy had come home to take his rightful place—a place that had been kept wide open and waiting for forty years.

"As lovely as miracles sound, we can't jump to conclusions," Gretchen said, picking her words carefully. "What if he awakens clearheaded and tells us he was merely passing through, that he's someone with a family who's missing him?"

"If he does, then I'll stop wishing for things I can't have," Abby replied, the strain in her voice all too apparent. "But until then, there's nothing wrong with hoping, is there?"

"No," Gretchen said, her heart nearly breaking. "I guess there's not."

Abby sighed and patted the arms of the chair before pulling herself upright. "You're right. I'm really tired. I think I'll hit the sack." She kissed her aunts on their cheeks before she gave Gretchen a hug. "How about I see you all in the morning?"

"Goodnight, lamb," Trudy said, and Bennie added, "Sleep tight."

Abby gave the unconscious man one final look before she left the room. A few seconds after, Gretchen heard the *thump-thump* of the suitcase as Abby pulled it slowly up the stairs.

"Good grief, aren't you going to help the poor girl with that? We'll stay with your patient," Bennie chastised her, and Gretchen scurried out of the parlor, pausing at the base of the steps.

"Abs," she called up, "you should let me do that!"

But her daughter had already ascended to the second-floor landing. "Can you get my bag?" she asked, peering down around the whitewashed balustrade. "I left it in the kitchen."

"Of course," Gretchen said as Abby disappeared around the upstairs railing, suitcase wheels clacking as she rolled it toward her old room.

Abby's heavy-looking satchel lay on the breakfast table, tipped on its side, spilling some of its contents. Gretchen righted it and began to stuff the loose objects back in: a black marker, several quarters, a tube of pale pink lipstick, and a paperback-size drawing tablet from which a photograph protruded.

Gretchen couldn't help herself. She slid the photo from the pages, and her heart leaped into her throat when she realized its subject.

"Sam," she breathed his name, seeing a sixteen-year-old version of the man who would eventually leave Walnut Ridge with his heart broken. It was a long time since Gretchen had glimpsed this image. She'd given the photo to Abby when the girl was in nursery school. Her daughter had constantly peppered her with questions about why all her classmates had a mommy and a daddy while she had a mommy and two aunts. "You do have a father, Abs, and this is him," Gretchen had fibbed.

She ran a finger over the slender face, his features frozen in time. Sam sat on the porch steps in his overalls, his long legs extended, an unruly black cowlick curled upon his brow. His silver eyes were bright though the curve of his mouth was barely detectible. The photo was limp from handling, faded in spots around the edges.

"Oh, Abs," Gretchen said and sighed gently. No wonder the girl was so taken with the thought of her father returning; she had never let the idea of him go.

Who was my daddy? Abby had asked so many times. *What was he like? Why did he leave? How did he die?*

"Sam was a lot like my own father, Hank," she recalled Lily Winston saying not long before she'd passed away. "He needed to make his own destiny, even if that destiny was ill-fated."

Lily was the one who'd first told her that Hank Littlefoot had been marked as a shaman, his own grandpa having been a tribal shaman before him. "He could have stayed and used his gift for the good of his people, but he didn't want to remain on the rez. He felt no real connection to the government land or even his people." Lily had then smiled one of her rare smiles. "Only when he settled here on the farm did he understand what having a home truly meant."

From that point forth, Gretchen had imagined Hank Little-foot as a medicine man, healing the sick, and she'd often wondered if he wasn't the reason why Sam had wanted to go to Africa to help those less fortunate. Sam liked looking out for the underdog, maybe because he'd always felt like an underdog himself.

"Gretch? Are you still in here?" Bennie's voice cracked her reverie, and Gretchen let the photograph slip from her hands.

"Just getting Abby's bag," she said, scrambling to pick up the picture from the floor near her feet. "A few things had fallen out."

"Well, Abby hollered down and asked for a glass of warm milk." Her sister began banging around, opening cabinets. "If you wait another few minutes, I'll send it up with you."

"Great," Gretchen said, her heart thudding. As quietly as she could, she flipped open the sketchbook, prepared to quickly tuck the photograph inside and be done with it. Only something else caught her eye, the pencil drawings themselves. She looked at one and then another, turning pages to peruse even more after that.

Oh dear, she thought.

Every rendering was some version of Sam Winston. Not just the gangly boy in the photograph, but clearly Abby's own ideas of what he could have looked like as he aged. There was Sam with short hair, long hair, in a baseball cap, and balding; his face both unlined and with sharp creases at the mouth and nose; bespectacled and bearded.

Indeed, it was the bearded drawing that made Gretchen's breath catch. The sketch of an older Sam with gaunt cheeks and facial hair looked very much like the man lying on the parlor sofa. No wonder Abby had gotten as carried away as she had. She doubtless felt like she'd seen a dream come to life.

Or a ghost turned to flesh.

Gretchen pressed the sketchbook to her chest and sighed deeply. She felt completely responsible for fostering Abby's obsession, for causing her daughter to wish for something that she'd never really had to begin with.

Because what Abby didn't know was that the lanky teen sitting on the steps in her treasured photograph—and the subject of all her fanciful drawings—was not the man who'd fathered her that summer night so long ago. That story was one Gretchen had never told to Annika or Sam's folks, not even her sisters. At the time, it had seemed far, far easier to lie about what had happened than to confess what a fool she'd been. Only suddenly it was beginning to feel an awful lot like that lie was coming back to bite her squarely in the ass.

The Gift

We must believe that we are gifted for something, and that this thing, at whatever cost, must be attained.

—MARIE CURIE

SIX

1930s

Henry "Hank" Littlefoot was a bona fide descendant of the Otoe-Missouria tribes—a full-blooded Native American and the grandson of a shaman. He was also Sam Winston's maternal grandfather. Born in 1915, Hank was one of a few hundred Otoe-Missourias still in existence; the tribes had been pushed out of land they'd once called home, resettled into the Oklahoma Territory.

A handsome boy who learned to read by age four, Hank began making up tales of his own once he'd read his way through the meager stack of books on the shelves of the reservation's one-room schoolhouse. By the time he had turned twelve, he'd become enraptured by the art of storytelling and regularly entertained the younger children, mixing ancestral folklore and yarns spun from his own imagination.

By his teens, he knew that he wanted to be on the stage, not exactly an aspiration that either of his parents seemed to understand. "You belong here. This is your world," his father had told him and looked him sternly in the face. "On the day you were born, the sky filled with lightning. A bolt struck the roof and nearly set the house on fire. It's the sign of a shaman," he'd insisted. "You have the gift, my son." With that, he'd gripped his son's shoulder, where Hank's skin bore a birthmark the shape of a teardrop. "My father had the mark as well. You're meant to heal, not to play roles on a stage." His pa had grunted unhappily, shaking his head. He was a mechanic on the reservation, which involved a different type of healing entirely. "You will be a voice to the spirits someday, whether you like it or not."

A voice to the spirits, eh?

Hank wasn't convinced. For much of his life, he'd watched his grandfather mix healing potions and pastes and perform rituals meant to cleanse evil spirits, draw the soul to peace, or cajole the forces of nature to aid in hunts or harvests. The more his grandfather gave, the more he suffered, and Hank wanted none of that, particularly when he realized the risks involved—when he understood that to cure sometimes meant great sacrifice, as when his grandfather contracted influenza from a family he'd tried to heal and the disease had killed him, taking Hank's grandmother as well.

But even those fears didn't lessen Hank's respect for the powerful acts he had witnessed. When his grandpa had performed his brand of "magic," Hank had believed as much as anyone else.

"I'm no shaman," Hank told his folks, because he didn't feel anointed by any gift save for his physical ones: the chiseled jaw; the strong, straight nose; the width of his shoulders; and his formidable height. If there was anything especially spiritual about him, he figured he hadn't grown into it yet. "I have to go," he'd insisted. "I don't feel like I belong here. I have to find my own way."

Sad as they were to see him leave, his parents did not stop him.

Hank didn't fancy living his life the Otoe-Missouria way any more than he wished to live the white man's way. He just wanted to do things *his* way.

So that was precisely what he did.

Since opportunities in the theater for men like him—meaning, with colored skin—were virtually nonexistent, he made a conscious decision to get his foot in the door any way that he could. After fruitlessly following leads in local news-papers and countless auditions with often cruel rejections, he met a man in St. Louis who managed a vaudeville troupe that traveled from the upper Midwest down to Texas, performing "Incredibly Entertaining Feats of Daring, Comedy, and Bur-lesque." *Wilbur Coonts's Caravan of Wonders*, it was called, hardly lacking in hyperbole.

Coonts had advertised for a thespian whose skills extended to wearing greasepaint and a headdress, portraying an Indian chief with a daughter who dances her way into the heart of a lonesome cowboy. Yes, the plot was trite, demeaning even. But Hank would have done just about anything at that point to get a toe in the door.

He showed up in ceremonial buckskin and turquoise beads for the audition, his dark hair braided and embellished with a single eagle feather, although his attire paled in comparison to the costumes worn by dozens of others, all Caucasians in "war paint," black wigs, and enormous headdresses. Hank watched from the wings as each actor took his place center stage, more than willing to spit out the "you, cowboy, me, Indian," routine.

When it was Hank's turn, he realized he couldn't do it. He couldn't utter the offensive dialogue without getting sick to his stomach. So he shucked the script, instead telling a vivid tale of his shaman grandfather who could make it rain and heal the ill. Then he proceeded to dance in a small circle, chanting words he'd memorized from childhood, doing an abbreviated and exaggerated version of the tribal rain dance.

When he was done, his face dripping sweat, Coonts was on his feet. His face beet red, he dismissed the others and waved Hank down from the stage. Hank braced himself, certain he was about to be browbeaten for refusing to play the part as written or, worse, for the color of his skin.

Instead, Coonts tucked his thumbs into his suspenders, rocking back on his spats.

"That was the bee's knees, kid," the stout, balding fellow told him and clapped him on the shoulder, grinning. "Better than anything I could have written."

"So am I hired?" Hank asked, hardly willing to believe it.

"Something like that, yes."

Coonts agreed to take him on for two months—at half pay—to see how things went. "As long as I'm happy, you'll stay," his new boss told him, and they sealed the deal with a handshake. Hank got his own act, aptly labeled "Chief Littlefoot's Authentic Rain-Making Ceremony," portraying an Indian shaman in the vaudeville show.

Of course, the main thrust of Hank's performance was making it rain in the theater, a bit that was full of pageantry and intensity, as well as smoke and mirrors. While stagehands worked the lights and sound to simulate the crackle of lightning and pounding of thunder, Hank shuffled in a circle on the stage, wearing buckskin and a full headdress—Coonts insisted on the latter—chanting the words he'd memorized from hearing his grandfather utter them time and again during droughts on the reservation. With the magic of dry ice and fans and an improvised sprinkler system rigged up above, soon a misty rain began to drizzle onto the tarp-covered boards. The audience ate it up, often giving him a standing ovation, even though they had to know the spectacle was merely sleight of hand, not a miracle.

"But you *do* make it rain, Hank," Nadya Celeste, the magician's doe-eyed assistant, told him one evening when he took her out for coffee at a twenty-four-hour diner after the show, requiring a shared umbrella as a light shower fell upon them from the evening sky. "Haven't you noticed it's always wet after your performance?"

"No," Hank told her, because he hadn't thought anything of it, not until she had pointed it out.

But when he began to pay attention, he realized she was right: every time without fail, no matter how clear the night was to begin with, it would be raining outside when the theater emptied. Sometimes it was no more than a drizzle; at other times, water came down in buckets. And it never seemed to reach more than a few blocks beyond the venue.

"It could be coincidence," he suggested, but Nadya didn't agree.

"What if it's not? Maybe what you do is more than an act. Maybe you have a real gift," she said, echoing what his father had once told him.

Hank didn't want to admit that he felt something quite beyond the ordinary when he did the rain dance, a kind of current rushing through him, a sense of being outside himself and part of the air around him. If he'd tried to explain that to Nadya, she would've thought he was insane.

So he just smiled and squeezed her gloved hand, thinking the only gift he truly wanted was to make enough money to buy some land, build a house, and ask her to marry him. Then he could wake up to her dimples and wide eyes every morning, and he'd never have to deal with Wilbur Coonts again.

When his probationary eight weeks had passed, Hank went to see Coonts and asked for more money, and not just the usual rate. He knew by the ads Coonts had been running in the newspapers that "Chief Littlefoot's Authentic Rain-Making Ceremony" was the show's biggest draw.

He even lied and told Coonts he'd had an offer from a rival vaudeville troupe, a remark that instantly quieted the man. His boss rubbed fat fingers together before nodding his double chin. "So long as the box office keeps coming in, I'll pay you what you ask. But the public's a fickle bunch, Littlefoot, and if they tire of you, your check will be the first I cut in half."

Hank was hardly worried about the crowds losing interest. In fact, they only seemed to swell, and Coonts added shows in Omaha and Springfield, Leavenworth and Salina, Peoria and Des Moines. Every night, Hank found more folks standing outside the venues, farmers in coveralls with grim faces who waited for him in the damp after the theater lights dimmed.

"We haven't had rain in two months," one would step forward and say. "My crops are turning to dust. I'll give you whatever I've got if you'll come do your tricks on my land and make the sky loosen up."

At first, Hank wasn't sure what to do with this newfound attention. He would mumble, "I'm sorry, but I can't help you," and hurry off with one hand clutching Nadya and the other his umbrella.

Then the letters started arriving, at first in a trickle and then in a flood so great that Coonts turned red-faced, stuck his thumbs inside his vest, and blustered at him, "For God's sake, Littlefoot, if you can make it rain outside the theaters every damned night we have a show, don't you figure you can give these poor bastards a shot?"

But the theater was the theater, Hank knew. Playing God with people's lives was something else entirely.

"I can't do it," he said, shaking his head, because he wasn't his grandfather. He hadn't even stayed true to his native roots. If his father realized what he was doing, he would doubtless be ashamed. Because what Hank did was pretend. He didn't know how to talk to the Great Spirit, to any spirit, not really. His gift was mimicry, not magic.

Then even Nadya began to nudge him, stroking his hair and whispering in his ear, "Aren't you curious, my sweet? Don't you want to see if you can make the sky listen to you speak?" She touched the teardrop-shaped mark on his bare shoulder. "If you can't do it, then at least you'll know for certain, yes?"

"But what if I flop? What if they see I'm a sham?" he said, because onstage he *performed;* he didn't control the weather. The fact that it was damp outside when he finished could be no more than dumb luck or coincidence.

"The only way you can know is to try," she told him.

"What if they put their faith in me, and I fail?" he asked.

She merely shrugged and smiled, assuring him, "Then I will love you still, no matter what."

So Hank bit the bullet and agreed to perform a ceremonial dance on a farm outside Jefferson City, Missouri, when Wilbur Coonts's Caravan of Wonders decamped there for a week of gigs at a theater in the state capital.

Though a solitary cloud hung over the downtown that evening, spitting out a hint of moisture as Hank left through the stage door and got into a waiting pickup with a farmer named Bert Peckinpaw, once they were a couple blocks beyond the venue, the sky was clear and full of stars.

The road out to the farm was all gravel and as bumpy as a camel's back. With the window rolled down to let in the hot breeze, Hank felt covered by a layer of silt by the time they arrived.

"Can I get you anything, Chief Littlefoot?" Peckinpaw asked once they'd exited the truck.

Hank cringed at being called "Chief" outside his vaudeville act. It felt downright sacrilegious. "No, just leave me be, and I'll find you when I'm done."

It was a sultry June night and dry as a bone, the ground so parched cracks ran through the dirt like empty veins. Hank did ask Peckinpaw to keep his kin and any curiosity seekers away. He hadn't even wanted Nadya to come along because he was too nervous.

Why was he even doing this? To prove something to himself? To see if he really had the gift as his father insisted, or conversely to prove his father wrong?

Whatever the reason, it was too late to turn back. Hank stood in the parched grass near the anemic-looking stalks of corn spread out before him in a gently undulating wall. He felt the scant breeze on his face and gazed up at the stars, knowing he had no props to make the weather change. He had only faith in himself, which was hardly unshakable. He hoped the Great Spirit would be generous and not dismissive of him for using the rain dance in his act for entertainment. If he could not provoke the thunder and lightning, he would fail, and that would be that.

With a sigh, Hank touched the single eagle feather woven into his hair to symbolize the wind and then the leather cord with the turquoise beads tied around his throat, the stones a symbol of the rain. Finally, he spread out his arms and took in a deep breath.

"Grandfather," he said quietly, "if you're in the clouds watching me now, please, don't laugh and think me a fool. I'd appreciate a little help, if you're not too busy. I just want to know if I have this great blessing my father talked about. If it's true, I need to use it."

The stars merely winked at him, and the warm air rustled through the field, setting the stalks of maize to whispering; but he heard no laughter, no sign that they were mocking him.

With a grunt, he began to shuffle, his feet light as they moved in a circle, stirring up dust from the dry earth. He chanted words he knew well, ones he'd heard in the ceremonies of his childhood, calling upon the spirits of the land and the heavens to bring the rain.

Hank fell into a trancelike rhythm as he danced, his thoughts becoming one with his intuition; his blood flowing fiercely through his veins, charging the air around him; his heartbeat pulsing outward as though speaking the language of the earth and the stars. A fierce connection gripped him, his soul attaching to the sky and the dirt; electricity surged through his limbs the more he moved, until he sensed something bigger than himself bubbling up. Beneath his doeskin moccasins, the parched ground trembled.

Then the sky darkened and crackled, rippling with the boom of thunder, powered by flashes of lightning so bright that Hank saw the silver bolts through his eyelids even when he closed his eyes. But when he opened wide and glanced up, there were no clouds in sight, nothing to obscure the same stars he'd glimpsed when he'd first arrived. The light and the noise may as well have been stage tricks.

It was as before: barely a tepid breeze to stir the heat, the chirp of crickets, and the anxious throb of his own heartbeat.

But nothing more.

Whatever caused the rain to come outside the venues when he performed—if he had anything to do with that at all—seemed not to be working here. Perhaps his only gift was in making a fool of himself.

Drenched in sweat, his dark hair stuck to his skull and neck, Hank gathered up his things and trudged back to Bert Peckinpaw's house. The whole family seemed to be waiting on the porch and each face looked crestfallen when Hank said to them, "I'm sorry. I did my best, but it didn't work."

"It's all right." The farmer shrugged. "I figured it was a long shot. So what do I owe you? It's only fair considering you came all the way out here for nothing."

All the way out here for nothing.

The words stung, but Hank kept his chin up. "You don't owe me a dime," he said and climbed in the cab of the pickup truck, hanging his arm out the window and feeling miserable as they headed back into town, to the rat-trap hotel where Coonts had put up the troupe.

They'd barely gotten a half mile down the dusty road when Hank felt the first plop of moisture on the back of his hand. And then another and another after that.

He turned his gaze toward the windshield and stared as drops began to quickly splatter, gathering force and turning larger until they were caught in one hell of a downpour.

"Holy cow!" Hank whooped and stuck both hands out the window, the wind rushing at him as he caught the rain in his palms and wiped the damp on his face. It shocked his system, feeling the wet, knowing it was real and that he was very likely responsible.

I did it, he said to himself again and again. *I did it!*

"Is that what I think it is?" Bert Peckinpaw said and started breathing roughly, like a man about to hyperventilate. "I can't goddamn see," he cursed, but he had a smile on his face as he pulled hard on the steering wheel, jerking the truck off to the shoulder of the road and hitting the brakes.

Hank threw his palms against the dashboard, fighting to stay in his seat, both of them breathing hard once they'd stopped. And still the rain sluiced down upon the truck, the steady patter sounding like a tap dance on the roof.

For a long moment, they just sat there in the truck's cab: Bert staring at the blur of the windshield, his noisy breaths steaming up the glass, and Hank shaking his head, equally stunned by the turn of events.

Then the farmer turned to Hank and blurted out, "My God, Chief, you did it! You goddamned did it! I knew you could. I knew it!" And he leaned over toward Hank, pulling him into a bear hug and patting his back so hard Hank felt the wind knocked out of him.

Finally the rain slowed to a drizzle, enough so that Bert could drive him safely back to his hotel in town. As Hank got out of the truck, the farmer said, "I won't ever forget this, Littlefoot. I'll be around the stage door tomorrow to pay you back."

"You don't need to give me anything," Hank told him, so drained that it was all he could do to shut the door and wave as Bert drove off. He dragged himself up the steps and through the dingy lobby to the second-floor room he'd been secretly sharing with Nadya. He saw the light beneath the door before he unlocked it and stepped inside.

"You did it, didn't you?" she said from the bed, where she sat, propped up against the pillows. "You made it rain. Geez Louise, you made it pour!"

"I guess I did," he replied and gazed down at the water spots on his buckskin, pulling the damp feather from his hair. He got his shirt off and swayed, suddenly dizzy, as the life seemed to drain from his limbs.

Nadya sprang from the mattress and grabbed him, holding him up as she walked him to the bed. "Are you all right?"

"I don't know," he mumbled, unable to focus. The room blurred before his eyes as he leaned back against the pillows. "I'm so tired," he whispered. "I feel like I've had my guts sucked out."

"Hank, are you okay? You're burning up. Hank?"

He thought he heard her saying his name, imagined he felt her cool hand upon his brow, but he fast sank away into nothingness.

As he slept, he had the most vivid dreams: of an eagle whose wings beat like thunder against the sky and whose yellow eyes shot bolts of lightning to the ground. He walked through a field of tall grass lit afire to find his grandfather awaiting him, dressed like a farmer in denim and plaid, feathers braided into dove-white hair, smiling at him, his weathered face cracking. "This is not a game," he heard him say. "Such power is not to be trifled with. Take it seriously, young one. Do not become greedy because of it. Know that it will take its toll on you until you have no more to give. Before it does, walk away."

And then his grandfather was gone, leaving Hank standing alone in the dark as the fires went out and rain began falling around him.

SEVEN

When Hank opened his eyes, a pink sky filtered through the flimsy shades on the windows. He grunted, sitting up, figuring it was dawn. He swung his legs around so his feet touched the floor, wincing as every muscle he moved throbbed and ached.

"You're awake!" Nadya was instantly beside him. Her brow was creased with worry. "I thought you'd never get up. I was getting scared. I nearly called for the doctor."

He touched her cheek. "But it's still early," he said. "Did you think I'd sleep the day away?"

"But you have," she assured him and stared, head cocked, as if he'd missed the punch line of a well-told joke. "The day is all but gone. It's already sundown," she said, and he realized she was wearing her corseted magician's assistant costume with the bustle, short enough to show off her long legs in fishnet stockings. "You've been out like a light for almost twenty-four hours. Even Coonts came in and tried to wake you. You missed the matinee, and he was furious! The crowd almost started a riot!"

"I missed a show? How could that be?" Hank had never missed a show in all the months he'd been traveling with Coonts's company.

Unnerved, he got up and switched on the bedside lamp. Then he turned and caught his reflection in the mirror. "What the devil—" he started to say, touching his head, his eyes widening at the sight of a white streak running through his hair from scalp to ends that hadn't been there before. And the teardrop birthmark on his left shoulder itched and appeared swollen. It was definitely larger than it had been.

What had happened to him? Was it the rain dance? Had it affected him physically, aging him as he'd slept?

"Are you all right?" Nadya asked, slim brow creased. "You're scaring me."

Hank wasn't anywhere close to being okay. Something had happened to him. He felt like he'd had no rest despite apparently having dozed through an entire day. But he gave Nadya a smile. "I'm fine."

"You think you can go on tonight?"

"Yes," he said without thinking, because he knew Coonts would can him if he missed the evening show, too, no matter if he was the rainmaker.

Despite the shakiness in his limbs and the fog in his head, he got up and showered, put some food in his belly, and donned his costume. By the time they left the room, Hank felt almost as good as new. The sidewalk warmed the soles of his shoes as he and Nadya set off for the theater, walking the handful of blocks through the thick summer heat. Hank could sense the lingering static in the air from the previous night; the vibration made his skin prickle.

As they came around the corner of the building, strolling hand in hand toward the rear entrance, Nadya nudged him, alerting him to the crowd of several dozen gathered there. Some were the grim-faced farmers he'd gotten so used to seeing, begging at once for him to save their drought-stricken crops, promising him everything from land to their daughters' hands if he'd do it. And there were others who shouted, "Where were you this afternoon, Chief? We paid good money to see you, and we had to watch a dancing dog take your place!"

The farmers may have looked desperate, but the disappointed ticket holders shook their fists and frowned. Money was so very tight, and they were clearly angry. He addressed them first.

"I'll get you tickets for tonight," Hank told them as he approached.

"It's sold out!" a woman cried. "And the troupe leaves tomorrow!"

"I'm sorry," Hank said, their scowling faces surrounding him. He touched his hair where the white streak had appeared. "I didn't mean to miss the show, but I was taken ill—"

"Leave the chief alone!"

Suddenly, there was the farmer, Bert Peckinpaw, pushing his way through the scrum, stepping forward in his overalls, his straw-colored hair askew, a grateful smile on his face. "Littlefoot saved my crops last night," he announced. "And I've come today with compensation for his services." He fixed his deeply lined eyes on Hank. "You never gave me a dollar sum, and we're a bit tight right now until the harvest. But I hope you'll take what I offer as a small token of my gratitude."

With that, he looked behind him and whistled. The crowd shifted as two boys came forward, one towing two goats on rope leads and the other holding a pair of squawking chickens by their feet.

Hank stood without speaking, uncertain of what to say. He thought of his grandfather and all the times his efforts at healing had brought him beaded moccasins, whiskey, woven blankets, and, even once, a half-tamed wolf.

"Thank you," he finally uttered, taking the tethered goats from one boy while the other proceeded to stuff the pair of chickens into Nadya's arms. "I'm honored to accept your gifts."

"Hell, Chief, you've given me a second chance," Bert Peckinpaw told him with a pat on his back. "You saved my family."

In that moment, Hank understood what his father had been trying to tell him before he'd left the reservation. The gift his grandfather had passed down to him was deserving of more than a few minutes in the spotlight of a vaudeville stage.

That night after his performance—when he'd left the theater with Nadya, sharing his umbrella in the rain—Hank realized with sudden clarity that his days with Coonts's traveling show were numbered. Over multiple cups of coffee, he and Nadya sat in a booth at the nearest diner and began to make plans, deciding they would stay on just long enough for him to visit more farms along the road, to see if what he'd done for Bert Peckinpaw could be repeated, to save enough money so they could begin a family. Hank wanted nothing more than for Nadya to put away the corseted and bustled costumes forever and marry him. He would take only enough money to plant the seeds for their new life. He would not become greedy, as his grandfather had warned in his dream.

Once he had squirreled away a sufficient nest egg, he could

retire his "gift" and settle down. He wanted nothing more than to be out of the public eye so he could own some land on which he could grow both a crop and a family.

But getting out from under Coonts's thumb might prove even more difficult than getting in.

EIGHT

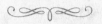

Six months later, after a hundred more vaudeville shows and a dozen privately arranged rain-making ceremonies in Kansas, Oklahoma, and Texas, Hank's black hair had gone completely white. The teardrop stain on his shoulder had become darker and larger, so much so that Nadya worried that it was infected. His taut cheeks became weathered, pinched at the corners of his mouth and eyes. He had the countenance of a much older man when he was not even thirty.

But Hank understood his power now. He knew what he could do and how to control it. He had learned how to call up the lightning and thunder, how to make a gentle rain or even a downpour if he so desired. And more amazing still, he had twice conjured up a beast of a storm, full of such fury that the wind spun in funnels, stirring black clouds that kicked up plumes of dirt where they touched the earth.

Had his grandfather been able to summon the spirits in such a way? Or were Hank's powers even stronger? Perhaps his gift was greater than he knew.

"You can't do this much longer. Your body can't take it," Nadya said one day, confessing her concern for him. "This isn't normal, Hank. Who knows what could happen to you?"

Hank didn't have an answer. Anything could happen. Nothing could happen. All he knew was that each ceremony took something from him that he never regained: a mix of his strength and energy, even his youth. Every rainmaking drained him beyond reason, and he would collapse afterward, falling into a weary stupor, sometimes for hours but often for days. The past few times when he'd awakened, he couldn't remember where he was or *who* he was. Even if Nadya reminded him, it was often an hour or more before the missing pieces returned, falling back into place. He understood all too well how much that worried the woman he loved. He had to admit that it worried him, too.

"Just a few more, and we'll be set," Hank assured Nadya and took her hand, squeezing. "I'm doing this for us, remember? For our future."

But she looked like she didn't believe him. "If you don't stop soon, I'm afraid it will kill you. There is nothing else to prove, is there? And we have enough money to leave. We don't need much to live on besides."

Hank knew she was right. These days, he hardly recognized himself in the mirror. He seemed to have turned into an old man overnight. And what *did* he have to prove at this point? He had become a big draw in the world of vaudeville, so much so that Coonts began dropping hints about giving Hank a show of his own, a Wild West troupe of which he'd be the star. But Hank wasn't about to sell any more of his soul, not even for buckets of money. It was more about getting his due and then getting out. He'd had stories written about him in small-town newspapers, had received telegrams from women he hadn't met proposing marriage, and had been presented with enough livestock that he could have populated his own farm. Instead, he'd sold each and every goat, pig, duck, hen, and burro, tucking away the cash in a leather belt he wore around his waist and rarely took off.

Inside the money belt, he kept something else as important: the deed to land in Walnut Ridge, Missouri, given to him by a grateful farmer whose crops he'd saved with a good hard drenching. "It's a parcel I inherited from a cousin, but I can't do nothing with it. I'm stretched enough as it is," the man had told him. "Besides, it's all I have that's worth something."

It was more than enough as far as Hank was concerned. It gave him the chance to make plans, real plans, which didn't include going back to the reservation. He had never fit in with his people; he'd always dreamed of leaving for somewhere better, a place he could make his own. Not only did the deed to the Missouri farm give him that, but he intended to take Nadya with him as soon as they could leave, especially since her costumes were becoming noticeably snug. When he helped to corset her in, he had to leave the stays wider and wider. She wasn't far along into the pregnancy—two months, by her best estimate—but then she was slender, leaving little room to mask her growing waistline. Soon it would be impossible to hide, at which point the jig would be up whether they were ready to leave the troupe or not. There was no room for a woman with a baby in vaudeville.

When morning sickness struck Nadya so badly she could barely stand and smile, faking her way through the magician's set without running off the stage to puke, Hank decided it was time to talk to his boss. On the morning after the first of three sold-out shows in Omaha, he determinedly knocked on Coonts's hotel room door, hoping he'd find him in a generous mood. He meant to ease into the conversation, but it didn't work out quite the way he planned.

"I appreciate my time with the show, but my run is nearly over," he said without prelude, instinctively touching the new-found lines on his face. "I can't keep up the pace, and I'm not sure I want to. I'm growing old before my time, and I need to live my life before it's too late."

"On the contrary, son, I believe your run with the show has barely begun. As for that white hair and shopworn look"— Coonts shrugged, hardly appearing as upset as Nadya about Hank's transformation—"they only make you appear more legit. It's time you let me convince you that this Wild West show is your future. *Our* future," his boss told him, flushed and bright-eyed from counting the previous night's receipts. "There's a lot of money to be made before the tide turns and the crowds want a dancing pig instead of a rain-making Injun."

Hank's mouth went dry. He didn't care about the money. He was tired, plain and simple: tired of performing and of using a sacred tradition as entertainment. Maybe it hadn't bothered him so much in the beginning when he was hell-bent on making a name for himself, but it weighed on him now.

"You have your dreams," he told Coonts, "and I have mine. They're not one and the same." He shook his head. "I'll stay with the troupe through this last leg and finish the dates, but that's it." He wasn't willing to risk any more than he already had simply to plump Coonts's bank account. "After Omaha and Des Moines, I'm done and so is Nadya."

"Is that right?" His boss clasped fingers over the straining vest buttons on his belly, his thick eyebrows coming to a peak as he stared at Hank point-blank. "Our deal was that you're in my act as long as I'm happy, and I'm happy as a pig in swill. We shook on it. You're not going back on your word now, are you, Chief?"

"But it was all on your terms! I don't remember getting a say in things," Hank said, frustration rattling his voice.

"That's right, boy. You didn't." Coonts's eyes narrowed on Hank, as if daring him to put up a stink. "So get any wild ideas of running off out of your head," he added, waving a hand dismissively. "You and your gypsy whore are staying put until I say otherwise. You got that?"

Gypsy whore?

"What did you say?" Hank blinked.

"You think I don't know what's going on with you two? Hell, boy, I've got eyes." Coonts laughed. "I know she's in the family way. She doesn't exactly fit her costumes the way she used to, and don't think I haven't noticed how green she is around the gills, too. I'm already casting for her replacement."

"You're firing her?"

"You heard me," Coonts said and smiled in a way that proved he'd gotten the reaction he wanted. "Pretty girls willing to show off their gams and hold magicians' props are a dime a dozen. I may just wake up tomorrow and decide she's out on the street. And if you don't want my lawyers dragging your red-cheeked ass into court for breach of contract, you'd better put up and shut up until I decide otherwise."

Hank stood mutely, so incensed he couldn't speak.

"Now get the hell out of here and grab some sleep." Coonts gave a nod, as if Hank's silence meant he'd given in. "I think we're done yapping."

Oh, I'm done all right, Hank decided and left the room, taking off as fast as he could before his heart leaped from his chest, before his hands somehow ended up around Coonts's neck. How had the fat man turned the tables so quickly? Instead of allowing Hank to peacefully resign, Coonts had made it all about control.

And Hank didn't appreciate being reminded that he wasn't the one who held the cards in this particular game.

Of course, he told Nadya nothing of the confrontation. Instead, he acted as if Coonts had given them both the green light to electively depart the caravan and start their new lives.

"I think we should pack our bags now," he said as she pressed her small hands to his chest, such an eager smile on her face that Hank hated to lie. "If all goes well, we may leave tonight."

That evening when he performed onstage, he was keenly aware of Coonts in the box seats on the balcony to his left. As he chanted and danced, the same anger that had arisen within him in Coonts's hotel room swirled inside his blood like a fever. The more he tried to bury it, the larger it got, until a mounting pressure swelled in his head as words came out of his mouth that he'd never meant to say, ancient phrases that came from somewhere deep in his subconscious, pleas for the sky and earth to feel the same fury he felt, for the spirits to rise up and assert their true power over man.

Answering his call, the theater lights began to flicker and

thunder rumbled through the building, swaying the lamps above and shaking the stage beneath Hank's feet. The audience gasped and applauded, awestruck, as if it were all part of the act, concocted purely for their enjoyment.

Until the air inside picked up strength and lifted paper programs and wayward kerchiefs, flinging them upward and rotating them like a twister. Above Hank's head, the velvet curtains billowed and the fog from the dry ice blowers dissipated in the swirl of wind. As a white-hot choler seared his heart, Hank begged the Great Spirit for lightning to strike Coonts's box. His final, unforgettable act.

Within seconds, a ball of fire appeared out of nowhere, hitting the pillar positioned just beneath Coonts's box. The flames licked at the painted column below, spitting upward toward the balcony as smoke belched and the audience coughed.

"Help!" people screamed, but Hank barely heard them. He focused solely on Wilbur Coonts, suddenly on his feet and backing away from the gray clouds billowing from below. The man's mouth moved, cursing him, but his voice was lost in the howl of wind and the frantic cries of the audience.

Hank willed the wind to toss Coonts over the brass rail and into the fire below. As he watched, an invisible hand bent Coonts over the banister while the frightened man desperately tried to hang on.

"Stop this!" Hands grabbed at Hank's arm, and there was Nadya's voice, sharp in his ear. "Please," she begged him, "stop it now!"

Somehow the touch of her hand and the fear in her tone doused the fury inside him, and Hank went still, breathing hard, the swirl of air settling down until the conflagration went out and the howling winds ceased. Though the panicked audience still cried out as they pushed their way toward the exit doors, inside Hank's mind, all went deathly quiet.

Though the silence existed only for a moment before Coonts began to shake his fist and yell, "You're done, Chief, you hear me? You're finished in vaudeville!"

Hank met Nadya's eyes, and his own filled with tears. "I'm sorry," he meant to say, only no sound came out. Still, she seemed to know just what he said.

"Let's go," she whispered and reached out her hand.

Hank nodded, doing as she bid and hurrying after her as they slipped out a side door to avoid any crowds gathered outside the stage door. Huddled together, heads ducked against the torrential rain, they hurried back to the hotel.

When he asked Nadya to grab her things and leave with him, she did just that, never questioning, simply trusting him.

Within minutes, they had gathered what they could carry and descended via the fire escape so as not to be seen. Once they'd reached the alley below, they scurried away from the dingy building toward the bus station. Hank bought two tickets on the last bus out of Omaha bound for St. Joseph, Missouri. They arrived just before dawn and changed buses en route to Kansas City.

By afternoon, they'd caught a train bound for Washington, Missouri, the closest spot to Walnut Ridge that Hank could find on a map.

By the time they arrived, the light of day was exhausted, the plum of dusk slowly staining the once-blue sky. With a bit of cajoling, they begged a ride in a hay-filled Ford pickup and were jostled atop the bales for several miles until they reached the outskirts of Walnut Ridge. The fellow dropped them off beside a decrepit wooden mailbox on the shoulder of the unpaved rural route.

"You sure this is the old Hansen place?" Hank asked the man, who gave him a solemn nod.

"It was, at least until a decade back when the Hansens died off and left it to some distant cousin. You the new owners?" he asked, squinting at them.

"Yes," Hank said, "I guess we are."

"Well, good luck then," the fellow grunted. "You'll need it if you aim to bring this place back to life. It's been nigh on dead for years." Then he took off, the thin tires kicking up a cloud of dust.

Hank carried their bags as they trudged down a weed-choked gravel drive on the patch of land that now belonged to him. From what he could see through the dusk, it wasn't much. The beams of a full moon showered gauzy light enough to discern a tiny house, barely more than a shack. Beyond stood the gnarled shapes of trees in what had to be the walnut grove. Why did everything look so sad and overgrown? Was it merely the night and fatigue warping his view? Or had nothing been cared for or loved in so long? Either way, he would find out in the morning, when the light of day showed him the truth about the farm.

He heard a series of soft clucks and wondered if any chickens had been left behind to fend for themselves, turning as wild as the rest of the farm.

"So this is ours?" Nadya asked.

"All twenty acres of neglect," Hank replied and tried not to wince, hoping she wasn't too disappointed.

When they reached the end of the private lane, when they stood at the foot of the broken-down steps leading up to the ramshackle porch, Hank felt gripped by a horrible panic. Was there still a working well so they'd have water to drink and cook with and clean themselves? Was there a chair to sit upon, a bed on which to sleep? He doubted there were electric lights or even rudimentary plumbing, at least not any that worked properly.

Though Nadya nudged him forward, Hank couldn't move. He set down their bags, truly wanting to weep.

"I didn't realize what kind of shape the property would be in. I didn't even think to ask—" he started to say, so disheartened he could barely breathe, only to stop short at the touch of Nadya's hand on his arm and the sound of her sigh.

"But it's yours and mine, yes?" she said again.

And he nodded, giving her a definitive "Yes."

He could see her smile through the dark. She reached for his hand and set it on the slight swell of her belly, holding it there. The warmth of her skin seeped into his. "It's our home, the three of us," she told him. "No matter what it looks like now, there's nowhere else I'd rather be."

Hank sighed, too grateful to speak.

"Come on." She drew him up the creaking steps and through the unlocked door, batting at cobwebs and bumping into the shadows.

NINE

Hank did the best he could that first night to make the place habitable. With only the glow of an oil lamp to guide them, he cleared debris and removed discolored sheets from the few pieces of furniture that remained. He beat the dust from the straw-filled mattress that sat atop the creaky springs of a paint-chipped iron bed.

Neither of them slept much. Instead, Nadya rested her head on his chest, and he put his arms around her as they whispered in the dark.

Once the day finally dawned, they got up quickly and dressed. While Nadya plundered cabinets in the kitchen, searching for anything canned to open for breakfast, Hank did a cursory walk around the grounds, poking his head into the broken-down barn, assessing the battered chicken coop, and taking stock of the barren-looking walnut trees before he headed the five miles into town on foot. Once there, he found the nearest church with a breadline and hired the first three men he met who said they were willing and able to work with their hands. Then he went to the general store and bought nonperishable foodstuffs for delivery to the farm, enough to last them several weeks. He purchased tools at the hardware store and wire to mend the chicken coop. Hank even found a donkey for sale, one that he was sure could pull the old buggy he'd spied half buried behind moldy hay bales in the barn.

On that day and every day after, he and Nadya labored from dawn to dusk: she scrubbed and sewed while he hammered, repaired, and painted. The small crew that Hank had cobbled together became indispensable, so much so that they set up bunks in the barn once that building got patched up so they could stretch their working hours.

Several months after, with the tiny house finally livable and bright and the barn nearly ready for livestock, the only trouble spots remaining for Hank were the walnut trees themselves. No matter what kind of advice he got—no matter that he pruned the old trees and planted seedlings to grow new ones—nothing seemed to flourish in the grove. The only thing he could see growing day to day was Nadya's burgeoning belly.

When he told her what he had to do, she tried to talk him out of it at first.

"You can't perform another ceremony," she said point-blank, pacing the newly sanded floor of their sparsely furnished parlor. "Every time you do, it drains the life out of you. What if you don't recover this time around?"

"I'm not going to leave you, if that's what you're worried about," he assured her as he wove an eagle feather into the single plait of his hair. "But I need to ask for help, more than anyone in Walnut Ridge can give."

"I don't like this," Nadya murmured, hands rubbing circles on her belly. "I don't like it at all."

"One last time, and then I'm through," he promised and finished fastening the strand of turquoise around his neck, giving her a thin smile.

"One last time," she repeated sternly and didn't smile back.

The deep purple of dusk filled the windows as he kissed her and left the farmhouse, his doeskin moccasins quiet on the patched porch steps, his movements blending into the shadows. He avoided the barn, where the laborers had settled for the evening, skirting the chicken coop as well to avoid unsettling the birds, which might in turn wake the hands. He didn't need the men spying on him and tattling in town that Hank Littlefoot was prancing around after dark, performing mystical mumbo jumbo, or whatever they might call it. He knew folks were already gossiping about the "pregnant gypsy woman" and the "long-haired Indian" who'd taken over the Hansen farm. For the most part, he seemed to get on well enough with those he encountered. No one in Walnut Ridge recognized him from his vaudeville days, and the last thing he needed was to draw attention to himself.

Hank moved unseen through the falling dark until he was amidst the gnarled walnut trees with their peeling bark and twisted limbs. For a while, he merely walked amongst them, touching their trunks with gentle hands and whispering reassurance, telling them not to be afraid.

"You will be reborn tonight," he promised them, and he didn't let himself believe otherwise.

What Hank desired most wasn't a heavy rain or winds. He needed lightning to hit the grove, not just once, but many times. His goal was not to burn down the barren trees but to give them a rebirth. He'd often heard his grandfather say that a lightning strike worked magic on the soil, causing plants to thrive and become greener and stronger. Hank figured the walnut grove was as good as dead, the earth unyielding as if it had been poisoned. If he and Nadya were going to support themselves on the farm, they needed a crop to harvest. It was up to him to make it happen, and he was determined that this was the path.

So Hank did what he had done dozens of times before. He began to chant and rhythmically shuffle in a circle beneath the stars, calling on the Great Spirit to send down lightning upon the land, to enrich the dirt and make the walnut trees flourish. He made an oath that he would care for the earth as if it were his own child, until he had no breath left in his body.

Please, he begged, *let me have this one last thing, and I will ask for no more.*

The chanted words and familiar motions soon put him into a trance so that he was unaware of the passage of time. He felt only the beat of his heart through his veins and the pulse of every living thing around him. The moon had risen high above and suddenly tugged at the air like a fierce ocean tide.

Hank ceased his dance at the first ripple of tension that whipped through the sky. As he looked up, sweat dripped down his brow and stuck the turquoise beads to his flesh. He swayed, so exhausted by his efforts he was sure his knees would buckle beneath him. But, somehow, he stayed upright.

In the heavens above, he saw brilliant veins of light pulse and disappear against the dark. Faint at first, their silver forks quickly lengthened and deepened, the electricity snapping and arcing, creating such a fierce illumination that Hank was temporarily blinded by the sight.

Thrown by an unseen hand, jagged spears of electricity shot to earth, hitting spots all about the grove, knocking Hank off his feet. He fell to the dirt just as a bolt split the gnarled tree nearest him and set its dry limbs ablaze.

The world seemed on fire around him, the air so alive that it breathed, brushing his cheek, tugging his hair, scattering sticks and twigs. A shadow winged its way past, and he blinked at the sight of an eagle, swooping down from the sky, eyes as yellow as the lightning.

"Grandfather," he said, and he smiled, sure the old man was there with him.

Hank could do no more. Now it was up to the spirits to finish the task.

He closed his eyes as the lightning strikes ceased and it began to rain, softly at first and then in earnest. He lay still as the water soaked through to his skin; he was too tired to move.

You have done your piece, he heard a voice say in his ear. *Now you are free.*

A heaviness washed over him, numbing his limbs and his mind, and Hank slid into a sleep so deep that three days slipped past before he awakened.

It was the noise of hammers driving nails that roused his senses, that and the smell of lemon and bleach, causing him to wrinkle his nose before he'd even opened his eyes. The bed springs creaking beneath him, he forced himself upright even though the fog had not completely lifted from his brain.

He ached something fierce, from his fingers to toes, and he realized the cause soon enough. Both his hands and feet were tightly bandaged in white cotton, salve oozing from the edges. Had he been burned?

"Hello?" he called out, his voice a mere croak. He tried again, hoping to be louder, but his dry throat merely turned the word into a whisper. "Hello?"

He momentarily panicked, heart racing; his gaze darted past the iron bed's foot-rail to the butter-colored walls and the simple oak dresser with the pitcher and basin atop it. Nothing seemed familiar. He had no clue how he'd come to be there or even who he was.

"Can anyone hear me?" he tried again, willing his aching body to move, but it didn't want to cooperate. Sitting up made him dizzy, and his shoulder throbbed. Grimacing, he turned his head to see a cloth bandage wrapped beneath his armpit and around his shoulder blade. The faintest tinge of pink seeped through the pale cotton. Had he been wounded there, too? "Please, is anyone here?"

It's okay, he told himself. *Someone's clearly taken care of you, dressed your injuries, and put you to bed. Wherever you are, you're in no danger.*

The thought calmed him down, and he eased back against the pillows. A creak at the doorway caught his ear, and he looked up to find a dark-haired woman approaching. She was barefoot and wore a simple cotton shift that did little to disguise the fullness of her belly.

Her face brightened at the sight of him. "Hank!" She said the name joyfully as she hurried over to the bed. "How do you feel? The doctor wasn't sure you'd pull through. He claimed your heartbeat was barely detectible and your blood pressure was frighteningly low."

Hank touched the bandage on his shoulder with similarly bandaged hands. "How was I hurt?" he asked.

"You were burned," she told him frankly, "on your palms and the soles of your feet. You were struck by lightning, we think. The doctor said it will be painful for a while, but your skin will slowly heal."

"And my back?"

"Oh, yes, that." The woman's sweet expression turned stony. "I told him to cut off the mole, the one shaped like a raindrop. It was so swollen and pus filled, and he was afraid it was infected." Her eyes narrowed. "I wanted it gone so you wouldn't be tempted to call the rain again."

"Call the rain?" he repeated, furrowing his brow. "Was I some kind of magician?"

"Yes," she said, "in a way, you were." She crossed her arms below the round of her belly, hugging herself tightly. "But I'm sorry, Hank, you're not anymore."

"So I am Hank, and I made the rain," he repeated, wondering why that didn't strike him any too oddly. It was as though it all made sense.

"You are Hank Littlefoot, and you have a gift like no other. You were out in the walnut grove three nights ago, summoning the lightning," she told him, cocking her head and watching him. "You don't remember?"

"It wouldn't seem like I should forget something like that," he said and gritted his teeth as he drew his legs over the edge of the bed. "Or that I'd forget a woman like you." He met her dark eyes. "You're my wife, I assume?"

"I will be," she told him, "whenever you get around to finding a justice of the peace willing to do the deed, hopefully before our baby arrives."

His gaze dropped to her swollen belly. "We're having a child, then."

"We are." She gave him a most tolerant smile. "I am Nadya, and this"—she placed her hands on her abdomen—"is Lily." Before a second passed, her smile vanished, and she sighed, impatient with him. "Try harder, Hank. You will remember us. You never forget for very long. Once you're up and about, the past will trickle back. It always has."

He nodded, wanting to believe her. Gingerly, he tried to move off the bed, but every muscle winced. Even his bones objected, aching at the marrow. Still, he forced his legs to bear his weight, his arms to push as he rose.

When he stood on the soles of his bandaged feet, he bit his tongue to keep from crying out. The pain was greater than he'd realized.

She had mentioned lightning in the grove, suggesting that he had summoned the spirits of nature and begged for aid to coax the walnut trees back to life. Perhaps if he could see, he would remember.

"Will you help me to the window?" he asked, wobbling.

She caught his arm, holding on. "Go slowly," she advised and held fast to him as he took an unsteady step forward and then another. "I was afraid you might not awaken this time," she confessed, not letting him go. "You should see yourself.

You could be a man of eighty. These ceremonies have aged you terribly."

He felt like an old man, one with atrophied muscles and brittle bones. He leaned on Nadya more than he would've liked, but it was the only way he could keep moving. His brow was slick with sweat, his heart racing, by the time they'd crossed the room. She let go of him to part gingham curtains from the window.

"I can stand," he assured her, and she nodded, backing off.

Hank leaned forward, catching his reflection in a pane of glass. It took all his might not to stare at the face looking back at him. The weather-beaten features, the white hair falling on either side of gaunt cheeks: all seemed to belong to someone else.

He was so certain he was staring at a man far older than he.

Ignoring the ghost in the glass, he gazed out, squinting past the thick grass and shrubbery. He glimpsed the side of a barn with bright red boards and, sloping away from that, the first few rows of trees.

Rather than seeing what was there, at first, he visualized the walnut grove, full of gnarled branches and skeletal limbs bare of growth, crooked toward the sky. They looked neglected, abandoned.

Dead.

He blinked to clear his eyes and realized that, in reality, the trees appeared anything but dead. "They are green," he remarked.

"Yes, very green," Nadya said, and he heard the gladness

in her voice. "The morning after the storm, they were covered with buds and, by the next day, they had leaves. You performed a true miracle, Hank. I'm not sure what gods you pleaded with, but they obviously listened."

His legs began trembling, and a question that seemed important popped into his head. "Are there walnuts?" he asked.

She nodded. "I saw them myself just before you awoke. They're ripening in their husks but they should be ready for a fall harvest, I'd think. Though what I know about walnut farming could fill a thimble."

He closed his eyes as a host of emotions and vignettes ran through him: elation at the rain falling down on him; awe at the silver flash of lightning against the black of night; bursts of orange as a tree was set on fire; warmth and affection as he held the hand of the dark-eyed woman who made his heart beat faster. He gasped for air as his forgotten past filled him up in a sudden rush.

I am Hank Littlefoot, grandson of a shaman, maker of rain, and I am right where I belong.

His knees began to tremble, and he bent forward, pressing his brow to the glass. "I remember," he breathed.

"How much?" Nadya asked.

"Enough to know that I am home."

He knew, too, that he'd pushed himself as far as he could go. His grandfather had warned him to stop before it was too late. Hank sensed that he'd narrowly escaped. What if he had died out there in the grove? What if he had left the woman he loved to raise their child alone?

"You are right." He found the strength to turn to her and gazed into her heart-shaped face, seeing tears in her wide-set eyes. "I'm a farmer now, and that's all I am."

"Are you sure?"

"Quite sure."

"And just in time, too." She sighed, fiercely clutching her arms around her belly.

He reached for her, his finger gliding along her cheek, marveling at the smoothness of her olive skin, without a single line. She looked more like his daughter than the mother of his baby. She would live for years and years beyond anything he would see, long enough to witness many walnut harvests. She would watch the farm prosper and their child grow as tall as the corn in the neighboring fields. No matter how weak he felt, Hank was determined to stick around for their first harvest and their child's birth. Beyond that, he could offer no promises, not to Nadya or himself.

It took another month till Hank recovered some of his strength and most of his memories. He resumed a few daily chores, such as gathering eggs and milking the cow, but he was far slower than he'd been and much less agile.

Hank was thankful that Nadya stayed with him regardless of the fact that she'd fallen in love with a young man who had, in a few years, grown old. It made him all the more devoted.

Before the autumn harvest, they found an open-minded justice of the peace to marry them so none could call their child a bastard. When Lily arrived all doe-eyed and dark-haired like her mother, Hank wept with relief not to find a single birth-mark on her body. He felt grateful that his child at least would live a normal life without the burdens he'd carried.

"You are blessed," he whispered to the tiny infant as he cradled her in his arms. "You're blessed to be just as you are. Because sometimes even the greatest gift can become a curse if you're not careful."

The Ghost

Of all the ghosts, the ghosts of our old loved ones
are the worst.

—SIR ARTHUR CONAN DOYLE,
The Memoirs of Sherlock Holmes

TEN

April 2010

Gretchen hardly slept a wink that night, too afraid to leave the Man Who Might Be Sam alone on the parlor sofa. She was terrified of losing him quietly in his sleep to some internal injury before he could even wake up and recall his name. If there was just a one in a million shot that this flesh-and-blood ghost was Sam Winston, she would not let him slip through her fingers. She had already lost him once. Twice would be unbearable.

And if he wasn't Sam, well, Gretchen believed there was still a reason she had found him in the grove. Some higher power had entrusted her with his well-being, and she wasn't inclined to fail. She considered him another challenge in a string of challenges that had consumed her the past forty years. First, she had raised Abby, giving the child all the affection and attention that Annika had never given her; living every day solely to mother her baby until Abby had grown up, gone to college, and started her own life in Chicago. Her second task had been taking charge of Winston Walnuts once Lily and Cooper had passed, though that had never been much more than a sideline with no actual walnuts to sell. And she'd kept an eye on Bennie and Trudy, as she'd promised her parents she would, although her sisters managed fine on their own. Indeed, they often roped her into their projects, like volunteering at the Walnut Ridge Historical Society, where Gretchen ended up sorting through hundreds upon hundreds of old newspaper articles and photos, while the twins translated captions and stories into Braille for the archives.

Staying busy had kept Gretchen from dwelling on the one thing she didn't have: namely, a hand to hold. Despite having been courted through the years by several perfectly decent men, she had never found love, not the soul-melding kind she'd felt for Sam—although she'd only realized years after Sam had gone how deeply she'd cared for him. She could still recall with blinding clarity a long-ago spring night in the cab of his pickup when he'd confessed that he loved her, and she'd shut him down with that kiss-of-death line about just being friends. No, it had taken losing Sam to understand that she needed him in the same way that fire needed air.

So was it wrong for her to assume that yesterday's storm had happened for a reason? Was she crazy to think that this man with Sam's eyes was meant to be here, if only to give her a chance at forgiveness, or to help her unravel one of her biggest mistakes? *Something* had caused him to appear out of nowhere—*something* had trapped him on the farm without a means of escape—and Gretchen felt compelled to find out what that something was.

Once she made sure that Abby had drunk her warm milk and gone to bed—her daughter so weary that she fell asleep the moment her head hit the pillow—and Bennie and Trudy had retired to their rooms as well, Gretchen had donned nightgown and sweater, taking a seat in the chair across from where the man lay. Armed with a pitcher of water and a damp cloth, she mopped his brow whenever he groaned, placed the quilt back over him when he tossed it off. She strained to interpret his delirious mumbles, but she could make out only a word here and there, things that didn't make sense: mutterings about water and flies and gorillas.

When the heat of his skin finally cooled and his twitching ceased, allowing him to peacefully rest, the barest hint of pale gray had just begun to permeate the darkness. Gretchen dared to close her eyes for but a minute and fell into an exhausted sleep.

When she awoke, the room was filled with light. Disoriented, she rubbed the crust from her eyes and got her bearings, seeking the fireplace across the room and the braided rug upon the floor before turning toward the Victorian sofa to find the injured man watching her with his silver-gray gaze. He sat silently, such intensity in his face, as though he were trying so hard to place her. *Do I know you?* his expression seemed to be asking. *Why am I here? What is this place?*

For a long moment, she simply stared back, sensing tiny prickles of awareness beneath her skin, wondering if he felt them too.

He was the one to break the ice. "Did you stay with me all night?"

"I did," she said, the directness of his gaze unnerving. She cleared her throat, glancing at her rumpled nightgown and tugging it down past her knees. Deliberately, she closed her cardigan and tucked wayward hair behind her ears. "I'm glad you're awake, Mr."—she hesitated, floundering—"I wish I knew what to call you."

"I'm not sure what to call myself," he replied, reaching up to touch his brow, which appeared slightly less swollen and less colorful than the previous day. "How did I get here?" he asked. "Did you find a car? Did I have a wallet? Anything to explain who I am and how I arrived?"

"I'm sorry, no," she told him, and he nodded despite his discomfort.

"Is it possible that I walked from somewhere?" He glanced down at the bare feet he'd settled on the rug. "My soles look so rough and scarred, and I'm missing my shoes and socks."

Gretchen hated to see the anguish in his eyes, the desperate need to know. "I wish I had answers," she replied, scooting to the edge of the chair. "But I can only guess that you got caught up in the storm and were swept onto the farm by a tornado. Whatever wasn't firmly attached was lost."

He pressed his fingers on either side of the bruise. "The only memory I have is a feeling of urgency, of desperately needing to be somewhere, but I don't know why or where I was headed."

Were you headed here? Gretchen nearly asked, thinking of Abby's assertion that her wishes had brought him back. *Were you desperate to come home and explain where you've been for forty years? Was it me you were looking for when the twister hit?*

He got up and glanced around him, one hand braced on the arm of the divan. "Can you tell me where I am? You mentioned a farm. So I'm in the country?" he asked.

How could he not remember this house, if he were Sam? Gretchen wondered. Sam had been born here, had let out his first cry within these walls. Was that something a man could forget?

"You're on the Winston farm, although it belongs to me and my daughter now," she said. "My name is Gretchen Brink, and I live here with my sisters." She watched the way his silver eyes flickered, scanning the room and trying hard to make sense of things. "We're about five miles outside of Walnut Ridge, Missouri. Does any of that ring a bell?"

"Should it?" the Man Who Might Be Sam replied, daring to let go of the couch. He walked unsteadily toward the stone fireplace, its rough-hewn mantel full of Gretchen's framed photographs. He braced his hands on the slab of maple, peering at the pictures. "Should I know who these people are?"

"Only if they seem familiar," Gretchen said, her eyes never leaving him. "You have to sort things out for yourself, or else how can you recognize the difference between your memories and something you've been told?"

"You're right." He nodded and pursed his lips, seeming to think for a minute. "Do you have a telephone?" he asked.

"Yes, but the line was dead last I checked." She started to get up. "If you'd like to try it yourself—"

He made a frustrated noise and tapped the mantel with a fist. "Even if it's working, I wouldn't know who to call or what number to dial."

"I'm sorry." Gretchen didn't know what else to say.

"It isn't your fault," he replied, turning away from the fireplace. He shakily made his way back to the sofa, grunting as he lowered himself to the cushions. "I feel like this has happened before, that it's not the first time I've forgotten things."

Did he have some kind of illness or dementia? Gretchen suddenly wondered, though he seemed coherent in all respects save for remembering his own past. "Are you sure you don't want a doctor? There's a tree blocking access to the main road, but I could walk into town and fetch—"

"No, no, I'm fine," he assured her. "Just angry at myself." He ran a hand over his face then through his long hair. He touched his beard and frowned.

Before he could inquire about where the rest of his beard had gone, Gretchen asked something else. "How did it feel," she began, "to ride a twister?"

He gave up scratching his grizzled jaw and let out a dry laugh. His pale gray eyes looked right at her. "I don't know about riding a twister," he said and raised his hands, turning them so she could see his reddened palms. "Though I think I know how it feels to be struck by lightning. I seem to recall a lot of blinding light and heat." He touched his forehead. "And one hell of a headache."

"That would explain a few things," Gretchen agreed.

"But not why I'm here," he said, and the hint of a smile touched his lips. "Unless this is Oz, and my name's really Dorothy."

"You're definitely not in Kansas," Gretchen told him, surprised that he could joke, or that he could summon up a literary reference but not where he'd come from.

"You figure if I click my heels together, I'll go home?"

Unless you already are home, she nearly said but bit her

tongue. Instead, she replied, "Don't you have to collect a scare-crow, a tin man, and a cowardly lion first?"

"Oh, yeah, that." For an instant, the worry left his face, brightening his eyes and taking years away. And like the sun coming out on a cloudy day, shadows were lifted and Gretchen quite clearly saw Sam in there, in the set of his jaw, the reluctant curve of lips, in the dry humor of his voice. Or was she seeing what she wanted to see, the very thing she'd accused Abby of doing last evening?

Unnerved by confusion, she rose to her stocking feet, hugging the thick sweater around her. "You must be hungry," she said, falling back on the old standby that if you fed everyone, they'd be all right. "Would you like something to eat? I could scramble some eggs. Would you prefer juice or coffee?"

He rubbed at his whiskers. "If you wouldn't mind, could I use the bathroom first? I'd like to clean up. I think I've got dirt in my ears and God knows what other nooks and crannies."

"Of course," Gretchen said, horrified that she hadn't offered. She motioned for him to remain sitting. "Please, stay here a moment, and I'll fetch you a few things."

"Just soap will do," she heard him say as she scurried from the room and raced about, pulling towels from the linen closet, gathering a spare toothbrush and travel-sized toothpaste, a bar of Ivory, a fresh razor (though she hoped he didn't mind that it was pink). The lot of it bundled in her arms, Gretchen took everything into the hall bath and left it there on the vanity. Then she stopped up the drain and caused the pipes to moan as she started the water, making sure it was neither too hot nor too cold.

Before she returned to the man, she dashed upstairs, peering into Abby's room, relieved to find her daughter sound
asleep, dark hair splayed across the pillow, softly snoring. Behind the closed doors to her sisters' rooms, she heard them stirring, as if they'd just roused.

Down the stairs she raced, checking the tub and finding
the bathwater midway up the sides. She shut off the faucet
before hurrying to the parlor, where she found the Man Who
Might Be Sam standing in front of the window, staring out.

"Are you ready?" she said, and he turned around.

Wordlessly, he took her arm.

She led him to the bathroom, making sure he had all the
necessities—and telling him to holler should he need her—
before she shut the door and left him to fend for himself.

For a few minutes, she hovered outside in the hallway, listening, afraid to go too far should he fall while climbing in.
But all she detected was the creak of the floor and a few gentle
splashes before quiet set in. As long as he didn't pass out and
drown he'd be fine, she thought, reassured enough to let him
be and head into the kitchen to start some breakfast.

She'd barely pulled the skillet from the cabinet and set it on
the burner when the noise of someone pounding a fist against
the front door made her leap.

"Gretchen Brink!" She heard Sheriff Tilby's muffled voice.
"Are you in there? Are y'all all right? If you can hear me, open
up!"

For heaven's sake, the next farm could probably hear him,
as loudly as he was shouting.

"Coming!" she replied and made sure her cardigan was

good and buttoned over her flannel gown before she unlocked the door and opened up.

"Thank God," he said when he saw her standing before him. He turned his hat round and round, clearing his throat before he explained. "I got a call bright and early from a cabbie in Washington who had a bad case of the guilts after dropping off a woman last night. From his description, I'm guessing it was Abby." At Gretchen's nod, he went on, "Fellow mentioned downed power lines and a big ol' tree blocking the drive. I tried to call before I drove over but you haven't got service. So are you and the girls okay?"

"We're fine," Gretchen assured him.

He ran his fingers across his slicked-back hair, lips pursed as he glanced over his shoulder, back toward the road half a mile away. "The rest of Walnut Ridge escaped with barely a drizzle. Nothing like what you saw here. It's as though the storm took aim at the Winston farm and only the Winston farm. You tick off Mother Nature or something?"

"Not on purpose," she said, feeling a familiar pull of tension; but there had always been such a strange tug of war between them. Once upon a time, they'd had what could only be described as a good old-fashioned flirtation, back when he'd been the cocky but charming son of the town sheriff and the star pitcher on the high school baseball team; back when she'd been too blind to see Sam Winston as anything more than her closest ally; well before she'd gotten pregnant with Abby and Frank had heard tell it was Sam's baby, causing him to up and marry the mayor's daughter, Millie, something for which Gretchen was now eternally grateful.

"Any leaks in your roof, or water in your basement?" Frank asked, tapping hat against belly and rocking back on his heels.

"Nope, we're dry as a bone." Gretchen knew that he was angling for her to invite him in, only she didn't intend to do anything of the sort. The last thing she needed was for Frank Tilby to find out she had a man—a virtual stranger at that—staying at the house. So she just smiled and said, "Appreciate your checking in, but rest assured, we're okay." Then she attempted to close the door.

Only he put out his big paw, pushing the door wide again, and ambled past her like he owned the place.

"I've got two deputies coming out with chain saws to cut up the oak," he told her as she followed him to the kitchen "and I've let the utility company know your electric cables got clipped. They should be around sometime today."

"Thank you, Frank."

He stopped as soon as he noticed the ceiling fixture was on. Except that the moment he stood beneath it, the lights flickered and dimmed, threatening to go off. "How is it that you've got juice?"

"Just lucky." She shrugged, not about to tell him the truth—or the truth as she saw it, anyway: that it had to do with lightning and a man who had fallen from the sky and who may or may not have brought the rain. That was hardly something any rational soul would believe.

"You have a generator?"

"No."

"Huh." He pursed his lips. "Well, that's quite a nifty trick."

The sheriff sniffed and set his hat down on the well-worn oak table. "Must be some kind of fluke," he decided and put his hands on his gun-belted hips as he began to take a walk around.

Before he could say more, the creaking floor announced the arrival of Bennie and Trudy in pressed shifts, canvas shoes, and combed hair, looking far more presentable than Gretchen.

"Is that the sheriff I hear?" Trudy asked.

"Of course, it is, sister. Who else would barge in without warning before breakfast?" Bennie remarked and made her way straight to the stove to fetch the teakettle, which she began to fill with water at the sink.

"Morning, Miss Bennie, Miss Trudy," Frank said, ignoring Bennie's sarcasm. "Sounds like you had a wild time out here yesterday what with the freak weather and Abby coming home for a visit. Did she bring her young man this time? What's his name again? Neville? Norton?"

"It's Nathan," Bennie corrected and put the kettle on the burner to heat. "And he didn't travel with her. She's come alone—"

"Well, not entirely alone," Trudy said with a sly grin, and the twins began to giggle.

Sheriff Tilby wrinkled up his face. "What's that supposed to mean?"

"Nothing," Gretchen said, quickly stepping in. It wasn't their business to tell anyone about Abby's pregnancy, and she wasn't about to let her giddy sisters spill the beans. "Abby took a few days off work is all. She was homesick."

"What rotten timing, her dropping in after the storm left

things a mess out here," the sheriff said, watching Gretchen so closely it made her uncomfortable.

"Abby's not the only one who dropped in out of the blue," Bennie offered and, before Gretchen had a chance to shush her, she added, "We've got another unexpected guest, too. Gretchen found him in the grove and dragged him inside."

"He passed out before we could speak to him," Trudy said as the teakettle began to whistle. "Poor man's sleeping in the parlor right now—"

"No, Trude, he isn't," Bennie interrupted as she pulled the china cups down from the cabinet. "Didn't you hear the pipes whistling in the downstairs powder room? Since Abby's still snoring away, and the rest of us are here, he must be taking a bath. It's the only thing that makes sense."

Trudy turned her guileless face toward Gretchen. "So then he's up and about? Did you find out if he's who we think he is?"

Aw, crud, Gretchen mused, *here it comes.* She watched Frank Tilby's face go from pink to bright red, his indignation puffing out his jowls so that he looked like an angry bulldog.

"There's a strange man in your bathtub?" The sheriff's voice rumbled, sounding positively apoplectic as he turned his narrowed eyes on Gretchen. "He stayed overnight on your sofa? Unchaperoned?"

Unchaperoned?

Gretchen wrinkled her nose at the word. Did Frank Tilby think it was still the Victorian era? Or, more likely, did he disapprove because he still wanted to keep such close tabs on her, even after all these years?

"He was injured," she explained, not sure she wanted him to interfere. "He was lying in the grove with a goose egg on his head and no shoes on his feet. What was I supposed to do? Leave him on the ground, unconscious, while I twiddled my thumbs and waited for help since I couldn't call out, or leave the property for that matter?"

Frank walked right up to her, arms crossed over his barrel-like chest, leaning in so they were nose to nose. "You should have told me."

"How?" She snorted, wondering if he'd forgotten the snapped utility cables dangling near the fence line. "With a tin can on a string?"

"I'll take him back to town in the squad car. I'll put him up in the bunk room at the jail," the sheriff said, arms crossed below the badge on his chest, the frown on his face brooking no argument. "He can't stay here."

"I beg to differ," Gretchen countered, heat rushing to her cheeks. "He's not well enough to go anywhere, and I don't want him staying at the jail, for Pete's sake. I spoke with him this morning, and he still can't remember who he is and where he's from, and he's frightened," she insisted, her pulse ratcheting up, not about to let Sam's ghost out of her sight. "He needs more time to recover. He's still weak and can't remember a thing."

"But it's not right for you women to keep a stranger in your midst when you're so isolated," the sheriff insisted, shaking his head with its careful pompadour. "No, ma'am, it's not right at all."

Bennie set a teacup into a saucer with a purposeful rattle. "We're not afraid of him, Sheriff," she said crisply. "In fact, just the opposite. We're not even sure he's truly a stranger, not after the walnuts falling—"

"And the scent of lemongrass," Trudy added before she'd finished. "Abby sensed something familiar about him, too."

"Hush," Gretchen hissed at them under her breath.

"So which is he, familiar or a stranger?" Frank Tilby asked and stared accusingly at Gretchen. "Why do I feel like you're talking riddles around me?"

"He's a bit of a riddle to us all," Gretchen admitted, which didn't seem to soften up the sheriff an iota.

"How about you just tell this fellow to come out so I can meet him." Frank Tilby pulled out a chair and took a seat at the kitchen table. "Matter of fact, I'll settle in and wait until he's free."

"That's not necessary," Gretchen started to say, but she was cut off by the groan of floorboards and the soft pad of footsteps as the Man Who Might Be Sam walked into the kitchen with a towel slung over his shoulders and another tucked around his lean hips.

His hair was dripping wet and his face was freshly shaven, his chin newly nicked with tiny bits of toilet paper sticking to it. His battered clothing dangled from his outstretched hand.

Above him, the lights that had flickered and dimmed in Frank Tilby's presence suddenly grew brighter.

The towel-clad fellow glanced around the crowded room, not saying a word to anyone before his gaze settled on Gretchen. "Forgive me," he apologized, "I didn't realize you had company. But you don't happen to have anything else I can wear, do you? I'm not sure these torn clothes are even good for rags."

ELEVEN

Frank Tilby gawked like a startled teenager as he watched Gretchen shepherd the man in the bath towel from the kitchen, all the while assuring him she had some clean things that would suit him well enough.

Unbelievable, Frank mused, shaking his head. *What in the hell is she thinking?*

He wanted to go after her and tell her this was nonsense. What woman with any common sense let a stranger into her house and put him up overnight? If he could have shaken her, he would've done it. But he knew that Gretchen Brink was about as stubborn as they came. Maybe she'd inherited a chromosome or two of crazy from her mother. Everyone in town who'd even briefly encountered the artistic and temperamental Annika had believed she was more than a little bit tetched.

While he waited for Gretchen's return, he paced the worn pine boards, the angry creaking beneath his footsteps attesting to his impatience.

" . . . she kept so many things, even his father's clothes and shoes, isn't that right, Trudy?" Bennie was saying across the table to her sister, quite loudly enough for Frank to hear if he cared to listen.

"She wouldn't get rid of them. Said it wasn't her place,"

Trudy agreed, and they both sipped their morning tea, as if having a half-naked stranger pop into the room wasn't anything out of the ordinary. "I think part of her always believed he'd come back so she hung on to them just in case."

"Whose things? Who's come back?" Frank finally stopped pacing to ask. "Well, aren't you going to tell me, or should we play twenty questions?"

For a long moment, neither twin reacted to his query. They merely gazed at each other with their milky eyes, teacups held so similarly in their right hands, pinkies crooked. Until finally Bennie—whom Frank had always found to be the more direct of the two—cocked her head in his direction and informed him, "It's not our business to tell you anything more, Sheriff Tilby. If Gretchen wants you to know, she should be the one to do it."

"Lord help me, but this is ridiculous," he mumbled, tugging his hat back on his head. Why was it like pulling teeth to get information from some females? "I'll be out on the porch, and I'm not going to leave till I have a word with Gretchen. Tell her that, won't you?"

"Will do." Bennie jerked her chin.

"So long, Sheriff," Trudy said, and then the pair bent their heads together, whispering in tones too soft for him to hear.

And he hadn't even left the room.

Frank made it a point to stomp out of the kitchen, grumbling to himself all the way to the door. When he yanked it wide, he nearly tripped over that damned skinny cat of Trudy's, which made a point of hissing up at him before it dashed through his legs and outside.

"And a good morning to you, too," he grumbled as the feline scampered down the porch steps and away.

Frank took a deep breath once he'd escaped, filling his lungs with crisp morning air. The whir of chain saws floated toward him from half a mile up the drive, and he nodded to himself, figuring the fallen oak would be little more than kindling soon enough. Then Gretchen would have no excuse but to let him ferry that gray-haired fellow away from the farm, and he could deposit the man a safe distance from the Brink womenfolk. Not that he thought the stranger posed a real threat. Hell, he looked nearly old enough to be Abby's grandfather. Mostly skin and bones, too, and slow on his feet like he barely had enough strength to stand upright. But if there was one thing Frank had learned from all his years as a second-generation lawman, it was that people were unpredictable and it never took much to make them snap.

Only two nights ago, he'd been called to a meeting of the Ladies' Civic Improvement League when Amanda Solomon and Hattie Daniels had nearly gotten into fisticuffs over what flowers to plant in front of the community center this season.

Still, he wished Gretchen had used her head. Taking in a stray cat was one thing, he mused, but *this*?

Until he'd settled down, Frank paced the porch and took lots of deep breaths, glancing out at broken branches littering the lawn, listening to a host of birds twittering high above him. He noticed the jumble of wicker furniture, tossed into a pile against the far railing, and he busied himself righting it all. By the time Gretchen finally appeared—her stocking feet jammed into her knee-high rubber boots—Frank was drying off a chair with his handkerchief.

"Ah, there you are," he said and patted the freshly wiped seat. He would stay calm if it killed him. "Sit down, why don't you, and let's chat."

"Can you make it quick, Sheriff?" she said, waving off his suggestion. "I'd like to get breakfast started before Abby wakes up."

Frank didn't want to make it quick. He liked to suck every moment that he could out of any encounter with Gretchen. Even as she frowned at him, he couldn't help but think how fresh and freckled her face seemed in the morning light. When he looked at her like this, he didn't see the fine lines that close to sixty years had etched into her skin; he saw the girl he used to know, a girl he still missed.

Because Frank Tilby had always been sweet on Gretchen Brink. He'd had so many dreams about her in his life that he'd lost count of them. They were as common to him as some folks' dreams of flying or being back in high school, taking a test for which they hadn't studied.

She'd never been conventionally beautiful but slender and fair, often smiling, with a complexion he'd heard referred to as peaches and cream. Every time she'd ever said hello to him, her pale eyes had radiated warmth and her nose had crinkled the tiniest bit. Gretchen was a lot like the sun, he decided. She seemed to glow from within, even now when she scowled at him.

Before he could stop them, words spilled out of his mouth. "You look good, even this early in the day," he said, even though he shouldn't have. He was a married man who knew better than to flirt with a woman who wasn't his wife. Still, he couldn't seem to resist. When he was around her, something odd happened to him. He felt like a teenager all over again. "You're blessed, you know. Every day that passes, you're an even more handsome woman, and you were already a good-looking one to begin with."

"Frank, please!" She blushed and touched her hair, once flaxen like a field of wheat and now more ashen, still thick enough that he imagined his fingers would get caught up in it good if he tried to run them through it. "I'm not sure any girl likes being called 'handsome,' you know, nor do we like to be reminded we're not exactly spring chickens," she told him, deflecting his compliment, looking back at the door like she wanted to bolt.

His stomach pitched. "I meant to flatter you, Gretchen. I'm sorry if I offended you instead. So handsome is a bad word? I need to make note of that." He pulled his tiny notepad and pencil from his uniform pocket, pretending to jot in it just for show, but it did the trick.

A smile settled on her lips, albeit a tense one. "It's that we don't want to think we look more like men the older we get. We want to feel like we can still turn a head every now and then, even if the plump's left our cheeks and gone straight to our ass."

"Is that so?" Frank couldn't help it when his eyes dipped toward the curve of her hip, the way even the bulky sweater and flannel nightgown couldn't disguise that she was very much a woman. She had a mighty handsome ass, he mused, but he wouldn't tell her that, even though he was sorely tempted.

She stepped forward to slap his shoulder. "Quit staring at me like that," she said. "What would Millie think if she knew you were standing on my porch right now, spooning out all kinds of sugar? And it's barely eight o'clock in the morning."

Frank was fairly sure that, if Millie had overheard, she wouldn't be too surprised. A man who talked in his sleep couldn't hide all that much from his wife.

"Look, Gretchen, I don't want to beat around the bush here, but—"

He bit his tongue before he said more. How he wanted to tell her then what he'd been holding in since high school, that if he'd had his druthers she would be sharing his bed, not Mildred. But all those years ago when he'd heard that Gretchen was pregnant and the baby was Sam Winston's, it had curdled his stomach. He'd felt betrayed, although there'd been no cause. Gretchen had never been his. She hadn't belonged to anyone back then, not really.

He'd had a knee-jerk reaction—that being asking Millie to marry him when he knew he didn't love her—and he'd been paying for it the four decades since. Not that Millie wasn't as loyal and kind as a cocker spaniel; she was, in fact, a most dutiful spouse. She just wasn't Gretchen. Sometimes, though, Frank found himself wondering if choosing a woman who *wasn't* Gretchen Brink hadn't inadvertently saved him from a deeper suffering. There were some in Walnut Ridge who saw the Brink women as completely unsuitable. "Consider that crazy Annika," they would say, "so blunt she drove her husband into the arms of a school librarian. Then Gretchen let Sam go off to Africa despite the child in her belly, and the twins never settled down despite having their fair share of suitors. No, some women are just better off alone."

"Whatever you've got on your mind, Frank, spit it out," Gretchen said, drawing him into the present, pulling his gaze back to her anxious face.

Instead of troubling himself even more by delving into the past, he merely groused at her, "Like I said, I don't appreciate that you've got a strange man staying here with you women. It's not seemly."

"He's completely harmless, I assure you," Gretchen said with a sigh. "I sat up with him all night. He was dead to the world till this morning."

"What did your sisters mean when they said you'd saved his father's clothes and that you'd hoped he'd come back?" As Frank repeated what he'd overheard, it suddenly dawned on him. He blinked, taken aback. "Aw, hell. You don't think that man's Sam? You can't possibly believe that."

But he could tell by the set of her jaw that she did.

"If I told you he has Sam's eyes, would you understand? I've never met another man with irises the color of a stormy sky."

Frank snorted. "He has Sam's *eyes*? Is that your only proof? Did you find his wallet or anything with a name on it?"

"No."

"And you didn't spot a car anywhere about, like the tornado tossed the thing around with him in it before it shook him out?"

"No."

Frank scratched behind his ear. "Call me a cynic, but it sounds awfully fishy. How do you know he isn't some con man, come to take advantage of your situation?"

"A con man?" Gretchen's mouth fell open before she snapped it shut again. She set her hands on her hips, and her nostrils flared as she challenged him. "And what situation do you figure he's ripe to take advantage of? You think he wants to steal the farm? You imagine he wants a grove filled with walnut trees that haven't produced in as long as Abby's been alive? Or that he's come to steal the tiny profit we eke out from the gallery, which covers utilities and food and little else?"

Instead of sniping back at her, Frank lifted his arms in surrender. "Okay, okay, I see your point. So let's say he's a helpless victim, not someone out to swindle the land from under your feet."

"Yes, let's say that," she answered with an irritated glare.

Frank sensed he'd lost the battle already. "So you honestly figure Sam Winston was somehow resurrected and a twister dumped him into your grove, is that it?" He found the idea so hard to swallow that it was tough to get the words out. "Though you've got nothing to confirm he's Sam but his eyes, since he doesn't recall his own name and looks a decade older than he should?"

"We don't know what happened to him all that time in Africa," Gretchen crisply replied. "We don't know what was done to him, how he survived. A lot of folks who've been through trauma age more rapidly than the rest of us."

"Since he apparently rose from the grave, I guess he could look a whole lot worse," Frank cracked wise, but Gretchen hardly seemed to find that amusing. He cleared his throat, shifting on his boots. "So what if he's not who you think he is? What if he's a stranger, pure and simple? Would you still want to keep him in the house with your blind sisters and your only daughter?"

"Whether he's Sam or not, he's got to remember who he is soon enough," Gretchen insisted. "And if, by the grace of God, it is Sam, he can't be in this place where he was born and where his parents died and not recall his past." She waved her arms. "There's too much of him here. A man never forgets where he comes from."

"I know a few drinking men who can't find their way home at night," Frank remarked, refusing to buy what she was selling.

"Somewhere inside, he knows," she insisted. "He can't forget his life forever."

"Aw, hell." The sheriff sighed and shook his head.

Gretchen gave him a long look. "If you've got a better way to rid a man of amnesia, let's hear it."

"Don't get all huffy just because I'm concerned for you," he said, and he meant it. He didn't like that she was getting so caught up in this wild daydream about Sam Winston returning. Seemed like she'd spent her whole adult life pining for the man until she made him into something no real man could live up to. Now she'd concocted this fantasy that he was back. Worse still, it sounded like she'd gotten her sisters and daughter wrapped up in it, too. It couldn't possibly be healthy. "Let me sit down with him alone," Frank suggested. "Let me ask a few questions, feel him out."

"I'm not leaving you alone with him! He doesn't need

threats." Gretchen's pale eyes narrowed. "You'll just push him around like you and your buddies did when we were kids, and I figure he's been through enough already."

"I'm not going to push him around!" Frank huffed.

But she squared her chin and didn't budge, clearly not convinced.

"All right, all right." He threw up his hands. "How about this," he said, realizing he had a very simple means to putting an end to any speculation. "I'll go back to the station and get my field kit and, when I return, I'll print him. If he's got any kind of record, we'll know it pretty quick."

"Your field kit?" Gretchen repeated. "You want to fingerprint him? Like he's a criminal?"

"Yes. I mean, no," Frank scrambled for the right words, not wanting to get into any more hot water than he was already in. "If we run his prints through the system and they come out clean, we'll know he hasn't been charged with a crime, not hereabouts anyway. And if he's ever held any kind of job where he's been printed, we'll find that out, too. One way or another, we'll learn who he is, or at least who he's not."

"Unless he isn't in the system at all."

"How about we cross that bridge when we come to it?" Frank said. "And in the meantime, I'll put out a BOLO locally for any signs of an abandoned car. Maybe we can see how he really rode into Walnut Ridge."

"I already know how he got here," Gretchen insisted, tightening the tuck of her arms beneath her breasts.

By hitching a ride on a tornado.

Okey dokey.

Frank sucked in his cheeks, not willing to touch that one. Gretchen had always been the fanciful type, prone to believe in fairy tales. "So if I leave without taking him with me, you won't make a fuss when I come back to print him. Deal?" he asked and extended his hand.

Gretchen hesitated but a minute before she reached out to shake it. "All right," she said as Frank held on to her smaller hand for several beats too long. "That sounds fair enough."

"Give me a couple hours, okay? Then I'll be back." With that, he tipped his hat and headed toward the porch steps, pausing just long enough to add, "If you need my deputies, remember they're just up the drive, cutting up that oak."

"Thanks, but I won't," she replied in that gentle way of hers before she turned on her heels and disappeared inside.

TWELVE

Abby always had the most vivid dreams when she came back to the farm, and this time was no different.

She was sitting on the back porch swing, gliding gently to and fro, humming a made-up lullaby, her arms cradling the engorged swell of her belly. She knew the baby inside her was a girl, and she marveled at the thought of pink bows and ballet slippers. "You'll be a strong woman in a long line of strong women," she whispered and rubbed a spot near her ribs where a tiny foot pressed hard against her. "No matter where you go, you'll always find your way back. And you'll believe in fairy tales, even if they don't make sense."

The baby kicked her again, as if agreeing, and she laughed.

Abby ceased rocking the swing and rose to her feet, holding her belly as she padded over to the whitewashed railing. From there, she could spy the red barn and the walnut groves beyond. She could see birds soar past, silhouetted by the fat clouds that lazily meandered across the sky.

She breathed in the sweetness of lemongrass as the wind picked up and tossed her dark hair, whipping strands across her face. She gripped the railing as it buffeted her body, and the baby suddenly began to kick more forcefully. A bird with the wingspan of a hawk swooped down upon her, coming near enough so she could see its yellow eyes before it flew off toward the grove, where it disappeared into the trees.

As the heavens rumbled, shaking the floorboards beneath her, a heavy wall of gray overtook the plump clouds until all the light had been smothered, like a fire being doused. As lightning cracked across the heavens and the rain began pouring down, she whispered, "It's just a storm, it won't hurt you. We're safe here," to comfort herself as much as the baby.

The air was so thick with the downpour that she couldn't see a thing beyond the railing. *Abigail,* she heard someone say. *Over here.* But she felt blinded by the rain, and the noise of it hitting the roof made the voice too hard to hear.

Then it stopped. Just like that. The dark clouds scuttled off, making way for blue skies again. The baby settled down in her belly, and Abby leaned against the damp railing, spotting a figure emerging from the fog of the grove. The sun shone down upon him as he walked toward her and lifted a hand to wave.

She felt compelled to run to him, but she couldn't; her legs wouldn't move. And though he seemed to be heading her way, he got no closer. They were so far apart still, too far for her to clearly see his face.

"Daddy?" she called out as tears splashed down, wetting her cheeks more fiercely than the rain. "Daddy!"

Bam bam bam! "*Gretchen Brink, are you in there?*"

Noises and voices seeped into her subconscious, and Abby stirred, a sob catching in her throat as she awakened, opening her eyes, damp with tears. For a moment, she lay there, willing herself to calm down and clutching at her dream although it had already started to fade. The more she tried to remember, the more it slipped away. But she did recall one thing: the tiny girl grown so big inside her, moving and kicking.

Beneath the sheet, she snaked a hand toward her belly, resting her palm on its gentle curve. She wasn't showing yet, but it wouldn't be long before she was. Nate would notice first, before anyone else. He knew her body nearly as well as she did. How much longer could she wait to tell him?

"It would be wrong to keep him from you," she whispered to the child who was little more than a cluster of cells and a tiny beating heart. "You don't deserve to lose your daddy, too."

She slowly got out of bed, leaving the covers in a tangle as she shed her pajamas and pulled on a clean sweater and her jeans from the day before. She shuffled into the upstairs hall bath long enough to squint at her bleary-eyed self in the mirror as she brushed her teeth and to draw her hair back with a headband.

Her steps quickened as she descended the stairs, thinking of the man on the parlor sofa, of how her mother had found him right after the storm, and she couldn't help wondering again if her father had finally come back. She hoped he could remember more about himself this morning, perhaps even who he was. Then the mystery would be solved, one way or the other.

She stuck her head into the parlor, ready to say, "good morning," only to find it empty. Even the quilt was folded up neatly and slung over the back of the couch.

Has something happened to him? she wondered, her heart pumping faster. Had he stolen away in the middle of the night, never to be seen again? Or was he merely part of the dream already lost to her?

She rushed into the kitchen, finding Trudy and Bennie sitting at the breakfast table, munching on buttered toast. The smell of eggs hung in the air, and it made her stomach curdle.

"Where is he?" she asked, trying not to sound as frantic as she felt. "Please, tell me he didn't leave already?" Then an even more frightening thought hit her, considering how exhausted she'd been when she'd arrived. "I didn't just imagine him, did I?"

"Abby?" her aunts said, nearly in unison, but it was Bennie who'd picked up on her frantic tone. "You didn't imagine anything," she assured her.

"So where is he?" Abby's mouth filled with the metallic taste of worry. "Is he all right?"

"Of course he's all right," Bennie told her. "Gretchen stayed up all night, watching over him like a mother hen."

"She's with him now," Trudy said, brushing crumbs off her hands. "So relax, dear girl. Anxiety is seeping from your pores like ammonia, and it's not good for either you or the baby."

"Your mom's got him outside," Bennie told her, "breathing in the fresh air."

Abby felt light-headed with relief. "So he's alive and well?"

"Even better, he took a bath," Trudy said.

"Thank God," Abby breathed, tugging at the cuffs of her sweater. "I was so afraid he'd be gone before I had a chance to find out if he really could be Sam."

"Sweetheart, you need to take a deep breath and slow down," Trudy advised, clucking softly. "We've all been jumping to conclusions since the fellow appeared out of nowhere, probably because we'd like to have a happy ending to a story that never had any real ending at all."

"But we can't make something be that isn't so," Bennie added, sounding perfectly reasonable, although Abby was hardly feeling very reasonable herself these days.

"You're right, of course," she agreed, though it didn't keep her from wanting a happy ending to this particular tale. "If he isn't Sam, he isn't Sam. Wishing won't make it so."

Her aunts beamed at her as they had so often when she was a girl and had done even the smallest thing to please them. *Yes, Abs, you have a wonderful ear! That is a cardinal's chirp. Good girl, of course, that's a honeysuckle vine, which has the most glorious, sweet scent.*

But identifying flowers and bird calls was easy. A honeysuckle was always a honeysuckle. A cardinal's chirp, a cardinal's chirp. Other things in life weren't so readily definable. Like the artwork she sold in the Lincoln Park gallery. Whether a painting was good or not was completely subjective. One patron might adore a collage and another might call it "trash." And what about love? The very subject that had caused such trouble between her and Nate. She knew what it meant for her—commitment and a real promise of a future together—but it appeared to mean something else entirely to him.

Not everything that was real came with proof. Sometimes, believing *had* to be enough.

"Abigail, are you sure you're okay? I can hear you grinding your teeth," Bennie said, her head cocked like a bird.

Abby breathed in deeply, relaxing her jaw. "Really, I'm okay."

"Would you like breakfast?" Trudy asked, getting up from her chair and dropping her napkin to the table. "You shouldn't have coffee though, should you? The caffeine wouldn't be good for the wee one. How about toast and eggs with juice? Remember, you're eating for two."

"Maybe some toast in a bit," she said, the thought of food making her queasy. "I couldn't swallow a thing right this minute."

"Morning sickness?" Bennie asked, and a knowing grin played upon her lips.

"A little," she admitted.

"Aha!" Trudy threw her hands in the air as she made her way toward Abby. "Your mother had it, too, for months and months." Her sensible shoes squeaked as she stopped and reached out for her niece, softly patting her arm. "Once she felt better, she had the strangest cravings, for peanut butter and cottage cheese and oranges."

"And fried chicken," Bennie added. "She ate that for dinner every night for weeks so the whole house reeked of it."

"Oh, and mashed potatoes." Trudy grinned. "We could hardly make enough!"

All the talk of food set Abby's stomach to lurching. She felt bile wash up the back of her throat and put a hand to her mouth.

"Excuse me," she murmured as she made a beeline for the mudroom, pausing long enough to throw on a windbreaker and slip her bare feet into a pair of gardening clogs before she scurried out into the cool morning.

She let the screen door bang behind her as she stepped out onto the porch, gulping in air to quell the queasiness. She bent over, hands on her knees until she felt less like something was going to come up. Once she could stand again, she eased toward the railing, gazing out toward the barn. That was when she heard her mother's voice mingled with the deeper tones of a man coming from just around the bend.

" . . . don't worry about him," Gretchen was saying. "He might growl like a bulldog, but he's completely harmless."

"He figures I'm up to no good, is that it?"

Gretchen sniffed. "He thinks everyone's up to no good."

Abby walked toward the sound of their conversation, rounding the corner of the house, the clomp of garden clogs on the porch planks inordinately loud against the quiet of the morning.

Gretchen glanced up from where she perched in a white wicker chair. She was still in her nightgown with a thick cardigan wrapped around her, not exactly high fashion when paired with her knee-high rubber boots.

"Hey, you're up!" her mom said, tucking messy strands of ash-blond behind her ears. "Did you eat breakfast yet?"

"My stomach isn't exactly ready for it," Abby replied as she went to kiss her mother's cheek. When she straightened, she turned toward the fellow swaying to and fro on the swing. "Hi," she said to him. "I'm Abby, the prodigal daughter from Chicago."

"Hello, Abby from Chicago," he replied and gave her a slow nod. He had his arms draped across the wood-slatted back and his legs extended as he rocked. "Your mother and I were just talking about the sheriff, who happened by a little earlier. I don't think he likes the fact that she's got a stranger hanging around."

"Frank Tilby's always been hot for my mom," Abby said, because it was the truth and had been forever. "So he doesn't like any man hanging around her."

"Abs!" Gretchen blushed, but she laughed just the same.

"Well, then it's a good thing he didn't haul me away in handcuffs." The fellow nodded and kept gliding, the chains creaking with the motion.

The sound was strangely comforting. It reminded Abby of all the spring and summer nights Gretchen had sat there beside her. Their bellies full from supper, they'd swayed back and forth, waiting for the sun to set or watching fireflies light up the dusk. Abby wondered how it would have been to have had Sam share in those moments with them. Even if she could get all that time back, it wouldn't be enough.

"You seem better this morning," she remarked and took a step forward, trying to look at him and figure him out without being too obvious. "Are you feeling okay?" She stopped shy of the swing. "I'm figuring you are 'cause you aren't unconscious and that bruise on your forehead has calmed down. It's no longer eggplant purple."

"Yes, I'm better, just plenty confused." His gray eyes squinted at her, like he was taking her in the same way she was him.

"That makes sense," Abby said, and she couldn't help adding, "Being dropped on a farm by a tornado would be pretty confusing, I'd wager, unless it's something you've done a lot before."

"Ah, so you figure I'm a professional tornado wrangler." A smile twitched at the corners of his mouth.

"You never know," she replied, feeling the weight of his

gaze. A shiver raced up her spine, despite the windbreaker. She hugged her arms to warm herself. "I grew up hearing stories about a man who could talk to the sky and make it rain."

"Is that so?" The fellow glanced at Gretchen, who hastily explained, "Abby's great-grandfather was something of a magician."

That wasn't exactly what Abby had referred to and Gretchen knew it, but Abby's mother had a knack for bending the truth. *Sometimes it's best to say what people need to hear instead of making them uncomfortable,* she'd once defended herself when Abby had called her on it.

As if afraid Abby might test the waters even further, Gretchen began nattering on about climate change and last summer's drought, asking the man if he was cold or hungry, whether he had thick enough socks with the borrowed shoes or if the shirt wasn't too big, all sorts of things to keep from tackling the elephant in the room. Namely, was he or was he not Sam Winston?

With a resigned sigh, Abby settled into the nearest wicker chair. She found herself watching the man, searching his face, looking for recognizable traits, bits of herself he'd passed on to her, things she couldn't discern in a decades-old picture. Like the way he cocked his head or scratched his nose. He'd cleaned up, she noticed, shaving off the rest of his beard, although his hair was still too long and shaggy. He had deep grooves at his mouth and eyes, making him seem older than he should have been. But forty years away was a lot, and who knows where he'd been or what he'd gone through.

He reminded Abby of the grandfather she'd barely known,

perhaps because he was wearing the obnoxious red-and-green plaid shirt that had belonged to Cooper Winston, one he'd worn on the first and last Christmas Abby had celebrated with him, preserved in Gretchen's treasured photographs. Her mom must have dug the shirt out of the cedar chest—along with a battered pair of Levi's and some navy blue Chris-Craft duck shoes—and Abby wondered if the clothes smelled of lavender and mothballs like everything old her mother tucked away.

Abruptly, the man stopped the swing's motion, rising slowly to his feet. "I think it's time I stretched my legs a bit, maybe took a little walk to see if I remember anything about how I got here."

"Are you sure you're up to it?" Gretchen asked, hopping onto rubber-booted feet. "I'd be happy to show you around the farm but only if you feel strong enough."

"I'm slow, but mobile," he assured her, taking a few steps to prove it. "Just a touch wobbly, enough so that I wouldn't mind an arm to lean on, if one of you kind ladies is amenable to joining me."

"Please, let me take him," Abby said, scrambling out of the wicker chair so hastily she nearly toppled it over. "A walk would do me good, too."

Gretchen frowned her disapproval. "I'm not sure that's wise. He's still weak, and you're—"

Pregnant, Abby figured was forthcoming.

"Exhausted," her mother finished diplomatically. "You only just got up, and you really need to eat."

"I'm fine." Abby didn't want to take no for an answer. In Chicago, she could hold her own with egomaniacal artists and art dealers, yet she fell so easily into the role of eager-to-please daughter when she was back in Walnut Ridge. "Are you all right with my being your tour guide?"

The man nodded. "Right as rain."

"Abs," Gretchen said in that drawn-out way so that even one simple syllable brimmed with concern.

"Please," Abby tried, all she had left. There was little she could do to persuade her mom to change her mind when it was made up.

"Oh, dear." Gretchen's face hid nothing well, and Abby could plainly see that she was nervous, undoubtedly worried that Abby might lose her mind and say something that would freak out their guest. Finally, her mother sighed. "All right, go on without me." She faced the man who now stood near the railing, one hand upon it for support. "Just take it easy, and don't go far."

"Easy is about all I can do at the moment," he replied.

"While you two wander about, I'll get dressed and rustle up some breakfast for Abby." Gretchen put a hand against her daughter's cheek. "I'll give a holler in twenty minutes if you're not back."

"Got it," Abby replied and added softly, "Please, don't worry."

The man offered Abby the crook of his arm. "I guess I'm all yours, Miss Abigail."

As her mom looked on, Abby touched him rather tentatively, wondering if she'd feel some kind of current between them, a physical sense of reconnection. Instead, when she grasped his elbow, she felt an ease that she rarely experienced with anyone but her aunts and her mother. Maybe that was sign enough.

They proceeded gingerly down the porch steps and away from the house.

He paused not far along the path toward the barn and tipped back his head, drawing in a deep breath. "It's good to be alive on such a pretty morning," he said, looking oddly relaxed for someone in strange surroundings.

"I guess it is," she agreed.

Abby led him on a path across the lawn, avoiding broken branches the storm had tossed around the grass like land mines. The lawn was slick, damp with dew; the earth still soft from the rain. But they were in no hurry, and Abby didn't mind the snail's pace.

"You grew up here?" he asked, stopping again to catch his breath as they neared the barn.

"My whole life," Abby said, nodding at the big red structure that once held goats and pigs, even a couple dairy cows. Now it merely housed old harvesting equipment that was probably as rusty as the exterior paint was worn and the boards warped. "I had a lot of freedom," she said, squinting at the rising sun peeking over the roof. "I used to run around barefoot and pretend I was a bird or a horse. I'm glad I grew up when I did. It was a different time, you know? There wasn't so much pressure to prove yourself or be someone you're not."

"You can only be who you are," the man said, making it sound so simple.

She put a hand on her belly, wondering what it would be like for her baby if it grew up in the city, raised in a world full of immediate gratification, communicating by instant messages, forgetting what it felt like to share real intimacy or to talk face-to-face.

"There's something about all this green," the man said, turning his head as he took in their bucolic surroundings. "And the blue sky's so close you could touch it. I'll bet you miss it when you're gone."

"I do," she told him. "More than I realized. My head feels clearer when I'm here, and not just because I can't use my cell or a laptop on the farm." She tried hard to explain. "I feel like time stands still, you know? Like I can pause and mull things over without the world passing me by while I make up my mind."

"Sounds perfectly reasonable to me."

"Do you recall anything about your home, even if it's just the feel of it?" Abby asked suddenly. "You must have some sense of where you're from."

He rubbed his jaw, a tinge of sadness softening his voice as he countered, "What if I don't? Am I lost forever?"

"No, you're not lost forever," she replied. "It's impossible to completely forget your roots."

"I hope you're right." He turned away from her, glancing around them. "Will you show me the walnut grove where your mother discovered me?"

"Sure, I'll show you the grove," Abby agreed. "Although finding the exact spot where my mom tripped over you is another thing entirely."

"Can't we just follow the Yellow Brick Road?"

Abby grinned. "Ah, a sense of humor in times of stress," she said. "I wish some of that would rub off on me."

"Maybe it will," he replied, but didn't return her smile.

He took her arm, and they continued toward the walnut grove in silence. There was so much Abby wanted to say but knew she couldn't. Instead, she allowed herself to do something she rarely did: stay in the moment, enjoy his company and even the weight of his body as he leaned against her. She might not know who he was, but she certainly hadn't imagined him. If he turned out to be Sam Winston, she would have more time with him to treasure. And if he wasn't, well, at least she would have this.

As they got nearer to the trees, his steps grew more hesitant. The ground beneath them seemed a movable thing, littered as it was with walnuts and twigs. Even Abby felt a bit clumsy on her feet.

"You doing okay?" she asked.

"Yes," he said, though his breaths became noisy as they drifted between the rows of trees, searching for something Abby couldn't see.

A light mist thickened the air around them the deeper they went into the grove.

Abby had a sense that the clouds had been hung too low that morning. The fog made it hard to tell where exactly they were, and she felt nearly lost in her own backyard.

"It's here somewhere," the man told her as they ambled up one row, cutting through to another, until he stopped abruptly and jerked Abby to a halt alongside him. He swiveled right and left until he seemed to zero in on something Abby couldn't see. "There," he said and grunted. "It's right in front of me."

"What's right in front of you?" she started to say, wondering if he'd received some kind of message from the trees. Otherwise, how could he tell? Abby could barely glimpse the tips of her fingers.

He released her arm and walked through the thick air, each stride filled with purpose. Abby scrambled over the walnuts, the world around her full of fuzzy shapes. She envisioned a blur rushing by her, felt something brush past her leg.

"Matilda?" she said under her breath, praying it was the cat and not a possum.

Abby ducked beneath branches to find where he'd ended up. As soon as she was nearer, she spotted him winding around the tree, pausing at times to squat, most likely searching for his wallet or another lost object that would point to who he was.

"Can I help?" she asked.

Instead of replying, he muttered, "Strange," and bent over, plucking up something from amidst the tree's roots.

"What is it?" she asked.

"I thought they were robin's eggs, maybe a nest knocked to the ground." He held his hand out to her. "It looks like turquoise. Do you recognize it?"

It was a necklace strung with pale blue stones on a leather tether. Abby gently rubbed away the dirt. "It's beautiful," she said, "but I don't know whose it is." She gave it back to him. "Maybe it's yours, and the tornado blew it into the grove along with you."

"Perhaps your mother would know." He slipped the beads into his shirt pocket before turning toward the tree itself. He stared at it, hands on his hips, before he approached, reaching out to touch the V where the trunk was split up the middle. "This is the place," he said, without a lick of doubt in his voice. "I was here beneath these branches when the lightning struck."

"Lightning?" Abby looked cockeyed at him. "You think you were under this walnut tree when it was hit?"

"I know I was," he said and wrinkled his nose, sniffing the air. "I remember the jolt and the smell of fire."

Abby bit her lip to keep from saying, *That's impossible.*

"I know it sounds crazy," he remarked as if reading her mind. "But it's there in my head like the slip of a dream. I'm sure it's true, but I can't make sense of it either." He held up the reddened palms of his hands, gazing at them as if he'd never seen them before. "I can feel the heat on my flesh, the surge of fire through my blood before I fell to my knees."

Abby still didn't know what to think. "You're sure it was *that* tree?"

"Yes," he said and touched the peeling bark. "This one."

But Abby wondered if he wasn't confused, his brain garbling truth and fiction, as the tree he indicated was one she knew very well from her childhood. She'd even named it, calling it "the treasure tree" because she'd delighted in climbing its gnarled branches and hiding objects in the deeply split trunk. She even knew the secret of how the tree had been nearly sliced in two, something that Sam Winston would have known as well, or *should* have known if he hadn't forgotten.

"That walnut tree was hit by lightning years ago, before I was born. Before *you* were born," she told him, because it was at the heart of a story her mother had recited, passed down from Sam's mother, Lily. When Sam's grandparents had just moved to the farm, a lightning storm had scorched the barren grove and made the earth come alive again. "So maybe you're mixed up," she began in the most sensitive way that she could, "because everyone knows that lightning never strikes the same place twice."

"Well, they're wrong." He slowly turned to her, and the furrows deepened in his cheeks. "It's not true that lightning can't hit the same spot. It does, all the time. Just like a lost love, it can find its way back if you give it half a chance."

Abby gazed at him, unblinking, her heart pounding something fierce. She was hardly a New Age crystal-wearing hippie who saw auras and took directions from her dreams. But something strange and complicated was happening here, and it had to do with this man who stood before her.

A sense of light-headedness overtook her, and she wobbled, a soft "oh" escaping her lips as she closed her arms around her belly. She felt a flutter inside, even though logic told her it was too early to feel the baby move within. "Quickening," the first movements were called, according to the pregnancy sites she'd scoured these past few days. At eight weeks, her baby was no bigger than a raspberry with a heartbeat. Still, what she'd sensed was very real, and she wondered if what she'd felt wasn't the baby at all but a sense of her own reawakening, like everything she'd loved wasn't really lost.

"You're expecting," the man said, and Abby realized he'd been watching her. The directness of his silver-gray gaze was unsettling.

She could have denied it. That would have been easy. Or she could have said nothing at all.

But a shaky "Yes" emerged before she could stop it. "I just found out. It's why I had to come home."

"Does the father know?"

She shook her head.

"Do you love him?"

What a strange question!

"Of course I do," Abby said, defensive.

"Then why?" he asked, his tone so raw that it made her want to cry.

Even his own eyes seemed to glisten, and Abby found herself wondering, if he wasn't her father, why would he care?

"He left before I knew about the baby," Abby admitted, willing herself to stay calm despite how her chest ached. "He wanted space to figure things out." She wasn't sure why she was sharing so much with him, but she couldn't stop herself. "I can't make Nathan feel the way I feel. He has to come back on his own terms or not at all. I don't want the baby to be why."

He sucked in his cheeks, making them appear even gaunter. "I understand how hard it is to find your footing when you're certain of your heart and the one you love isn't sure at all."

"It stinks," she said, the mere thought of Nate's indecision tying her stomach in knots. "I just want to be with him."

"Then don't let so much time and space come between you that, when your minds are made up, it's too late."

She shivered, suddenly wondering if coming home and putting distance between them only pushed Nate further away. Had she made a mistake?

"You'll do the right thing," he said, giving her arm a nudge.

"How can you be sure? You don't even know me," she said, and a sob caught in her throat, despite how she tried to be strong.

"What I know is that you have a very kind and generous mother." He turned toward the scarred walnut tree, catching thumbs in his jeans pockets. "Surely the apple didn't fall far from the tree."

"I wish you were him," Abby found herself saying, under her breath, so she thought.

But somehow he heard. "Who's that?" he asked and looked at her.

How tempted she was to blurt out: *my father.* Instead, Abby told him, "Sam Winston. He was an old friend of my mother's, and this farm was once his. No one's seen or heard from him in forty years."

"Hmm" slipped from his lips like a breath. "That would explain it."

"What?"

He shrugged. "Just something your mother said when I was looking over some photos on the mantel. I got the sense she hoped I'd recognize somebody in them. Could be she wishes I were this long-lost friend too."

Abby nodded, saying nothing.

He glanced around him with an uncertain expression, as if absorbing the red of the barn, the blue of the sky, and the green of the grass, perhaps trying to remember or maybe just soaking it all in, imagining what his life would be like if he truly were Sam Winston. "This would be a hard place to forget," he said.

Abby sighed. "You're right, it would."

He shot her that barely there smile, and she felt her spirits lift just as the fog began to lift from the air around them.

"Shall we go back before your mother has to holler?" he asked.

"Yes, let's not make her holler. It isn't pretty," Abby said and accepted the arm he offered without hesitation.

With so much weighing on her mind, it didn't register until they were out of the grove altogether that the once-bare branches of the walnut trees harbored tiny green buds.

They had come alive again.

THIRTEEN

Gretchen hovered over the sink, gazing out the window, resenting the appearance of the mist that kept her from seeing past the barn to the walnut grove. She was second-guessing herself, wondering if she'd done the right thing letting Abby take the Man Who Might Be Sam on a walk alone. Although Abby seemed better this morning, more her rational self, Gretchen couldn't stop thinking of the old photograph tucked into the pages of Abby's sketchbook and all the pencil drawings of an ever-changing Sam.

"She's in such a fragile state," Gretchen said aloud. "I shouldn't have left them to wander off alone. I should have gone with them."

"They're fine," Bennie remarked from the breakfast table. "You can't worry about what may happen between them. What will be, will be."

"It's true, you can't fight fate," Trudy concurred, causing Gretchen to sigh for the thousandth time.

The twins had eaten already but had stuck around, keeping Gretchen company while she fidgeted. Trudy busily knitted a baby hat for Abby's unborn child. Yellow yarn unfurled from the ball in her lap while her needles busily clicked.

"They should be back by now," Gretchen said, leaning over

the counter and so near the glass her breath clouded the panes. "It's been nearly twenty minutes."

She was getting ready to head outside and yell for them to come in for breakfast when she spotted the pair trudging toward the barn, their arms intertwined.

"Here they come," she announced and wiped her palms on the thighs of her jeans, trying not to jump out of her skin. Quickly, she concerned herself with heating the skillet, adding a pat of butter before she cracked half a dozen eggs into a bowl and began furiously beating them.

She was pouring the eggs into the skillet when she heard the slap of the screen door, then the more solid click of the mudroom door. Suddenly Abby burst into the kitchen, her cheeks flushed and eyes bright.

"Hey!" she said and rushed up to Gretchen, giving her a hug. "You're not going to believe this! But the walnut trees have buds!"

"Buds? Are you sure?" Gretchen stared at her daughter, concerned that a gush of pregnancy hormones was making Abby see things. "But that's not possible," she said and peered out the window to find the fog lifting; but there was still too much mist for her to make out anything but the ghostly shapes of the trees.

"I'm not kidding." Abby sounded just a little out of breath. "The walnut grove seems to have risen from the dead."

"Could be the lightning's responsible," the man offered, coming up beside Gretchen, their arms brushing as he washed his hands. "Some folks think that a strike can make bad soil turn fertile again."

That sounded an awful lot like something Sam would say, Gretchen thought, and her gaze met his. For a second, it seemed that her heart had stopped beating. If he *was* Sam Winston, had he created the storm that brought him home and conjured up the lightning to bring the grove back to life, just as Hank Littlefoot had years before him? Was that why he couldn't remember anything?

"I'll believe it when I see it for myself," Gretchen replied.

"Would I lie to you?" Abby said with a laugh, and she squeezed between Gretchen and the Man Who Might Be Sam to wash up before breakfast. Then she caught her mom around the waist and bent toward the stove. "Careful or you're going to burn our grub!"

"Out of my way, child," Gretchen teased and nudged the girl aside. She took a spatula to the skillet, pushing the eggs around and, every now and then, glancing out the window. Something had happened to the farm since the twister yesterday, that she couldn't deny. Exactly what, she wasn't sure, but there was nothing logical about it.

"Can I pour you a cold one?" Abby was asking the man as she lifted the pitcher of juice from the counter.

"Make it a double," he said.

Chairs scraped and old wooden joints creaked as Abby took two glasses of juice to the table, and she and the Man Who Might Be Sam sat down alongside Bennie and Trudy.

"Did you show him around?" Gretchen asked, forcing a calm she didn't feel as she slipped bread into the old toaster.

"Yes, ma'am, I sure did," Abby said, a brightness to her voice that made her sound like a kid, one without the weight of the world on her shoulders. "We went to the very spot in the grove where you found him. I think Matilda was out there, or at least I hope it was her. Something brushed against my leg and ran off."

"Matilda can come and go like a vapor sometimes," Trudy quipped.

"Oh, I found something out there, beneath the tree where I was struck down," the man said and got up from his chair, plucking an object from his shirt pocket. He brought it round to Gretchen at the stove and held it up so she could see. "The stones feel so warm, as though the sun's been shining on them."

But it was foggy outside, Gretchen mused, taking the beads from him. She felt the warmth he described only for an instant before the turquoise turned cool in her hand.

"Does it belong to him, or is it something you lost?" Abby asked as Gretchen stared at the necklace.

No, it wasn't hers, Gretchen knew, looking at the pale blue beads in the light of the kitchen window. A knot tied itself up tight in her belly as she recalled the last time she'd seen the necklace. Sam had been wearing it around his throat. "Do you mind if I keep these for now?" she got out, never answering Abby's question.

"Of course you can," the man told her. "I found them in your grove."

Gretchen nodded and quickly pressed them into her jeans pocket, wiping her hands on the dish towel, feeling even more discombobulated than before, if that was possible.

"Oh, and don't freak out," Abby piped up, "but I told him the truth."

"The truth about what?" The skillet clattered against the burner as Gretchen dropped it along with the serving spoon, a smattering of scrambled eggs showering the stovetop.

"That he reminds us of the man whose family owned this farm," Abby said, giving her a pointed look. "A long-ago friend of yours named Sam Winston."

"You told him about Sam?" Gretchen's tongue seemed to stick to the roof of her mouth. "How much?"

"Enough," the man said, and he wrinkled his bruised brow. "It explains why you were so quick to take me in." He shook his head. "Maybe it would be easier if I were this fellow Sam instead of having no clue who I am or why I'm here. Why can't I remember such a simple thing as my own name?" He hit the table with his palm, rattling his glass so it slopped orange juice onto the table.

Gretchen jumped as the toast took that moment to pop out of the toaster.

"Give yourself a chance," she heard Abby saying to him. "Even Rome wasn't built in a day."

"And it took the town nearly six months to get up a new bridge over the river," Bennie added in her crisp voice, and Trudy's knitting needles stopping clicking long enough for her to add, "Though I think the Walmart in the next county went up in about two weeks. They don't mess around, do they?"

Heaven help us, Gretchen thought, drawing in a deep breath.

She managed to keep her composure long enough to fix two heaping plates of eggs and toast, taking them over to the table and plunking them down before her daughter and the Man

Who Might Be Sam. Then she took a seat across from them both, watching as they dug in. It was like viewing her life the way it should have been if Sam Winston had never left Walnut Ridge. If she'd asked him to stay. If she had known then that she truly loved him. If he had actually fathered Abigail.

All those *ifs* had haunted Gretchen for years and years, especially as Abby had grown up, asking so many questions. Until Gretchen had finally packed up all those *ifs* and stored them away, like the boxes of Lily and Cooper Winston's old clothes up in the attic. But clearly residual emotions couldn't be so easily contained by plastic bins filled with lavender and mothballs.

"Mom? Did you hear me?" Abby asked, and Gretchen shook aside her thoughts to listen. "You really need to give him a haircut. He's definitely looking better without that horrid beard, but he's got a mullet straight out of the eighties."

"A mullet?" the Man Who Might Be Sam repeated and picked up the butter knife, trying to catch his reflection in the blade. "What's that? It doesn't sound good, whatever it is."

"It's when your hair's all business in front and a party in the back," Abby told him matter-of-factly. "It's very old-school Billy Ray Cyrus."

"And that's not acceptable?" the man asked, eyebrows arched against his bruised forehead.

"Nope," Abby got out as she swallowed a piece of toast.

Gretchen sat like a spectator at a badminton match, surprised by the rapport between Abby and the Man Who Might Be Sam. He even seemed more relaxed since the walk, less unsettled. Abby, too, appeared to have let go of her worry. They were good for each other, Gretchen mused, but found herself thinking nonetheless, *Please don't break Abigail's heart.* What if this stranger who'd fallen from the clouds left their lives just as suddenly? Gretchen worried about Abby. It was so early in the pregnancy, and she was already under so much stress with Nathan walking out two weeks before. She couldn't fathom the kind of pain Abby would feel if she were deserted by another man, equally important. To Gretchen, this baby was Abby's miracle, just as Abby had been for her all those years ago, even if she'd been too young to know it at the time.

"So will you do it?" her daughter said and got up, rounding the table to hug Gretchen from behind, pressing her cheek in Gretchen's hair. "Will you give him a trim? I'd offer to do it, but the last time I cut my own hair I had bangs that were insanely cockeyed. Took two years to grow them out."

"I'd be happy to volunteer," Trudy cheerfully offered, "except that he might not appreciate that Bennie and I use the mixing bowl for guidance when we give each other a snip."

The man repeated, "You use a mixing bowl?"

Abby laughed. "He'd look like one of the Beatles."

"So?" Bennie sniffed, feigning offense as she shook a finger in her niece's direction. "What's wrong with the Beatles? Particularly since you were named after *Abbey Road.*"

"I was?" Abby drew away from Gretchen, loosely shaking her shoulders. "You never told me that."

"That's because I didn't—" Gretchen started to protest, but Bennie talked right over her.

"It's a well-known fact," the older twin announced, "that Sam Winston couldn't go anywhere without whistling a tune from the Beatles' last album. Whenever he came by to fetch Gretchen from our house in town, it was 'Here Comes the Sun.' Dear Lord." Milky-blue eyes rolled heavenward. "I could hear him from two blocks away, sometimes three. It used to drive me batty."

"No wonder you played Beatles songs so often when I was a kid." Abby crouched beside Gretchen's chair, giving her a look. "Why didn't you tell me?"

"The truth is I just liked the name Abigail," Gretchen said, which was only half right. Yes, Sam had been a Beatles fan from early on. Lily Winston frequently had their LPs playing when Gretchen would visit. She would sit with Sam on the back porch, the music flowing through the opened windows, while Sam perched on the top step with a sharp-bladed knife, carving tiny shapes out of errant blocks of walnut. "I think I like Paul best," Gretchen had said once to make conversation. "Or even Ringo. He's kind of like a big puppy." But if Sam had a favorite, it was George Harrison, which made sense as George was the quiet one, the contemplative one, much like Sam himself. *Abbey Road* had come out the year before Sam left with the church mission, and every time Gretchen heard those songs she thought of him. But that had nothing to do with her naming Abby, she reminded herself, at least not consciously. It was simply a rather neat coincidence.

The Man Who Might Be Sam sat quietly, hands in his lap, watching Gretchen with those familiar eyes and listening.

"So what else don't I know about my roots?" her daughter asked, rising to her feet and walking back around the table. She gripped the back of her empty chair with one hand, waving the other as she spoke. "I came home to figure out what's best for me, but how can I decide if I don't know everything about who I am?"

"Who we were once doesn't always define who we've become," Trudy said and stopped knitting for long enough to count stitches with her fingers. "Don't you agree, Gretch?"

"I do." Gretchen had spent way too much time ruminating over the choices she'd made. It had taken years before she'd finally accepted that Sam wasn't coming back, that Annika had flown the coop, and she was on her own, caring for a child, a farm, and her sisters, too. *Must we live our lives in hindsight?* she wanted to ask. Wasn't it enough to be right where they were, to accept their lot and move forward? Or was she lying to herself, believing she could ever forget the mistakes she'd made and never ever dwell on the past?

"Why do I feel like you're being evasive?" Abby asked, staring solemnly at her.

"I'm not," Gretchen insisted, her mouth tasting sour. "I just don't seem to have the answers you want to hear. There's a difference."

Her daughter sighed petulantly and, for an instant, Gretchen saw a twelve-year-old Abigail, pouting in pigtails, not a thirty-nine-year-old woman who ran an art gallery in the big city. Why did it always seem that when her daughter came home, she turned into a kid, all tangled hair and endless questions?

"Can we talk about this later?" Gretchen murmured as she got up and began to collect empty plates. "Let me clean up first," she said and wished her heart would stop beating so wildly, "then I need to find my sewing scissors so I can cut our guest's hair. That is, if he's willing—"

"I am," the man said, although he didn't sound as sure as he looked.

"We'll take care of the dishes," Bennie suggested, pushing back her chair. Trudy set down her knitting on the table and quickly followed suit. "You take care of Billy Ray Cyrus."

So while the twins cleared the table—with a bit of help from Abby—Gretchen left the room to fetch her sharpest sewing shears, a comb, and a towel. She took a deep breath before reentering the kitchen and instructing the Man Who Might Be Sam to drag a chair to the middle of the floor.

While her sisters and daughter busied themselves at the sink, scraping plates and washing dishes—and pretending not to pay attention—Gretchen sat the man down and draped the towel around his shoulders.

"Be still," she told him, hoping he couldn't see her fingers tremble as she combed out his salt-and-pepper hair, snipping a bit here and a little more there. Hadn't she done this once before with Sam years ago, when he'd asked her to chop off the ponytail he'd grown before he'd left for Africa? He'd told her there might be times he couldn't wash for weeks, and he wasn't game for dreadlocks. Gretchen had gone whole hog, nearly giving him the buzz cut of a marine. When she'd finished, he'd blinked, looking dazed for a full five minutes before he'd started laughing. "If Hank Littlefoot could see me now," he'd said, staring in the mirror and touching the back of his newly naked neck. "I just hope I don't lose my superpowers," he'd joked, "like poor old Samson."

"Hey." Strong fingers grasped her trembling hand to still it. "Are you all right?" the man asked. "You're shaking."

"I'm sorry." Gretchen realized she'd been holding the scissors awfully near his earlobe. "I promise I won't cut off your ear."

"Just don't take it too close," he remarked, his gray gaze following her as she began to snip at the nape of his neck. "I'm not sure I'd recognize myself scalped."

"You don't even recognize yourself now," Gretchen said, trying to joke, but he didn't laugh.

"You're right." He tugged at the towel around his neck, clearly uncomfortable. "Until I can remember my past, all I've got is the present. Kind of like you were talking about with Abby earlier."

Gretchen put a hand on his shoulder. "When it comes down to it, that's really all any of us have got, isn't it?"

He gave a quick nod. "Yes, I guess it is."

Trudy was wrong, she decided. He didn't smell like sorrow and lemongrass. He smelled like a man—one scrubbed clean with Ivory soap—but a man nonetheless, all woodsy and warm. And he was solid and real, not a vaporous specter.

Gretchen touched his cheek to angle his head, and a shiver went through her. "Hold still, please," she said, knowing that, whoever he was, there was something compelling about him, a kind of current emanating from him. She could feel it thrumming from his body and through her hand. Even when she drew her fingers away, she could sense it, buzzing like an insect in her ears.

"Is there a problem?" he asked as she hesitated.

"No," Gretchen lied, "there's no problem at all."

It took little more than fifteen minutes for her to clip his hair to a reasonable length, hardly the flattop she'd given Sam that summer day long ago. When she removed the towel from his neck and brushed the loose hair from his collar, she saw something that stopped her heart again: a dark brown mole low on the back of his neck. It appeared swollen, like a puffy teardrop. A bit dry and scaly. Was it not a birthmark at all but a scab from his bout with the storm? She had glimpsed other scratches on his arms and legs when he'd come out of the bath in his towel. This could be one of them.

But if it *was* a birthmark, well, such a thing—such a small thing—would be another piece that fit into the puzzle. Sam Winston had been born with a teardrop-shaped mole at the base of his neck, one that seemed to get darker whenever he was out in the sun. He had hated the thing and had wanted it removed, but Lily had steadfastly refused to let that happen. "It's a sign of your gift," his mother had told him. "A connection to your past, to your grandfather and your great-great-grandfather as well."

But the older Sam got, the more he'd seemed to resent the burden this legacy had placed on him. "Someday," he had told her, "I just want to forget it all and be free."

So are you free enough now? she had asked in the first letter she'd sent to him in Africa via the church's care package. Only she had never heard back from him, not a peep.

"We're done," Gretchen said, slipping the scissors into her back pocket.

"That was painless enough." The man reached up to touch

his newly trimmed head. "I feel ten pounds lighter already."

Gretchen opened her mouth, tempted to ask about the mole, to see if he'd had it his whole life, only she never got the words out.

"Oh, heavens, he's back," Bennie said quite plainly, shutting off the tap and cocking her head toward the front of the house. "I can hear his plodding footsteps."

Trudy dried her hands on the dishtowel, leaning near the screen of a half-opened window and inhaling deeply. "Pine tar soap," she said, which was as good as agreement.

There came a sudden and very loud pounding at the door. "Gretch? It's Frank Tilby. I'm back. So c'mon and open up!"

"The sheriff?" Abby said, turning questioning eyes right on Gretchen. "What's he doing here again?"

"I don't know," Gretchen said. "I'm sure it's nothing," she added, though she knew that was about as far from the truth as she could get.

FOURTEEN

Frank Tilby considered himself an honorable man in that, no matter how he screwed up sometimes—well, he *was* only human—he always kept his word. When he'd told Gretchen he'd return within a few hours, he did exactly that. Setting down the case in his hand, he pushed up his hat, wiping sweat from his brow with his sleeve. He took a deep breath and raised a fist to soundly knock on the door of the farmhouse before hollering through it: "Gretch? It's Frank Tilby! I'm back. So c'mon and open up!"

While he waited on the welcome mat, he whistled tunelessly, the noise dying on his lips at the click of the lock and a swift squeal of hinges.

"You're here again so soon?" Gretchen said, suddenly standing before him. She was dressed more presentably this time in jeans and a pale linen blouse, her hair neatly drawn back into a ponytail. She wore a nervous frown on her lips.

"As promised," he said and, with a soft grunt, picked up his field kit. "I've got everything we need right here."

A soft "oh" escaped her mouth and her gaze fell to the aluminum briefcase clutched in his right hand. "If I didn't know better, I'd figure you'd brought a backgammon set."

Only they both realized what was inside the case, and it was hardly a game.

"May I come in?" he asked, plucking off his cap and tucking it beneath his arm. He felt sweat trickle down his face despite the cool morning. He'd walked the half mile from the dirt road again, which had him breathing hard. The overhang of belly atop belt attested to the fact that he wasn't used to regular exercise, not anymore. Sometimes even he found it hard to believe that he'd been an athlete back in high school. The years may have been kind to Gretchen but they'd definitely sucker punched him.

"How long will this take?" she asked, not looking happy about the whole thing, or perhaps just her part in it.

"Five minutes tops," he said.

"Then you'll leave the poor man alone?"

"I'll have no cause to bother him if he's done nothing wrong," he assured her. "And if it turns out he's Sam Winston, hell, I'll be the first to welcome him back from the grave."

"For goodness' sake! The things that come out of your mouth." Gretchen's face looked pinched, and she seemed about to turn him away.

Although she had to know it wouldn't have done any good. Frank Tilby had been a small-town sheriff for twenty years, ever since his election to the post after his dad had retired his badge. So he was rarely deterred by a door in the face. Like sweet ants in the summertime, he'd just keep coming back. That was his M.O., always had been.

"Made up your mind?" He shifted on his feet, wishing he could scratch his back as perspiration slid down his spine.

"As if I have a choice." Gretchen sighed. "Just be quick about it." She waved him inside.

He nodded, telling her as he entered, "The boys are making good progress on the oak. They should at least have enough of it cut by later this afternoon so a car could get in or out."

"Terrific," she said, hardly sounding like she meant it.

Frank tried not to think that she might actually enjoy being stranded out here with a man who reminded her of an old flame.

"Oh, hey, and the power company's arrived, too," he went on as he followed her into the kitchen. "They're aiming to fix the broken cables by day's end. Although"—he hesitated as he glanced up at the brass fixture, its bulbs abruptly flickering—"I'm not sure that'll make much of a difference since you seem to be powered by magic."

"What about the phone company?" Gretchen asked. "Will they repair the line?"

"They should be on their way." The sheriff stepped around the oak table. "Is it okay if I set up shop?"

"Just don't get black powder all over everything."

He laughed. "You've seen too many bad movies, young lady. I'm not going to dust for prints. I'll just be using my neat little ink pad. A two-year-old could do it."

"A two-year-old, huh? Well, in that case," she said, giving him a look.

He ignored her sarcasm because she'd been giving him guff since they were teenagers. He liked to tell himself it was her way of keeping a safe distance between them.

"Can you fetch Sam Winston's ghost for me, then? The

sooner I do this, the quicker I'm out of here," the sheriff said, plucking his hat from beneath his arm and catching it on the back side of a chair. He set down his field kit before running a hand over his sweaty pompadour. "That's assuming he's still around. He hasn't taken off, has he?"

"No. He's still here." Gretchen had sent him upstairs with Abby, suggesting her daughter show him around the farmhouse. "I'll go get him," she offered, but she made no move to leave.

Despite her irritation, Frank could tell she was anxious. He imagined she was chomping at the bit to get the dirt on whether or not the prodigal Sam had returned. What if her mysterious houseguest didn't recall who he was for weeks or even months? What if no one came looking for him, and they never really knew for sure if he was a soul come back to life or a con man with Sam's gray eyes?

Frank only hoped she understood that his solution was the most logical one, and all he had to do was take some prints then run them through the computer to find a match. If all went well, they'd be able to identify the man in a virtual snap.

"It'll be okay. Trust me," Frank said and reached for Gretchen's hand, giving it a damp squeeze. "You don't have to look so petrified. It'll be utterly painless," he added, assuming that was the cause of her hesitation. Though why she was so concerned with offending a stranger who was taking advantage of her kindness, he wasn't sure.

She tugged her fingers from his grasp.

"Give me five minutes," she said, leaving the sheriff alone to wonder about the look he'd seen in Gretchen's eyes. It was as if the woman was letting herself get attached to this guy.

"Nearly forty years gone, and he suddenly comes back," Frank murmured to himself. "If he's really Sam Winston, I'll eat my hat."

FIFTEEN

Gretchen smoothed her blouse, steadying her nerves, before she headed up the stairs. She skimmed her palm along the well-worn banister, remembering how it had felt to move in with Sam's parents when she was pregnant with Abby, once Annika had forced her out after chastising her repeatedly for being a disappointment and a dreadful example to her younger sisters.

Gretchen had felt nothing but welcome living under the Winstons' roof. Lily and Coop had treated her as kin from the moment they'd agreed to take her in. It was a magical time in so many ways, despite the worry. Sunshine had spilled through the windows most every morning, and each breath she took smelled as crisp and fresh as summer grass. Lily and Cooper Winston had inherited the farm from Lily's parents, had added on to the tiny house, had hoped that someday Sam and his wife would make their home inside these walls, too.

But once that pastor had told them, "I'm sorry, Sam is missing and believed dead," everything had changed and there was no going back. Gretchen had stayed that night with the Winstons, sleeping on the daybed in the tiny sunroom, awakening in the dark to the crash of thunder and lightning. A fierce storm had whipped through the farm with such anger that it had decimated the walnut grove. Lily described peering out the window and seeing walnuts raining from the sky. Gretchen had gone out with Cooper the next morning to find the ground littered with green hulls. The winds had sheared the leaves from every branch, and the walnut trees had never borne fruit again.

Like the trees, something in Lily and Cooper had died that day as well. Their hearts profoundly broken, their health had swiftly declined, Lily suffering chest pains and Cooper uncontrollably high blood pressure. The only thing that seemed to keep them going was knowing there was a grandchild on the way, and both held on long enough to see Abby's birth. But before Abigail had turned one, Lily and Cooper Winston were gone, passing in their sleep, Lily just two days after her husband. "Heart failure," the town's doctor, who was also the coroner, had decreed. Gretchen figured that was about as good a way to describe it as any.

Because Lily and Cooper had no one else close, they had deeded the house and the farm to Gretchen and Abby, lock, stock, and barrel. Not long after, Annika showed up on the porch with Bennie, Trudy, and two suitcases and a few boxes. "Your father deserted me and so did you, the day you showed up pregnant," she'd announced. "Now that you're a mother, you'll be stuck here in the middle of nowhere until the child is grown. You might as well tend to your own sisters, too, while I go do what I've always wanted. I'd say it's high time I lived life for myself." With that, Annika had left the twins and headed to an artists' colony in Key West. Gretchen had never heard from her again. Perhaps even worse, she did not miss her.

Her father no longer kept in touch either, having replaced

his family long ago once he'd married Miss Childs and she'd given him three new daughters. He'd had a thriving veterinary practice in Bozeman, Montana, according to a Christmas newsletter from years and years before, though Gretchen imagined he was probably retired by now. Perhaps even deceased. It was strange, she thought, how sometimes blood mattered less when it came to family than who loved you enough to stick around.

". . . yes, those arrowheads belonged to Sam Winston, and the feathers and the geodes. You can hold them if you'd like. I used to believe they had special powers, like they could transport me to somewhere else. Maybe they'll spark your memories if you let them . . ."

As she stepped up to the second floor landing, Gretchen could hear Abby's animated voice, telling the Man Who Might Be Sam about various objects cluttering her old room—once Sam's room—that she'd never been able to part with.

". . . I love the finger paintings that Sam did in grade school. They're really quite good and the use of color is amazing . . ."

Gretchen hung back, listening to the warm tones of the man's voice as he turned the focus to Abby, inquiring about her work and her own ambitions. Abby was soon rattling on about the gallery in Chicago and a series of acrylics she'd started, all scenes that related to rain.

"It's symbolic of our emotions, don't you think?" she was saying. "How we can be mad one moment, our hearts rumbling like thunder, a storm raging inside, and, with one kind word or a gentle touch, it can all blow over in a second. The next thing we know, the sky has cleared, our pulse downshifts, and we feel like we're given a clean slate to start again. Even the drops of rain left behind sparkle in the sun like diamonds."

"Water's worth more than currency in some places," Gretchen heard the man remark. "People fight over it, die for it."

"Is that something you remember? Being in a war zone?" Abby asked as Gretchen quietly approached the half-opened door, hanging outside to hear his answer.

"What I do recall seems more like random thoughts and ideas than anything concrete," he answered. "There's no rhyme or reason. They seem to come and go at will."

"Maybe some of those thoughts will be about your past," Abby suggested. "Maybe your brain is working to put the pieces together."

"We'll see about that."

Gretchen took that opportunity to knock, pushing wide the door and announcing herself with a "Hey, you two, I need you downstairs, okay? Sheriff Tilby has to get something from—" She paused and looked straight at him. She had nearly called him "Sam."

"Me," the man filled in for her and rubbed at the back of his neck. "What could I have that he wants?"

Gretchen noticed then that the swelling on his brow was even less than it had been that morning. What was once a purple goose egg now appeared as a smaller pink bump. He certainly appeared to heal very quickly.

"The sheriff's here for your fingerprints," Gretchen said point-blank, avoiding any whitewash. With Frank Tilby downstairs waiting, there was no way around it besides. "He'd like to help figure out who you are."

The man cocked his head, eyes narrowed. "You sure he's not back to arrest me, maybe for trespassing or loitering? Just to keep me away from you?"

At that, Abby snorted. "He can't arrest you for being somewhere you're wanted, and we want you here with us. So he's got no cause."

"I appreciate that," the Man Who Might Be Sam said and touched Abby's arm.

The way Abby looked at him with such hope in her face made Gretchen's heart hurt. What would Abby do if the truth wasn't what she'd dreamed? What if this man wasn't Sam after all? On the other hand, what if he was and what if he soon recalled enough to explain to Abs that he'd had no part at all in creating her?

Either way, it would be a blow. Abby would be furious with Gretchen for lying to her, and Gretchen would risk losing Sam again as well.

"Come on," Abby said, tugging at the man's arm. "Let's get this over with. Think of it as pulling off a Band-Aid. It hurts more if you do it slowly. It's quicker and less painful if you just yank."

"Yank, don't pull. Got it," the fellow repeated. And though he still appeared guarded, the hard look on his face softened slightly. "This may be the only way to get to the bottom of things. If there's anything I've done that I should regret, it's best to find out now."

"I can't imagine that," Gretchen said, and Abby chimed in, "Of course you haven't done anything wrong."

The man ducked his head, though his expression remained

worried. "It's nice to know you don't share the sheriff's assessment that I might be a criminal."

"I don't share Frank Tilby's opinion on much," Gretchen said and gave him a reassuring look. "You ready for this?"

"As I'll ever be."

Abby was the first out the door and the Man Who Might Be Sam followed closely behind. He brushed past Gretchen in the doorway, causing the hairs on her arms to prickle. Though Gretchen may have seemed calm on the outside, her insides had tied themselves into knots.

Bennie and Trudy had made their way to the kitchen already, settling into chairs at the round table, opposite where the sheriff sat. Gretchen put her arm around Abby's shoulders as they stood a short way back.

"Just tell me what needs to be done, and I'll do it," the man said, approaching the sheriff. "I'd like to know who I am as much as anyone." His brow creased and lips pursed, concern written there for all to see.

"This won't take but a few minutes," Frank Tilby told him, rising to his feet as the man stepped forward. "Give me your left hand, if you would, and we'll get to it."

Without a word, the man reached out his arm, and the sheriff proceeded to roll each finger and thumb over a tiny black ink pad. Then he guided each digit toward a white card lying on the table.

"Normally when we print subjects at a crime scene, it's to eliminate them as suspects," Frank explained as he positioned the pad of each fingertip onto a particular square, gently rolling and leaving behind a black smudge. "In your case, we'll search the database for matching prints for identification purposes."

Gretchen felt Abby's fingers reach for hers and squeeze. She squeezed back. For the next few moments, no one spoke.

When he was done, Frank Tilby ripped open a packet no bigger than a matchbook and pulled out a moist towelette.

"This should get most of the ink off," he said. "The rest will come off in time."

"So that's all there is to it?" the man asked, seeming surprised.

Before he answered, Frank picked up the card with the black smudges from the table. He walked toward a sunny window, tilting the paper toward the light and squinting at it as if his life depended on it. A noise escaped his mouth, rather like a disapproving sniff, before he patted his chest pocket, retrieving a pair of spectacles that he plunked on his nose. Then he squinted some more through his glasses, eyeing the smudges outlined by the black boxes, and he sniffed again.

Gretchen didn't like the sound of it.

"You are done, right, Sheriff?" she repeated, sensing something was very, very wrong.

"Well, we would be, if the circumstances were ordinary," Frank replied and looked at her over the rims of his specs.

"And by ordinary, you mean what?" Gretchen wanted to strangle him. This was hardly a time to be cryptic. "Is something off?"

"You could say that," the sheriff replied, walking back toward the table and setting the card down with a flick of his fingers, as if it were meaningless. He crossed his arms, screwed up his face, and looked over at the Man Who Might Be Sam, busy cleaning his hand with the towelette. "What I'm wondering is how in the hell it so happens that our friend here's got no discernible prints."

No prints? Gretchen tried to digest what that meant.

Abby instantly jumped to the man's defense. "He was struck by lightning during the storm! His hands have been burned."

"Makes no difference," Tilby told her. "Even if the burn is severe, the whorls should regenerate."

The Man Who Might Be Sam stopped wiping the ink off his fingers, the tips of which now appeared a deep purple. His expression stoic, he bluntly asked, "What exactly do you want me to do, Sheriff? Clearly, I can't give you something I don't have."

"He just wants to scare you," Abby said and took another step toward Frank Tilby, anger turning her face beet red. "You don't really care who he is. You just don't like that he's here with my mother."

"Now hold on there, missy!" The sheriff shook a finger at Abby. "I'm just doing my job—"

"Don't you speak to her in that tone, Franklin Tilby," Bennie sharply uttered.

"You bully!" Trudy shook a knitting needle at him, warning, "If you can't behave, you can leave."

"For God's sake," the sheriff muttered, "I'm only trying to do what's right and proper—"

"Okay, enough," Gretchen interrupted, waving hands in the air. She could hardly hear herself think, her pulse throbbed so loudly in her ears. "Everyone calm down. Frank"—she looked directly at the sheriff—"come with me to the parlor, if you would. I'd like to talk privately. The rest of you, stay put."

Gretchen swept an arm before her, urging Frank Tilby to precede her. As he scowled and clomped out of the kitchen, she followed on his boot heels. Once in the front parlor, she directed him to sit on the sofa, precisely where the Man Who Might Be Sam had slept the previous night, but she didn't take a seat herself. Unable to stand still, she took a few steps to the left and then to the right, all the while telling him, "I had a bad feeling about this from the moment you brought it up."

"Don't blame me for the fact that the man's prints don't exist," the sheriff grumbled. "Although we could try to ink one of his feet. The county hospital should have his birth records—"

"The soles of his feet look burned, too," Gretchen cut him off. "I noticed when I found him. It's like he's been walking over coals."

"Or he's a human lightning rod." Tilby ran a hand over the shoe-polish black of his hair. "The whole thing's just plain weird."

"Have you found a car abandoned anywhere nearby?" she asked, keeping her voice low, concerned that the others might overhear.

"Not yet."

"Any bulletin about a missing person matching his description?" she asked.

Tilby shook his head, rubbing his big hands on his dark-polyester-clad thighs. "No, ma'am, nothing."

Gretchen exhaled gratefully and crossed her arms over her chest. "So what do you suggest we do now?"

The sheriff cleared his throat, tugging at his collar, eyes narrowed. "The only way to know for sure if this man is Sam Winston is to get some blood or spit from him and Abby so we can run DNA," he was saying, but Gretchen didn't let him finish.

"DNA from Abby?" she breathed, her knees threatening to buckle.

"Without prints to prove identity, it's the only shot we've got, and it's a surefire one. If the results show he's Abby's father, well"—Tilby shrugged his wide shoulders—"we'll know he's Sam. Case closed, end of story. Millie's cousin works at the county lab. I'll give her a call, see how much they're backlogged. We should do it soon though, because results can take weeks—"

"No," Gretchen blurted out, feeling sick to her stomach. She sank into the armchair where she'd dozed off only hours earlier. "No, it's not possible."

Tilby's wide brow creased. "And why's that?"

Because it won't match, she wanted to shout at him. *Because Sam's not Abby's father.*

But even as the words formed in her head, she couldn't say them. She wouldn't.

After so many years of living a lie, Gretchen had come awfully close to believing it. Lily and Cooper Winston had died knowing in their hearts that Abby was Sam's child. Even Annika, who lived and breathed the truth, had never questioned it.

"No," Gretchen said again, this time more quietly. She went to the window, touched her fingers to the glass, remembering the relaxed look she'd seen on Sam's and Abby's faces as they'd come back from the grove. The way they seemed to connect. Gretchen was not going to be responsible for snuffing out her daughter's most heartfelt wish just like that.

"I understand you're feeling mighty confused by this fellow turning up the way he did," Tilby started in, "and how much you want to buy into the dream that he's Sam. But don't you owe it to Abby to find out if he's the real deal?"

"Abby's pregnant, Frank," Gretchen confided in a rush, brushing at the tears that sprang to her eyes. "She's only two months along. She could lose the baby if anything rattled her. She's thirty-nine. This could be her last chance. If we do anything more to add to her stress, she could miscarry," she added, and her voice shook just to say the word, as it was hardly fiction. "It's not worth the risk."

Frank's bulldog face crumpled. "I'm sorry, Gretch," he said, sounding truly contrite. "I didn't know."

"Well, you do now."

The sheriff rubbed his jaw. "I guess we'll have to figure something else out."

"Yes, something else," Gretchen said, pressing fingers to temples, feeling like she'd narrowly escaped a storm of another kind entirely.

Seeds

A tree is known by its fruit;
a man by his deeds.
A good deed is never lost;
he who sows courtesy reaps friendship,
and he who plants kindness gathers love.

—ST. BASIL (329–379)

SIXTEEN

1952–1956

Sam Winston was conceived on the cusp of spring in 1952.

"A miracle," most called it, considering Sam's father, Cooper, had a bad bout with the mumps as a child, rough enough that the town doctor swore he'd been left impotent. Since the whole of Walnut Ridge knew everyone else's business, folks had naturally assumed Coop was out of commission in the baby-making department. So when word got out that Lily Winston had a bun in the oven, not a few neighbors looked upon the mother-to-be with a bit of a jaundiced eye, whispering that she must have let someone other than Coop dip his ladle in her gravy in order to concoct a fertilized egg. After all, Coop was often gone for weeks at a time, driving a long-haul truck. Still, all one had to do was glance at the couple to see their devotion. The way Lily gazed at her husband—and he at her—made every wagging tongue stop cold. The quiet, dark-haired daughter of Hank and Nadya Littlefoot had eyes only for one man. Soon enough, gossip about the pregnancy died down and any errant speculation about the baby's parentage was considered utter hogwash.

It was an ordinary enough pregnancy at the start, so smooth that Lily would hardly have been cognizant of anything blooming in her belly except for the difficulty in getting her blue jeans to button up. A true farmer's daughter, she liked working outdoors, quitting only when the sun went down and her muscles ached. She'd spent her girlhood at her father's knee, learning how to manage things. She took a tight grip on the reins after her dad had passed, barely loosening that hold once she'd married Coop and her new groom became her partner in life and in business.

But when she'd digested the fact that she was with child—and the town's general practitioner harangued her about her tipped uterus and ordered her to take it easy or risk miscarriage—Lily agreed to cut back on her hours and left the grunt work to Coop and the farmhands. For the first time in her life, she became an observer rather than a participant, watching from the sidelines as the clouds of straw were removed in late spring from where walnut seedlings had been planted, supervising the fertilization of the grove with rich manure instead of getting her own hands dirty, and directing the careful pruning of dead and broken branches instead of climbing ladders to clip them herself.

When the warm months had bled into the fall, she witnessed the harvest from the back porch, knowing she could neither handle the heavy machinery nor pick up the hulled nuts after they'd been shaken to the ground. Cooper had made her promise to forgo lifting anything heavier than laundry to the clothesline and soon enough she would stop doing that as well.

"How're you holding up?" Coop would ask her now and again, worried she was going stir-crazy.

But Lily always assured him she was fine, no matter how antsy she felt. "It won't be forever," she would remind him, because there wasn't anything she wouldn't do for their child.

Though she had never been cozy with the women of Walnut Ridge, never joining the Ladies' Civic Improvement League or bonding over Bible study, Lily agreed with their assessment that the baby in her belly was a miracle. She wasn't religious and didn't attend the Presbyterian Church on Sundays with Cooper, but she did have a deep faith in the spiritual. Before his death, Hank had taught her to be mindful of the earth and to respect the spirits who looked out for creatures great and small. She wasn't sure if it was God or Mother Earth who'd given her the gift of this new life inside her; but she did take her role as its guardian very seriously and wasn't above asking for guidance now and then.

So concerned was she about protecting the child that she quit driving into Walnut Ridge with Coop to see the doctor, afraid of the long, bumpy ride in their truck. She found a midwife named Delia Boggs who made weekly trips out to the farm, and she followed all of Delia's advice to the letter. She slept as much as she could, napping whenever fatigue struck. Even if Coop complained of falling behind, she didn't volunteer to muck the stalls or wade in the slop to feed the pigs. She'd been warned to stay away from animal dung and furred and feathered coats that might breed ticks or bugs, so Lily even ceased chores like collecting eggs from the hens or milking Mildred or Mabel, their two dairy cows. And though she still tended her vegetable garden—until the point when she couldn't bend over—she refused to do any more vigorous work. Her hands, callused from a lifetime of manual labor, began to soften and her blunt nails to grow.

"How does it feel to be a woman of leisure?" Cooper teased one night after dinner when Lily pricked her thumb for the umpteenth time trying to embroider a bib for the baby.

"If this is how gentrified ladies of Walnut Ridge spend their days," she told her husband, "then I can see why they're always sipping gin."

She felt guilty, leaving more for Cooper to do. She rarely saw her husband from dawn until dark, except when he returned to the house to eat, wash up, or rest. But they both realized all would return to normal once the baby was born. Since the child meant everything to them, neither did much complaining.

Fiercely swollen by her seventh month, Lily began to sit often with her feet propped up, sometimes reading novels and other times darning Cooper's socks. On a particularly gray October morning, she felt an itch to do something she did very rarely: she drew a bubble bath, easing her swollen body beneath water that was warm but not hot. Leaning her head back so her neck rested against the curved lip of the claw-foot tub, she closed her eyes and dozed off for a few minutes, awakening to the pounding of rain against the glass. Beyond the windowpanes, the sky had turned a nasty shade of gray so that it seemed more akin to night than day.

A rumble of thunder shook the house, rattling the floorboards beneath the tub and setting the bathwater to rippling. Before Lily could get herself out, an ear-splitting crack rent the air and a flash lit up the window so brightly it momentarily blinded her. Tucked beneath the eaves as she was, she felt the force as lightning struck the roof, causing the room in the attic to shudder as if the clapboards holding it together might break apart.

Fearful of falling, Lily grabbed the sides of the tub, sliding onto her behind as suds sloshed around her. Lights flickered and then went dark. A startled "oh" escaped her lips as a current rushed through the water, racing over her skin and setting her arms and legs to furiously tingling.

Oh, please, she prayed as tears filled her eyes and her hands went to her belly, *please, let the baby be unharmed.*

She pressed her palms against her rounded flesh, willing the child to kick or somersault, something to confirm he was unaffected. "Are you okay in there?" she said aloud, terrified the surge that had gone through the water and into her body had stopped the tiny heart from beating. How could this have happened when she'd been so cautious? It was as though a force of nature far greater than she was reminding her who was in charge.

Don't let me lose him, she continued to beg. *He means everything to me.*

Lily found herself holding her breath until—there!— she felt faint movement inside her, a sensation akin to a fish flopping in water. She saw something, too, as she spread her fingers wider across her belly, absorbing each solid motion. Though her eyes were wide open, she watched the flicker of a daydream unfurl within her mind, what her father would surely have called a vision. Smack in the center of a field of tall grass stood an old man with a feather in his braided hair and turquoise beads around his neck. He looked very much as she remembered Hank Littlefoot, and he cradled a cooing baby, raising it up to the heavens. He smiled proudly and said, "Your son has been blessed. Samuel Henry has the gift and, if he honors it, someday he will become a force of nature."

Lily gasped as the lights came back on and the gray skies swept past, sunshine again filling the window as if the storm had never happened.

Footsteps thundered up the stairs as Cooper appeared, wet from the rain and out of breath, calling out, "You're not hurt? And the baby?"

"We're fine," Lily murmured as he rushed on about the roof being struck and there being a fire, one that had been put out by the sudden downpour almost as fast as it had started.

As she stood there shivering, Cooper reached for a towel, never pausing as he described how the clouds had blown in, turning the air pitch-black and stirring up rain and wind. "The lightning was brighter than the sun, and a bolt shot down on the farmhouse like someone had taken aim at it. Then the storm disappeared into the heavens again, as quick as it came." He let out a low whistle. "It was the damnedest thing I've ever seen."

Lily closed her eyes, hugging the towel around her as Coop patted it with his big hands. Her legs trembled, and she could hardly speak for her chattering teeth; but there was something she had to tell him and it wasn't about the current that had run through her or the baby's wild kicks.

"I s-saw my f-father," she stammered, recalling the scene clear as day. "He s-spoke to me."

Cooper stopped rubbing her arms and looked her in the eye. "You saw Hank Littlefoot? Maybe you fell asleep in the tub and dreamed about him before the storm shook you awake?"

"No, it w-wasn't a d-dream. I was w-wide awake," she assured him as water dripped from her long hair onto her breasts. "He was h-holding the baby, and it was a boy," she explained, the shivering gone as she began to warm up. "He called him Samuel Henry and said he was blessed. So that," she told her husband, "will be his name."

Cooper stared at her like she'd gone crazy.

"It's a sign," she insisted, not about to ignore it. "We have to listen."

"All right," her husband said, tugging the towel close around her and hugging her tightly. "If you believe, that's good enough for me."

And Lily did believe, as fiercely as she had ever believed anything in her life.

In the days and weeks following the lightning strike, Lily was afraid that the baby might stop moving, damaged somehow by the incident. But Sam only seemed to get stronger, kicking harder in her belly so that she could see the movements lift and ripple her skin.

"You can't come out yet, little one," she would tell him, softly rubbing around her belly button in circles. "You have to stay inside until you're big enough to face the world."

Lily felt more at peace somehow, as if someone were watching over them. She had no nightmares when she went to sleep, only gentle dreams, of blue skies and soft breezes, of eagles soaring above as she held her son's hand. She never saw her father's visage again, but she didn't expect it. He had told her what he needed to tell her. If he had anything more to say, he would find a way to give her the message.

Winter arrived in a blanket of snow several days before Christmas, and Samuel Henry Winston arrived as well after a quick and uneventful labor. He had grown big enough to face the world, indeed, at eight pounds and six ounces. Dark-haired and dark-eyed, the boy looked much like his mother, although she insisted he favored his grandfather. "He already looks wise beyond his years," she said, although Cooper remarked that "every baby looks like a wizened old man."

While Lily rested with Sam bundled beside her, Cooper ran around town with cigars, proudly announcing the birth of his son. A steady stream of visitors made their way out to the farmhouse, wishing to see the child and present Lily with a host of handmade baby gifts. "They feel guilty," Lily told her husband behind their backs, "for the seeds of doubt they sowed in the beginning." Even the cruelest hearts melted once they met the boy. He was a good-natured baby, calm and quiet, so peaceful in fact that sometimes Lily had wondered if there wasn't something wrong with him.

"Maybe he's just stoic, like his mother," Cooper suggested. "He's got a quarter Otoe-Missouria in his blood, you know."

"I do," Lily said, "and someday he will know it, too."

Sam had also inherited a birthmark shaped like a raindrop. It sat at the nape of his neck, and Lily thought of it as a kind of talisman, passed down from her father. Hank had once borne a similar mark on his shoulder, or so Nadya had told her, though

Lily only remembered a scar where a mole had been removed. "It brought him luck at first," her mother had said, "before it caused us almost unbearable grief."

Lily hoped that the birthmark would be a blessing for Sam, a tie to past generations. How she wished her parents were around for her son. But Hank had died far too young, not long before Lily and Coop had married. "He gave too much of himself, trying to help strangers and make a life for us. It turned his body old beyond his years," her mother had said by way of explanation. Nadya hadn't stayed at the farmhouse much beyond the wedding. She'd departed soon after, heading back to her village in Bulgaria to live with her widowed cousins. "They are like sisters and they need me. This farm and the house belong to you now," she had told Lily with tears in her eyes. "Fill it with laughter and love, and never waste a precious moment wanting anything more than you have."

Lily missed them both, but she felt her father's presence. She knew without a doubt that Hank's spirit had protected Sam the night of the lightning strike and would continue to watch over him. The birthmark, she decided, was simply a reminder of that.

By the time he was six months old, Sam's eyes had turned the color of pewter, and that wide silver-gray gaze seemed to intently watch everyone and everything as he took in the world around him, often putting a tiny finger to his chin and pressing his rosebud lips together as though contemplating something far too powerful for one so young.

When he was old enough to walk, Lily would take Sam outside, where he would toddle beside her around the farm.

She liked to point out the bright red cardinals pecking at seeds, the caterpillars creeping across fallen leaves, and the row upon row of walnut trees that had been in the Winston family for two generations. Sam would listen as she shared stories about his grandfather Hank, who wore an eagle feather in his hair and turquoise around his neck. "He needed to make his own mark on the world, so he left the reservation to perform on the stage," she told her young son, even if he couldn't yet understand. "It was said that he could make it rain, just like his grandfather before him."

Little Sam would clutch her hand, never smiling and rarely blinking, simply staring up at her as she spoke. When he seemed tired from walking, she would spread a blanket on the grass near the duck pond, where he would sit and contemplate the boat his father had carved him from the wood of a walnut tree. He would glide his fingertips across it as though memorizing the knots and the grain and the grooves dug by the blade.

"Do you know what that is?" she would ask, and he would nod. "It's a boat," she would prompt, "B-O-A-T." Which only made him cock his head and give her a funny look as if to say, "Of course it's a boat," although he said nothing.

"Our boy's a thinker," Cooper remarked to his wife, neither of them entirely sure if that was a good thing or a bad thing, considering they were farmers and not philosophers. But they loved him with every fiber of their being.

When he began to speak, it was hardly the unintelligible babbling of most children his age. Sam parceled out his words, using them only when he had to, mainly when he needed assistance. "Cookies," he would say to his mother and point to the green glass jar on the counter. Or, "Pencils, please," when Lily had put them away in a drawer too high for him to reach.

When Sam was four years old, he would often slip out of the house unnoticed, and Lily would go on a mad hunt for him, afraid he'd gotten into a pen with the pigs or fallen into the pond, chasing after the ducks.

Soon she realized what he liked most to do was visit the walnut grove and sit beneath the trees. Sometimes he would fall asleep leaning against a trunk. When she found him curled up amidst the roots, she would gently shake him awake and ask, "What're you doing out here, baby?"

He'd say simply, "I was talking to them, Mama."

Lily would ask, "Who?"

Sam would inevitably answer, "The birds," or occasionally, "The trees."

"And do they ever talk back?" she would inquire.

He would bob his dark head, his gray eyes so earnest. "Yes," he would answer as Lily brushed dirt from his knees and bits of bark from his hair. "They tell me how happy they are that I'm here."

"They do?"

"Yes, and they give me things."

"What things?" Lily had wondered. That was when she had learned about Sam's secret hiding place. He had apparently been stashing his treasures in the burned-out hollow at the base of the walnut split by lightning years ago after Hank and Nadya had first moved to the farm.

"See," Sam said as he stuck his hand into the hollow, withdrawing the bright blue shell of a robin's egg, a slightly battered but intact cardinal's nest, and a large white feather that surely had come from a hawk or an eagle.

Lily felt a catch in her throat as she held the feather. "Which of your friends gave you this?" she asked.

"The wind," he replied before he took it from her and tucked it away. "Sometimes it even whispers my name."

"I see."

Had Lily been any other woman—had she been raised by any father other than Hank Littlefoot—she might have merely believed her son had a fanciful mind and liked to tell tales. But Sam had no ordinary lineage. Maybe the gift Hank had mentioned in her vision was an ability to communicate with nature. Whatever it was, Lily wasn't about to pooh-pooh it.

"Do you ever notice, Mama," he went on as she took his hand and led him toward the house, "that if you're sad, the sky will turn gray?"

"No," Lily said, surprised that a boy of four could utter such a statement. "Does that happen to you?"

"Sometimes," he said solemnly, squishing up his face. "Like when Toad got run over by Daddy's truck. I cried and cried and so did the sky."

Lily blinked, recalling the morning several weeks before when the big toad that lived in their front yard—and which Sam had adopted and named—had met his untimely demise. And, yes, Sam was right. It had rained that day. She had consoled her son with a Popsicle on the back porch, and as he'd sadly licked the icy treat, the sun had disappeared behind a bank of gray and a soft drizzle had fallen, strumming on the roof and plopping into puddles near the railing.

He squeezed her hand, having noticed the frown on her face. "Don't worry, Mama. The sun always comes back out when I find something else to be happy about," he professed and let go of her to race toward the house, leaving Lily to stare after him, wondering just how much of his grandfather's and great-great-grandfather's blood he had flowing through his veins.

SEVENTEEN

1960–1965

The first time young Sam Winston laid eyes on Gretchen Brink was during Sunday school at the Presbyterian Church in Walnut Ridge on a sticky and overcast summer morning, though he had been made aware of her existence well before that. Her father, Dr. Brink, was the only farm veterinarian within a fifty-mile radius and came out to the Winstons' place whenever they needed help delivering a calf or inspecting a sickly hen. Sam genuinely liked the doc, who always patted his head and acted amazed at how tall he was getting. He also knew that Gretchen had two blind baby sisters and that her mother was, according to gossip, "a sharp-tongued harpy." Sam's own mom would sometimes come home from town and mention to his dad that she'd bumped into "that awful Annika Brink. She's so brusque with those poor little girls. How does her husband stand her?"

Sometimes when Dr. Brink visited the farm, Sam tagged along so he could hold the vet's black bag or, if he was lucky, watch him check a horse's teeth or rub salve on a cracked hoof. "You remind me of my Gretchen," the vet had told him one day. "She's an observer, too, and quite compassionate."

Sam was older than Gretchen by a year, seven to her six. Though there were a dozen children in the Sunday school class that mixed first and second graders—four boys and eight girls—Sam spotted Gretchen right off the bat. She had the brightest blue eyes he'd ever seen and a riotous tangle of golden curls, but that wasn't what made him pay attention.

When she turned her smile upon him, even in passing, it was like bathing in the brightest light. And just the way she said, "Hello, how are you?" seemed less akin to lip service than actual kindness. She even inspired apparent politeness from the rowdiest boys in class, the ringmaster of them being a kid named Frank Tilby, whose dad was the town's sheriff. While Frank unmercifully tugged the other girls' pigtails and untied neat bows on the backs of their dresses, he curiously left Gretchen Brink alone.

Sam wondered if it was Gretchen's sweet demeanor that kept her untouched by the cadre of unruly boys, or if the other kids were just giving her a chance to blend in. Perhaps she'd get her pigtails tugged once the newness had worn off.

On the first day that Gretchen appeared, their teacher, Mrs. Macabee, whom they all called Mrs. Mac, strolled into the church's basement wearing the most hideous bird's nest hat, causing the other kids to titter. Gretchen merely smiled angelically and offered up, "Why, that's the prettiest hat I've ever seen."

Normally, Sam would have pegged such a remark as a lie but it wasn't, not the way that Gretchen said it. He could tell that she meant the *feeling* behind the words, if not the words themselves. When Mrs. Mac beamed and said, "Why, thank you, sweetheart," Gretchen looked as pleased as if she'd won a prize at the county fair.

Sam usually avoided making friends. He liked being alone. But he was magnetically drawn to the soft-spoken girl with the magical smile. After several Sundays of observing her, he'd hoped to find a way to casually sit beside her. But Mrs. Macabee insisted on arranging them in half circles around the chair from which she read them Bible stories, and the boys never settled on the same side as the girls. Though he was hardly a chicken, Sam's palms got clammy at the thought of being the only male seated somewhere between all those ruffles and bows.

Sam did pick a wooden chair as far away from the other boys as he could. He didn't like how they acted like clowns the moment the teacher left the room. They would gang up on each other, punching arms until one of them turned red-faced and teary-eyed and cried, "Uncle!"

Though they rarely, if ever, picked on Sam. It was more like they avoided him altogether. He figured it was because he was taller by half a foot and unflinching. There wasn't much that scared him, not loud noises like fireworks or thunder and lightning. Not even the snakes or spiders that made his usually composed mother shriek, "Cooper! Come get this thing out of here!" No one really talked to him unless they had to, and he didn't worry about that.

Sam actually liked listening to Mrs. Macabee when she read them the fantastical tales that sounded less like truth and more like fiction. It reminded him of the stories his mother shared before his bedtime, most of them involving animals, like wolves, eagles, and bears, many with human characteristics. But then, they were mystical spirits.

When Mrs. Mac began describing the Garden of Eden, Sam closed his eyes, picturing Adam and Eve with the snake slithering down from the tree, whispering to Eve that she should eat the forbidden fruit.

"Why didn't the snake talk to Adam?" Sam asked when Mrs. Macabee paused for a breath, causing all the children but Gretchen to snicker.

Mrs. Mac gazed at him slightly cross-eyed through her rhinestone-studded horn-rims. "Because it was Eve the devil wanted to tempt," she explained, hands clasped above her ample bosom. "After all, she was the weaker sex, born of Adam's rib."

"What if she was just hungry?" he suggested.

Mrs. Macabee opened her mouth to respond, but Gretchen shot up out of her seat, making a statement of her own.

"My mother says that men are the weak ones," Gretchen announced with a shake of pale curls as the rest of the class grew hushed. "They don't like hearing the truth, and they're never satisfied with what they've got. You know the commandment that says, 'Don't want what your neighbor has'?" she asked, and Mrs. Macabee nodded, big hat bobbing like a boat caught in riptide. "Well, my mama says that men do it anyway, especially if the neighbor has a car that's extra nice or a wife with very large bosoms—"

"That's quite enough, Gretchen," Mrs. Macabee interrupted, and she waved a paper fan across her bright red face. "Your mother certainly has an interesting take on the Lord's word."

"Her mom's a crackpot," one of the boys blurted out, the

one called Bobby with red hair and freckles whose own mother always made him wear a bow tie.

"Now, Bobby, that isn't nice at all," Mrs. Macabee said in a feeble attempt to shush him.

"Well, the Bible says we shouldn't lie, doesn't it?" Bobby remarked with a smirk. "And everyone knows her mom's a nut."

Gretchen Brink screwed up her face, rosebud mouth puckered like she'd sucked on a very tart lemon. For an instant, Sam imagined she was going to walk over to bow-tied Bobby and punch his lights out. Instead, she quietly sat back down and placed her hands in her lap, crossing her feet at the ankles.

Sam was impressed. There weren't too many folks he knew who could take their anger and switch it off like that. But he wasn't surprised either. Just as he'd arrived at the church that morning, he'd witnessed her saving the life of a daddy longlegs from the ill-tempered Bobby, who'd decided to poke the creature with a stick. Gretchen had walked straight up to him, ordered him to "cut it out," then had picked up the spider with her bare hands, taking it away a safe distance. If Sam had stood openmouthed, it was only because he'd never seen a girl touch a bug before, not in all his seven years.

"Mrs. Mac, is there a commandment that says something about 'Thou shall not be a fruitcake'?" Bobby asked, unwilling to let it go and obviously enjoying the cackles from his buddies.

Still, Gretchen stared at her lap, saying nothing.

But Sam wasn't about to let it be.

He rose to his feet and turned his steely gaze on Bobby. "You take that back," he said. "You apologize to her or else."

"Or else what?" Bobby replied, and his comrades nudged

him, egging him on until he stood up to Sam. His freckles seemed suddenly dark against pale skin though he raised his chin, clearly wanting to save face in front of his friends. "Are you going to scalp me?" he remarked, his voice starting off squeaky until the other boys' laughter emboldened him. "I'm not afraid of you, Winston, not even if your grandfather really was an Indian medicine man."

Sam knew an ignorant remark when he heard it, and Bobby's stupidity wasn't worth the consequences of fighting in Sunday school, he told himself. But logic didn't keep the anger from rising inside him, swirling in his chest and thundering in his brain. Within moments, the still air began to move, wind blustering through the opened windows and stirring up the coloring books on a nearby table, tearing the paper fan out of Mrs. Macabee's hand.

"Heavens to Betsy! I think a tornado's brewing!" Mrs. Mac declared as her voice trembled and the wind tugged at her bird's nest hat. But she pulled herself together to hop to her feet, clap her hands, and shout, "Children, hurry, get beneath the tables, hands clasped above your heads, just like during the drills!"

The girls in the class squealed, scrambling from their chairs as their hair bows were tugged into disarray. Bobby stumbled backward into his seat, pinned there by an unseen hand, even as his friends leaped up and deserted him, diving under the nearest wooden table.

"Take it back," Sam said, holding his ground, even as Bible pages flapped and papers swirled about him. "Say you're sorry for everything."

Bobby shouted, "Okay, okay, I'm sorry!"

"Did you get that?" Sam asked Gretchen, who had come up beside him and tugged at his arm.

"Yes, I heard," she said. "Now, c'mon!"

Sam took a deep breath, slowing down his pounding heart, giving in and allowing himself to be pulled to a spot beneath a desk where a handful of girls huddled. As his anger eased, the winds began to die down along with it, until the room was still again and the stifling heat resumed.

"Is it over? Is it gone?" the children asked, one girl sniffling back sobs.

"It seems so." Mrs. Macabee crawled out from her hidey-hole, and the kids followed suit.

Beyond the basement windows set high up in the walls, the sky appeared calm but overcast, much as it had looked when Sam and his dad had arrived at church a half hour earlier.

The Sunday school teacher straightened her cockeyed hat and asked, "Is everyone all right?"

After a chorus of, "Yes, Mrs. Macabee," she nodded, remarking, "I do believe we're safe now."

"I think we always were," Gretchen whispered so that only Sam could hear.

He blushed but said nothing.

Gretchen smiled at him knowingly—as if they shared some deep, dark secret—then she dusted off her pink dress before joining Mrs. Macabee in righting the chairs that had toppled. Sam peeled his eyes off Gretchen long enough to assist the others in picking up papers from the floor. When the room seemed put together again, she beckoned Sam to take the empty seat beside hers.

From the center of the circle, Mrs. Macabee cleared her throat and trilled, "Now, where were we? Ah, yes, Adam and Eve in the Garden of Eden . . ."

When Sunday school ended that day, Gretchen dashed out of the basement room before Sam could follow. Ignoring Bobby's hissed "You're a sideshow freak, Winston," he headed outside to the usual spot to meet his dad at the bottom of the church steps.

As it so happened, Cooper Winston was chatting with Dr. Brink. Sam appeared in time to overhear Gretchen's dad remark, "If you wouldn't mind, I'd like to bring her out to the farm one of these days. She needs to be around a woman like Lily, one who's strong but sensitive. Anni can be so harsh sometimes."

"Hello," Sam said as he shuffled down the steps, his hand on the slab of stone at the base of the railing.

"Ah, good timing," his dad said, gesturing him nearer so he could sling an arm about his shoulders. "What would you think of having a friend to play with now and then? Dr. Brink has a daughter who'd like to spend some time on the farm. You could show her the walnut grove and the barn and the pond."

Sam tried to act nonchalant. He shoved his hands in his trouser pockets, glancing up at the cloud-draped sky, fighting to contain his excitement. "Yes," he said carefully. "I guess that would be all right."

Moments after, Gretchen emerged from around the stone building, her golden curls in their usual chaotic state, a smudge of dirt on her cheek and hands behind her back.

At the sight of her, Sam's heart swelled until it felt too big for his chest.

"This is for you," she said, approaching him, and pressed a large orange day lily into his hands. It looked like the ones that grew at the back of the church, and it still had a bit of its roots attached. "You didn't have to stick up for me, you know, but I'm glad you did." She smiled at him, and he tried his best to smile back.

"I would do it again," he murmured, holding the green stalk of the flower against his chest and feeling his cheeks heat.

She cocked her head. "You know what?" she said. "I like you, Sammy. You're different from everyone else, and, even better, you don't seem to care that you are."

She likes me? Sam thought and his toes began to tingle, a warmth spreading upward to the rest of him.

Then as had transpired so many times before when happiness overcame doubt or sadness within Sam's head and heart, the sun began to wink through the clouds, melting them away until the heavens turned a blue as cheerful as a robin's egg.

"See you later, Sam," Gretchen said, waving at him as her daddy took her hand and led her off to their car.

"That's my boy," his dad leaned down to whisper, nudging him, and Sam suddenly felt a foot taller.

He knew somehow that having Gretchen Brink in his life would change it forever. The boy who liked to be alone had made his first true friend.

That next weekend, Dr. Brink brought Gretchen out to the farm, and then she came again with him several weekends after. It wasn't long before he was dropping her off every Saturday morning even if he didn't stay, which pleased Sam to no end.

He could hardly sleep Friday nights, he was so bottled up with excitement at the prospect of spending hours and hours alone with Gretchen, collecting geodes and arrowheads from the creek that ran through the farm; catching frogs and butterflies just to view them up close and then letting them go again; climbing the walnut trees and seeing who could get the closest to the sky.

"You are more than my friend," she told him one day when they'd taken a break in the pasture, picking clover and making long strands of it, which Gretchen wrapped around her neck like they were pearls. "I have Trudy and Bennie, but they're sisters. So I imagine this is exactly what having a brother should feel like."

Sam beamed as brilliantly as the sun overhead, secure in the notion that they were as close as family, and family meant forever, didn't it? "Blood is thicker than water," his mother had told him.

Until the years slipped past, and Gretchen turned eleven. Without explanation, her regular visits became more sporadic. When she didn't show up with Dr. Brink for a third Saturday morning in a row, Sam frantically asked Gretchen's dad, "Is she okay? Is she sick?"

Dr. Brink put a hand on his shoulder. "She's not sick, son." He shook his head, sounding as unhappy as Sam when he explained, "It's just that her mother decided that she's a young woman now, and it doesn't become her to run around a farm all day, getting dirty britches."

"Doesn't Mrs. Brink like me?" Sam asked, because he sensed in his heart there was more to it than that.

"You shouldn't worry about what Mrs. Brink thinks." The vet ruffled his hair. "You're a great kid, Sam, and anyone who can't see that has rocks in her head."

But Sam did worry, and he pined for Gretchen. He missed having her around so much that it hurt. He even went so far as to take his pocketknife to the back of the walnut tree in the grove's center, the one split at the trunk by lightning. He carved something deeply into its old bark, something that made him feel at least a little bit better. It was a heart with "S + G" inside it.

Maybe he didn't know what real love was at that point, but Sam did know for sure that he had a deep and abiding affection for Gretchen.

The next week, he made it a point to track her down at school. Lily even dropped him off early one morning so he could wait outside the door of her classroom, eager for her to appear. When she saw him there, her big blue eyes lit up.

"Sam! I'm sorry I haven't been out to the farm in a while," she said as kids pushed around her to get into the room. "But my mom's been on a tear. She doesn't believe I should spend so much time running loose with a boy like—" She stopped herself. "Never mind. I'm just sorry is all." She bit her lip, looking down at her feet.

A boy like him? Is that what she'd been about to say? Sam had a feeling he knew exactly what Mrs. Brink meant. Her aversion to him couldn't be because he lived on a farm, as half the population of Walnut Ridge did. It was more likely because he had Indian blood running through him. Lots of the kids had made digs about that in the past—some still did—and his parents had told him that such thoughts were passed down from parents who didn't know better. Sam was just glad that Gretchen *did* know better than that.

"I feel awful, Sam, honestly. My dad stuck up for you, but Annika put her foot down. And when she does that, it's not worth fighting over," she whispered, pressing against the tiled wall and leaning toward him. "No matter what, you will always be my best friend. I'll see you around school, right? And one day, I'll be old enough that Annika can't keep me from doing whatever I want." She squeezed his hand. "You trust me, don't you?"

He could do little but nod.

"Good!" She smiled at him, but it wasn't quite as bright as usual. Then she slipped into her classroom, and Sam shuffled off to his.

That night as he lay in bed, something pained him terribly, an ache in his chest that made it hard to breathe. All he wanted was to be with Gretchen Brink. It seemed like such a simple thing. He turned on his side and pulled his knees to his chest, balling up in frustration, wondering if his head might explode with all his pent-up angst.

Outside, the wind picked up, banging the shutters against the clapboards and moaning through the eaves, the sky as bottled up as Sam, the air emitting a low rumble as if the clouds were as fit to burst as he.

EIGHTEEN

1970

Sam had been in love once and only once.

He knew that some folks were geared toward trial and error, the whole "plenty of fish in the sea" approach to relationships. But at seventeen, he was already sure of where his heart belonged. No one else he'd ever met—or had yet to meet—could make him feel as good as Gretchen.

But he was aware that the sixteen-year-old Gretchen had her share of suitors, not the least of whom was Frank Tilby, son of the sheriff of Walnut Ridge. Even though Sam had caught Gretchen blushing at Tilby's macho attempts at flirtation in the hallways of the high school, and even though he realized she showed up at Tilby's baseball games to cheer him on from the stands, something inside Sam couldn't imagine Gretchen ending up with anyone but him. They had been best friends since Sunday school, even if they didn't see each other as often as they used to. But that bond between them meant something, didn't it? She had told him before that she loved him, though maybe that kind of love was more brotherly than he now hoped for. But feelings could change, couldn't they? He had heard his mother say that the most enduring affection started out slowly and burned more deeply as time passed. Love that came too quickly was more like a flash fire, there and gone in the blink of an eye.

Which gave Sam a ray of hope, and he hung on to it.

Oftentimes in the late spring when the weather was neither too hot nor too cold, he and Gretchen would prepare a late-night picnic, and he'd borrow his father's truck to drive to an open field. He'd park smack in the middle, lower the tailgate, and they'd sit with their legs dangling over.

They would eat first, usually something like cold fried chicken and coleslaw with lemonade. Once they'd filled their bellies, they'd push the basket deep into the bed so they could spread out a quilt and lie flat on their backs.

Then Sam would tell Gretchen to close her eyes, even if she giggled because the whole thing seemed silly.

"Okay, Galileo, what's in the sky tonight?" she'd ask him on cue.

Gazing above them, he let his eyes inhale the landscape of the night just as his lungs took in a deep and cleansing breath. Carefully choosing his words, he described to her exactly what he saw there. "The Milky Way is so bright that each star shines like a white diamond on black velvet, winking at us like they know so much we'll never know. The gases they release create an insanely vibrant aura, a bit like I'd imagine halos must look on angels."

"It's not often that gas can do that," she teased with a grin, and Sam cleared his throat. "Oh, wait, I'm interrupting, sorry. What else do you see?" she said, playing along and keeping her eyes closed.

"The aurora borealis," he told her, "sweeping across the

dark with a vaporous chartreuse cloak, illuminating the pitch with such quick strokes, first that limpid green and then lavender . . ."

"Vaporous and limpid!" she repeated with a soft *oooh*. "My God, Sam, you sure know how to paint a portrait with words. Annika paints with a brush, but she's always so heavy-handed that mostly things end up looking like an angry blob of mush."

"I'm sure my perspective is very different from hers," Sam remarked, knowing he had little in common with Gretchen's mother.

"Ain't that the truth." She sighed and placed clasped hands atop her flat belly, which gently rose and fell as she breathed. "You see things differently than everyone, Sammy. Other boys would just say something like, 'Yep, it's pitch-black, and there's stuff twinkling,' but you make it sound like poetry."

"The night sky *is* poetry," Sam quietly insisted.

She opened her eyes and turned her head to look at him. "You do realize that you're connected to the world in a way the rest of us aren't, right? You always were."

"Hmm." Sam wasn't sure he agreed entirely. Gretchen was as sensitive as anyone he knew. She would no more squash a bug than he would. Life was precious to her, too, and she was incredibly empathetic.

"I'm sure you must feel a part of what's around us," he said to her, inching nearer so their shoulders touched. "Most people don't take the time to notice the colors, the sounds, the way the air feels on their skin. But you and I both do."

Gretchen unclasped her hands and reached for his. "I don't

imagine anyone feels what you feel or sees what you see, not even me. That's what makes you special."

Sam swallowed hard, wishing he could describe how he felt about her as easily as he could describe the stars. But he let that moment pass as he had so many others, telling himself, *Next time, I will do it.*

But it would be weeks after that before he screwed up the courage.

Not long after Gretchen's father had walked out on Annika, moving away from Walnut Ridge with the school librarian, Miss Childs, Gretchen phoned the farm, asking if they might have another evening picnic. "Please, Sam, I really need to get out of the house. If I don't slip away for a while, I'll go mad, I swear it."

"Are you sure you're all right?"

"I'll be fine," she replied smoothly enough, but he could tell from her voice that she was lying. "Being with you is the perfect medicine."

"Good." Sam felt exactly the same.

So that Friday night, he packed some of Lily's brisket sandwiches, pickles, and potato salad, and he picked Gretchen up at her house in town, idling the pickup out front and giving two quick toots of the horn as she'd instructed him so that he could avoid a confrontation with Annika. "She's still really angry at my father for leaving," Gretchen explained. "Actually, she's angry at all men, so it's best if you keep a distance."

He watched her fly out the front door of the neat gingerbread house and race toward him through the dusk, her cornsilk blond hair bouncing in waves on her shoulders. When she hopped into the cab beside him, she leaned over to peck his cheek before she settled in. Sam inhaled the scent of her, as fresh as the sky after rain and as sweet as a daffodil.

"What are you waiting for?" she asked and thumped a palm on the dash. "Let's get out of here before Annika appears and drags me back inside, kicking and screaming."

The tires screeched as Sam hit the gas and took off, Gretchen laughing through the open window, hair blowing in the wind.

The truck bumped along the country road that took them outside of town, the pop of gravel a constant under the wheels and the sound of cicadas spilling through the opened windows. Sam liked riding in silence. It felt companionable, like they didn't need to talk to fill the space. But Gretchen apparently didn't agree. She sighed and turned on the radio. Sam had an eight-track tape pushed in, and it started playing in the middle of the Beatles' "Something," right where he'd left off with George Harrison asking when would his love grow and replying, "I don't know, I don't know."

Gretchen reached over and popped the cartridge out, hitting the buttons for the AM radio instead, switching from crackly station to station—although there weren't many to choose from—muttering about "stupid farm reports" until she found Patsy Cline singing "Crazy" and left it there. She let out a doleful moan and settled back in the seat, resting her arm on the door.

"How can a man who once loved a woman enough to marry her and have three daughters fall out of love so easily?" she asked, her mood downshifting. "It doesn't make sense."

How was Sam supposed to answer that? He was hardly a fount of knowledge when it came to relationships. The only member of the opposite sex who interested him sat three feet away, and he could hardly begin to understand how *her* mind worked.

So he fell back onto facts, with which he felt far more comfortable.

"Does it make sense that a dragonfly only lives for a few months?" he said, the first thing that came to mind. "Or that when a worker bee stings to protect its hive, it instantly dies? And you don't even want to hear about the poor mosquito fish. It only lives about a year, but has something like a hundred babies before it croaks."

"Oh, Sam!" The way she said his name was like a sob.

"What is it?" He took his eyes off the headlights skimming the road to glance at her sideways. She had her hands on her face and, for a moment, he thought she was crying. Great balls of fire, what had he done?

"Gretch?"

She surprised him when she began to giggle, the noise bubbling up from within. It sounded less like amusement and more like hysteria.

"What is it?" He wondered if she was losing it, having a nervous breakdown or something. Everyone in Walnut Ridge talked about how Annika had gotten even crazier since Dr. Brink had run off with Miss Childs, and Gretchen was undoubtedly bearing a lot of the burden. Just to be safe, he pulled the truck over, barely keeping it on the shoulder and avoiding the ditch. He jerked to a stop and threw on the brake so he could face her.

"What's going on? What did I do?"

"You didn't do anything, Sam! You're the only one who hasn't messed up my life completely," she told him, her voice too high-pitched. "No, I take that back, what you've done is absolutely everything!"

Gretchen suddenly scooted over, setting her head on his shoulder. Sam could hardly breathe.

"What you did," she said, her voice softer and less frantic, "was the perfect thing. Compared to the poor mosquito fish, maybe my parents splitting up isn't so bad."

"You'll get through it." Sam let go of the wheel and reached for her hand, which rested on her thigh. It felt cool against his warm skin. "I'm sure your father didn't mean to hurt you."

She lifted her chin, looking straight at him. They were practically nose to nose. "I feel like he deserted all of us, not just my mother. Me and Bennie and Trudy."

"He probably didn't see it that way at all." Sam defended her father, although he wasn't sure why. He had always liked Dr. Brink very much, but he didn't admire him for ditching his responsibilities, even if the poor man had felt trapped with a shrew like Annika. "Sometimes the path we take isn't clear-cut. Sometimes it forks, and we have to make hard choices."

"Shouldn't we make the choice that hurts the least amount of people?"

"That sounds real nice, but I don't think it always works that way."

She didn't respond for a moment, just stared out the windshield. He hadn't cut off the headlamps, and bugs danced in front of the lights, batting at each other and against the truck grille.

"Promise me something?" Gretchen tightened her grip on his fingers. "Promise you won't ever abandon me, Sammy?"

"I won't." He swallowed hard, his muscles tightening. "Not if I can help it."

"You'll always be there for me, right? My best friend through thick and thin?"

"Yes," he said, nodding so hard it hurt his neck. "As long as you want me to be. Until you tell me to scram."

Despite the knot in his gut and the breathless race of his heart, he shifted his weight so one thigh pressed into the steering wheel. He had to see her face full-on. He had to see her eyes. "I—" He stopped and swallowed hard, starting again. "I love you, Gretchen," he got out in a rush. "I mean, I really love you. I think I always have. You must know that by now."

She smiled gently, but it was enough to light up the dark like bright moonbeams. Still, there was a glisten in her eyes, a sadness that he wasn't used to seeing. "I love you, too, Sam," she said. "You're my rock. You're like a bro—"

"Don't say it." He cut her off, putting fingers across her lips because he didn't want to hear the word *brother* come out of her mouth. He couldn't bear it. "What if I don't want to be that anymore? What if I want something else?" he whispered, hoping her answer wouldn't tear his heart in two. He was risking everything, being so sincere, but maybe it was time he took the risk.

"Oh, Sam." She sighed, and her hand slipped away from his.

She touched his arm, the gesture sweet but platonic. "I don't know how to put this, but I'm just not sure that I feel *that* way about you . . . about us."

Sam could hardly speak. He ground out, "You could try."

"Please," she said, laying her palm against his cheek. "Please, don't do this. Let's pretend we never had this conversation. I don't want to lose you, and romance is the quickest way I know to kill a friendship."

But it was too late.

He had told her how he felt, and she'd shot him down. It didn't even matter how kindly she'd done it. The whole world Sam had built in his head, his entire existence, had been suddenly squashed like a bug against the truck grille.

"Sam? Talk to me."

Instead, he murmured, "Leave me alone for a minute."

He turned his back on her, fumbled for the door handle, and pushed his way out. Before she could follow, he slammed the door in her face, shutting her in. Then he stood there beside the cab, hands curled into fists, his face turned toward the heavens, wondering what he had done to deserve this. He'd been her playmate, her shoulder, her rock, everything but what he wanted.

The thunder came first, a low growl that rumbled across the night and shook the earth, sending a tremor rattling up Sam's skeleton. Next came the lightning, which turned the black sky a brilliant silver, cracking like an angry whip.

When the rain fell, it fell hard, pounding at the earth around them, drumming loudly on the metal body of the truck so that it drowned out all other sounds. And still Sam couldn't move, even as the drops hit him hard in the face, so sharp they felt like they would slice him to ribbons.

They never made it to their picnic spot, never saw the stars that night. Sam took Gretchen straight home, his eyes on the road all the way back to town. He didn't say another word, not even when he let her out in front of the gingerbread-trimmed Victorian.

Lily was waiting up when he arrived at the farm. His father was already in bed, tuckered out from a long day in the groves. His mom looked up from her book as he leaned into the parlor to say good night.

"Oh, Sam." She sighed and set the book aside. She doubtless wondered why he was dripping wet, hair plastered to his head, his face loudly broadcasting his dejection. She grabbed the knitted throw from the back of the sofa and held it open to him. "Come here," she said. "Come dry off and sit down for a minute."

Reluctantly, he crossed the room, stiffly perching on the cushion as she tossed the throw over his shoulders and began to rub. He kept his hands on his knees the whole time, avoiding her eyes.

When she finally stopped ministering to him, she drew back and asked, "What happened? Is everything all right?"

"Yeah, it's fine." He began to nod and then it turned into a shake of his head. "No, it's not," he confessed, because he couldn't lie, not to Lily. "Nothing's right, as a matter of fact. I did a dumb thing tonight," he went on. "I told Gretchen how I feel, and I thought she'd feel the same."

"But she doesn't?"

"No, she doesn't." Sam bit his cheek hard, struggling to keep his composure.

Lily made a sympathetic noise, though she didn't console him or coddle him. She didn't even reach out to hug him. That wasn't her way. Instead, she got up and went to the fireplace mantel, lifting the lid on a carved wooden box and removing something from within. She returned to the sofa, telling him softly, "I know Gretchen's a smart girl, Sam, but what does any sixteen-year-old know about love? True love, I mean. With one so young, it's all about emotion and desire, all highs and lows. Real love needs time to settle and grow. Some folks go a whole lifetime without being sure of what it feels like. Everyone wants fireworks. Few can appreciate the stillness that comes with the deepest kind of connection."

Sam knew she meant well, but it didn't make him feel the least bit better to hear it. "And how's that supposed to help me now?"

His mother smiled at him, a rare grin that crinkled the corners of her eyes and softened her usually stoic face. "You must *believe*, Samuel Henry. You must have faith that true love will find you when it's ready," she advised and pressed whatever she'd retrieved from the box into the palm of his hand. "This belonged to your grandfather and to his grandfather before him, and he'd want you to have it," she said. "It's believed to have mystical qualities."

Mystical enough to make the woman he loved love him back? Sam wondered and stared at the turquoise beads that snaked across the leather cord. His first thought was that the blue stones were the very color of Gretchen's eyes.

Then he noticed something else, how his hand warmed where the beads touched his skin, a heat that slowly spread up his arms and through the rest of him.

The room was not cold—and neither was he—but still Sam shivered.

"Know that Hank's spirit is always with you," Lily said. "Even before you were born he was watching out for you. Everything will be as it should be." She rose from the sofa and set her hand on his damp head. "Give it time. That alone can make all the difference."

"I'll try," Sam said and curled his fingers tightly around the old choker.

Time was all he had.

Faith

Faith is an invisible and invincible magnet,
and attracts to itself whatever it fervently desires
and calmly and patiently expects.

—RALPH W. TRINE

NINETEEN

April 2010

By the time she herded the sheriff out the door for the second time that day, Gretchen was exhausted. Between the tornado, finding an injured man in the walnut grove, a pregnant Abby dropping in, and Frank Tilby turning up twice, she had nothing left to give. She certainly had nothing left to say to the sheriff, no more theories or conjecture. The Man Who Might Be Sam had done nothing wrong, and neither had she by taking him in. At this point, she'd had enough.

"He's been through the wringer already, don't you think? So why don't you leave us in peace to figure things out for ourselves?" she had suggested before she'd shut the door in his face.

"He'll be back, you know," Bennie said, even as Gretchen went to stand beside Abby at the window overlooking the front porch, making sure the sheriff really left the property. "He's a persistent cuss."

"That he is," Gretchen replied, watching as Frank Tilby walked away from the house, shifting the metal case from hand to hand, glancing back a time or two as he lumbered up the gravel drive.

"I'm sorry for the trouble I've caused you."

Gretchen turned her head at the masculine voice, tinged with equal parts frustration and contrition.

The Man Who Might Be Sam ran fingers through his newly clipped hair. His sturdy features showed agitation in the set of his chin and twitch of muscles at his jaw. "Maybe I should just go and save you the trouble of another of the sheriff's visits."

Abby voiced a panicked "No, you can't leave!"

Gretchen more sensibly asked, "Go where?"

He shrugged, his slim shoulders lost within the oversize plaid shirt. "You're right. I don't have a wallet so I don't have a means to pay for a room in town. I have no car to drive there besides. And I don't know anyone else who'd take me in the way that you all have."

Crossing the kitchen toward him, Gretchen said, "You're welcome to stay for as long as it takes."

"Thanks for that."

She thought she saw a blush in his cheeks and was tempted to hug him but touched his arm instead, allowing her hand to rest there a minute if only to reassure herself for the umpteenth time that he was real. No matter how the sheriff pushed or how many questions still hung overhead, she wasn't about to let him disappear from her life as easily as Sam Winston had.

"You *will* remember what's important soon enough," she assured him. "You just need a chance to heal. Until then, you're our guest, and we want you here."

"Yes, please, stay," Abigail echoed, pushing dark hair behind her ears, an angry frown on her face. "As far as I'm concerned, Sheriff Tilby can stick his field kit up his fat—"

"*Abs*," Gretchen hissed her name, cutting her off, and Abby sighed and crossed her arms.

"As long as you're sure." The Man Who Might Be Sam shifted on his feet, the rubber soles of the borrowed duck shoes squeaking. "I don't want to disrupt your lives any further."

"Disrupt away," Trudy trilled, patches of rose on her smiling cheeks. "It was awfully quiet around here before the storm."

Bennie nodded agreeably. "I find it preferable to have a house filled with noise."

"So it's unanimous." Gretchen patted his arm. "And that's that."

The man set his hand atop hers to still it, such gratitude in his gaze. "Whoever Sam Winston was, he was certainly lucky to have inspired such devotion."

Gretchen wasn't sure how to respond to that. She just stood there, sensing something true passing between them, something too real to be imagined.

Perhaps her sisters sensed it, too, as Bennie cleared her throat, her chair creaking as she rose and reached for her sister. "Come on, Trude, let's go out for a bit. Abby, join us, won't you? I'd like to find out how far the sheriff's deputies have gotten chopping up that old oak."

"That's a grand idea, Ben," her twin said, arms outstretched to feel her way, their shoes clip-clopping across the planked floor as they scurried out of the kitchen, calling out, "Abigail!" in their wake.

"Okay, okay!" Though Abby dragged her feet a bit, she tagged along behind them.

Gretchen drew apart from the man and busied herself by

making them each a cup of tea. "Let's go into the parlor," she suggested, and there they went, settling on the claw-foot sofa.

But he seemed unable to sit for long. He got up almost immediately and headed straight for the fireplace. He skimmed his fingers across the framed photographs lining the mantel as he'd done that very morning. On occasion, he leaned nearer to study one of Abby riding a pony on her eighth birthday or a teenaged Gretchen with a swaddled Abigail in her arms. He paused the longest on the faded black-and-white shot of Hank and Nadya Littlefoot holding Lily.

"I feel as though I've seen this man before," he said and picked it up, turning around so that Gretchen could watch the struggle of emotions on his face. He went a few steps closer to the lamp, shedding more light on the grainy details. "Who is he?" he asked. "He looks a bit like me."

"His name was Henry," she told him. "Henry Littlefoot, but he was called Hank. He was"—she hesitated—"Sam Winston's grandfather." *Your* grandfather, she had nearly said.

"So this was his house once upon a time?"

"It was."

"I see," he replied, still gazing at the photograph. "Was Hank a Native American?" he asked, pointing out Hank's dark, braided hair and the strength of his features.

"He was descended from the Otoe-Missouria tribes, although he left the reservation when he was very young. He had to follow his own path," Gretchen told him, just as Lily had once told her.

"He looks so much older than his wife, or is that his daughter?"

"His wife. Her name was Nadya. The baby is Lily Winston, Sam's mother. She was like a mother to me in so many ways. My own left a lot to be desired." Gretchen held the cup of tea in her palms, grateful for the warmth seeping through the china to her skin. It made her feel far calmer than she actually was.

"What happened to this Hank?" The man glanced up from the photograph. "Was he ill?"

Gretchen wasn't certain how to answer that except to explain what she knew of Hank Littlefoot. "He used to perform some kind of rain-making act on the vaudeville stage and then ended up going from drought-stricken farm to farm, enacting his ceremony to save the crops in the fields. Apparently, he had the magic touch. Only each time he succeeded, it beat him down physically. So that by the time Lily was born, he looked more like her grandfather than her daddy."

"He really made it rain?" The man returned the framed picture back to the mantel. "So it wasn't some kind of trick?"

"Nadya swore to Lily that Hank single-handedly brought the walnut grove back to life by causing lightning to strike," Gretchen continued her story, setting her teacup into its saucer with a gentle clink. "The trees were barren when they took over the farm back in the late 1930s." Her eyes met his. "As dead as they were before the storm that brought you here."

He touched his bruised brow and blinked. She could see so many things sifting through his mind, and she wondered if any bits and pieces were coming back to him. Or if he was just as confused as ever.

"So what about this Sam fellow," he remarked, looking at Gretchen so seriously. "What kind of person was he?"

"A very good man," Gretchen said without hesitation. "The best."

"Was he kind?"

"I've never met anyone kinder," she replied, hoping he couldn't tell that his nearness made her breath quicken and her hands tremble the tiniest bit.

"You were in love with him?" he asked suddenly, seeking truth in her eyes.

Gretchen blushed. "That's not fair," she said, shifting in her seat, her skin so warm she felt feverish. "What Sam and I had was very complicated."

"Why?" He cocked his head. "Either you loved him or you didn't. It seems pretty straightforward to me."

She nervously reached for her teacup, then reconsidered, clasping fingers in her lap. The question wasn't tricky to answer because she hadn't loved Sam but because she *had* loved him in so many different ways throughout the years, until what she felt for him comprised so many layers that it went beyond any simple definition.

"Sam and I began as friends," she explained, avoiding his eyes. "We used to play together when we were children. My father was a veterinarian, and he tended to the Winstons' farm animals. He'd bring me out here with him so I could run around with Sam. It was the most wonderful part of my growing up."

"So were you in love with him?" the man repeated, soft but insistent.

Beautiful memories engulfed her, and Gretchen smiled,

looking up from her hands. "He was the first boy who ever said he loved me."

"I hope you said it back."

Gretchen laughed, but it was strained. "Spoken like a man."

He rubbed a palm over his craggy face, shaking his head. "You still haven't answered my question."

"Yes," she said, and even more honestly, "I loved Sam Winston. I still do, perhaps more now than ever."

His taut expression relaxed. "Not sure why that was so hard to admit."

"You don't understand," she started out, surprised by the catch she felt in her chest. "I didn't say the things he wanted so badly to hear. I think I broke his heart, maybe more than once. He's probably never forgiven me."

The man grunted. "You were young and foolish. Time can make all the difference."

"I just wish I'd had more of it with him," Gretchen added wistfully. "Time, I mean."

How strange it felt, saying those words aloud. How she wished she'd stopped Sam from leaving all those years ago! Why hadn't she asked him to stay? He would have done anything for her, she was sure of it. But she'd been too blind, too flighty, too wrapped up in her own melodrama. She hadn't realized until he was gone just how insanely she loved him. He was her other half, her better half, the only one who understood her, who saw her flaws and adored her regardless.

A tiny sob escaped her, and strong hands quickly covered her own.

"I didn't mean to make you sad," the man said, his graveled voice incredibly tender.

"I don't like looking back," she confessed, and weary tears fell unguarded.

"You can't beat yourself up over choices you made so long ago." He squeezed her fingers, catching them up in his.

"It feels like I was the one who was lost, even though I stayed behind. Sam's the one who traveled halfway around the world." She brushed at the tears, tasting salt on her lips. "I wish I could talk to him, find out what happened, where he was all that time, how he died."

"Would it change anything to know those things?" he asked, rubbing her hand, the scars on his palms rough against her softer flesh.

"I'm not sure," Gretchen said, her mind spinning. She'd never thought about it like that. She'd always assumed that having answers would make it better somehow, would give her some kind of closure. But would it?

"So much of the world is illogical," the man went on, impassioned. "Take the salmon who kill themselves swimming upriver to spawn in the same spot every year, or dragonflies with their gossamer wings whose lives span only a matter of months. Does either make sense?"

"What?" Gretchen stared at him, her own world screeching to a sudden halt. "What did you just say?"

"About the salmon spawning or the dragonflies?" he asked, salt-and-pepper brows furrowed.

"The dragonflies," she told him, barely breathing.

"Let's see what I recall." He cleared his throat, squinting

up at the ceiling. "The adult dragonfly only lives an average of two months. Although if you count the nymph stage, it's more like a year."

Dear God.

Gripped by a fierce wave of déjà vu, Gretchen tugged her hand from his, setting it against her heart, feeling the wild palpations. *Does it make sense that a dragonfly only lives for a few months?* a teenaged Sam Winston had said to her ages ago. She'd been crying then, too, upset over her parents' divorce, and he'd talked off the top of his head, trying to calm her down.

"Did I say something wrong?" the man asked her.

"No," she told him, but she looked at him differently, sure that a part of him was starting to remember even if he didn't realize it yet. He had been out to the grove, had meandered by the barn, had touched the arrowheads in Sam's old room—he was wearing Sam's father's old clothes! Surely some of who he was had sunk in by now. *You're in there, Sammy, aren't you?* "I'm just wondering how you can recall such odd facts without re-membering other things."

More important things, she almost said.

"I don't know." He shrugged. "It's a bit like chasing fireflies. Some light up in the dark, and those are easy to catch. Others flicker and fade before I can get near them."

"Aren't there any memories you can catch? Any faces you can see?"

His gray eyes filled with frustration. "I know what you're thinking, and I wish so badly I could say what you want me to say, that I remember being on this farm, that I'm the man you loved and not a stranger. But I can't lie to you, Gretchen. I won't do it."

"So you're telling me there's nothing there?" she asked as a tightness deep within her began to loosen, the lock on her most guarded emotions slowly opening up; she felt so close to breaking. "You don't feel bound to this place in ways you can't explain? You don't feel a sense that you belong?"

She was pushing it, she knew, something she'd discouraged Abby from doing. So much for taking her own advice.

He said nothing at first. Then he reached up to touch her cheek, and Gretchen instinctively leaned into him, pressing against his scarred palm. She closed her eyes, frightened by how much she wanted this, how desperately she needed him to be Sam, all in one piece, the past forgotten, ready to move on together.

"I was wrong," he said in a rough whisper. "There is something here, and I do feel it strongly, whoever I am."

She wanted to tell him she was sorry, if she needed him to be someone he was not. But as she parted her lips to speak, he kissed her with such unexpected gentleness that the dam within her broke.

"Oh," she breathed, and her arms went round his neck, her fingers catching in his hair as she kissed him back.

The moment didn't last long, and when they drew apart, she felt as muddled as if she'd awakened in the middle of a dream. She didn't want to open her eyes. She wanted to keep them closed so she could imagine she was sixteen, kissing Sam in his truck, steaming up the windows and telling him, "I love you," over and over instead of pushing him too far away to reach.

"... so are you leaving some of the wood with us? Because I would think you should, since it was our tree," Bennie lectured one of the sheriff's deputies, both of whom had shut off their chain saws to entertain Abby's aunts' questions.

At least it appeared that there would be room to get a car through the driveway soon enough, as long as Bennie and Trudy didn't talk the men's ears off so they could get back to work before the sun went down.

Abby was honestly glad she'd come out with them, since neither woman used a cane and there was still storm debris everywhere. When she'd needled them about that, Bennie had sniffed. "What good would it do when we know every inch of this place by heart?" Then the pair had steadfastly made their way up the drive, walking arm in arm, chattering and finishing each other's sentences.

"Be mindful that the ground is littered with branches," Abby had said, certain that even Trudy's keen sense of smell and Bennie's acute hearing couldn't detect every husk and twig. "Those kinds of things can trip up people with sight."

"That's why we have you," Bennie had declared, squishing up her right eye in what passed for a wink.

"Perhaps we should contact the lumber mill or call for

a wood chipper," Trudy piped up, sticking in her two cents' worth. "We should call Walter and see if he can come help us clean up besides."

"Then you can get more practice flirting with the handy-man, eh, Trude?" Bennie teased.

Figuring her aunts were too preoccupied to go anywhere for the next five minutes, Abby drifted away, moseying toward the rural road that ran perpendicular to the dirt drive and straight into town. The road was empty save for the dust kicked up in the wake of the utility truck that was heading off after fixing the cables. There was a pickup on the shoulder that Abby figured belonged to one of the deputies. Otherwise, all was clear.

She allowed herself to roam beyond the property line, across the unpaved lane to where a host of black-eyed Susans tipped their petals toward the sun. A carpet of violets had sprouted beneath, entangled with the clover.

How pretty that would be to paint, she mused and plucked a yellow flower, twirling its stem in her hand. In the city, there weren't such colorful weeds. If she wanted to see flowers, it meant a walk to the florist or to the Lincoln Park Conservatory, where blooms could hardly be plucked at will.

She wondered if her baby would be happy here, if this would be a better place to rear her than Chicago. So much open space, wildflowers in abundance, bugs and toads and more birds than she could count on all her fingers and toes.

"How would you like to live here?" she asked down to her belly. "Maybe you'd like growing up on the farm as much as I did."

Abby bit her lip at the idea, knowing she'd seriously have to think about it, depending on what happened with her and Nate. *I would feel safe here,* she knew. *I would feel loved.*

She meandered back across the road to the mailbox, its post engulfed in wild honeysuckle. The painted black box still said WINSTON FARM on the side. Although the name had faded through the years, Gretchen had never seen fit to change it. The metal door hung open, looking very much like a panting dog's tongue. Abby reached out to shut it, remembering a time when she was a kid and had opened the door to find a bird trapped inside. With a squawk and a beat of its wings, it had swooped out, scaring her half to death.

Zzzzz. Zzzzz.

Startled, Abby dropped the black-eyed Susan she'd been holding, feeling her right butt cheek begin to vibrate. She'd stuck her cell phone in her rear pocket before they'd left in case she'd wanted to check her messages. Even a yard or two outside the fence was far enough away from the farm to get a signal.

She glanced at the familiar number and braced herself as she answered, barely getting out a civil "Hello, Nate" before he laid into her: "What the hell were you thinking, leaving Chicago without telling me? Haven't you checked your voice mail? I've left a million messages!"

"You know I don't get reception down here," she reminded him, shoulders stiff, already on the defensive. "And the landline's been out since yesterday's storm."

"If I hadn't gone back to our place to get fresh clothes, I would never have seen your note. Why didn't you tell me what you were up to? Am I supposed to be telepathic?"

"First off, I'm not *up to* anything." Abby bristled. "And, second, I didn't figure you'd care. Remember, you were the one who needed space," she said, trying not to get worked up, thinking of the tiny baby in her belly and hoping it couldn't sense her anxiety. "You're the one who walked out, not me."

"You're the one who pushed me out—oh, for crying out loud," he grumbled, and she could sense his reluctance to keep fighting. "Look, I'm not calling so we can rehash our argument."

Then why *was* he calling?

Her eyes misting, she glanced up at the sky, which suddenly filled with a noisy murder of crows that decided to settle nearby on the repaired utility lines. How lovely it would've been if he'd told her he missed her, if he'd said he couldn't stand another day without her. Instead, the first thing he did was lay into her about her trip to Walnut Ridge. Was this the kind of man she even *wanted* to help her raise her kid?

She drew in a deep breath and dared to ask, "So what *do* you want, Nate? And if you so much as raise your voice again, I'll hang up," she said, glancing back across the fence to see Bennie staring in her direction. She wondered if her aunt could hear her every word, no matter how quietly she spoke.

"What do I want?" he said, and he took a noisy breath. "I want to know why you're keeping something from me, something I have every right to know."

"And what would that be?" She stopped moving, though her pulse did the opposite, picking up its pace.

"Are you pregnant?" he blurted out, and Abby nearly fell over. "I found instructions for a pregnancy test in the bathroom," he proceeded slowly, managing not to holler, "right there on top of the wastebasket. You must have ditched the sticks somewhere else because I couldn't find them."

"Oh," slipped out of Abby's mouth, and she thanked her lucky stars she'd put the test sticks and box into the pharmacy's plastic bag before tossing it down the apartment's garbage chute. She hadn't realized she'd missed the directions. Although maybe it was one of those subconscious "accidentally on purpose" things.

"I just can't believe you'd do that," he went on, and she envisioned him pacing with his cell in one hand, tugging at his ear with the other. "Why would you keep this a secret from me?"

Abby wondered if it made her a bad person to feel good that he was angry, like at least she wasn't the only one confused and hurting.

"Let's not talk about this now, Nate," she told him, lowering her voice. "We can discuss it when I'm back in Chicago."

"And when will that be?"

"I don't know," she admitted. She hadn't planned to stay home more than a few days to talk to her mom and clear her head, but that was before she'd met the stranger who'd fallen from the sky, a man who might very well be her dad. "I still have things to sort out," she added.

"I'm not kidding, Abby. Tell me the truth right now," he said, his voice rumbling like distant thunder, "or, I swear to God, I will get in my car and drive down there this minute."

"Sure you will," Abby said, finding that hard to believe. He'd moved out two weeks ago, had not made any attempt to see her, had not said one kind word to her in this entire phone conversation, and she was supposed to buy that he'd drop everything and road-trip five-plus hours to Walnut Ridge to grill her on whether or not she'd seen two pink lines on a plastic stick?

If Nate had that kind of initiative, she'd love to see it.

"Don't tempt me, Abby, because I will skip my afternoon meeting for this new app I've been working my butt off to finish, and I'll leave Myron high and dry even though I promised we'd go out to dinner this evening—"

For crying out loud!

"Then do it," she said with a hiss, losing patience with his threats. "For once in your life, Nathan March, quit making excuses! Just decide if I'm important enough and commit!"

Before he could sputter any kind of response, Abby ended the call and strode through the split-rail fence, her heart slamming against her ribs, trying hard not to hyperventilate.

Once she was back on the farm, she glanced at her phone to see zero bars, which was exactly what she'd expected. She had lost all reception. So if Nate wanted to reach her again, he'd have to phone the house—if the line was working—and deal with her mother first.

"Your call, Nate," she said, feeling strangely liberated as she tucked her cell away.

TWENTY-ONE

The phone rang, quite out of the blue.

Gretchen jumped at the noise. She hadn't even realized the line was reconnected. She'd just shown the Man Who Might Be Sam to the sunroom, giving him clean linens for the day-bed since he'd be staying there for a while more. "I wouldn't mind a lie-down right about now," he'd confessed, touching fingers to his bruised forehead, and she'd left him alone to take a nap.

She was heading through the parlor, thinking about going upstairs for a rest herself, when the black beast began to trill. She quickly picked up the handset and said, "Hello?"

"Gretch? It's Sheriff Tilby. Hold on to your hat 'cause I've got some mind-blowing news on that fellow you've taken into your house like a lost pup."

Aw, shoot.

Gretchen sank down on the sofa, twirling the cord around her finger, a ball of tension knotting up in her belly. "Spit it out, Frank," she demanded, despite the cotton dryness of her mouth.

"We found a 1974 Oldsmobile Cutlass half submerged in Fork Creek, just under the bridge. Driver must've lost traction when the storm hit, unless he'd already shucked the car to lie down in a ditch. Could be the twister tossed it when it was empty."

He paused, and Gretchen wondered if he were waiting for applause. Instead, she begged, "Do go on. There's more to this, I assume?"

"Yes, of course, there is, sorry," he mumbled, and she heard the rustle of papers. "The plates were expired and rusty, like somebody had kept the car in an old barn for a spell. But we managed to trace the VIN." The sheriff dramatically cleared his throat. "The car is registered to someone named Henry Little."

Henry Little?

"So?" Gretchen felt a pounding at her temples. Why did Frank Tilby persist in playing guessing games? Did he do this with his deputies, too? If so, she was surprised they hadn't shot him by now. She hardly knew what to say, and she very nearly plunked the telephone receiver back into its cradle. Bennie was right. He was persistent, worse than a stray dog with a bone. "What are you implying?"

"Wasn't Sam Winston's grandfather's name Henry Little-foot?" the sheriff asked, and she could hear the smirk in his voice.

Gretchen sighed. "Good God, Frank, everyone in town knows about Hank Littlefoot. And if there's an ignorant soul who doesn't, all he'd have to do is check the archives at the Historical Society. Sam's family tree is not a secret."

"No, it's not a secret, is it?" the sheriff agreed. "Nothing that's ever happened in Walnut Ridge is."

"Could you just tell me what you're getting at?" Gretchen

twisted the phone cord around her finger until the tip turned white. "I've got better things to do than speculate about a car in a creek."

"Hold your horses, missy," Frank said, sniffing impatiently. "So I ran the name Henry Little through the system, and he was apparently a bona fide weasel. He racked up a long list of warrants in his prime. His full name is Henry Stewart Little, and he was a preacher out of Oklahoma who put down stakes in the Show Me State for a while. In fact he spent a few weeks right here in Walnut Ridge."

"What's that got to do with me?" Gretchen asked, having had just about enough. She untangled her finger from the cord. "Get to the point, or I'm hanging up."

"Hear me out," the sheriff growled.

Gretchen gritted her teeth, but she stayed on the phone.

"Henry S. Little was an evangelist who traveled around the Midwest, pitching a tent, and putting on a show. He took a lot of money from people who couldn't afford to give it. Some of their families got wise and claimed fraud, trying to recover anything they could get." He paused for air but picked up again before Gretchen could give him any flack. "Preacher Little told his flock he was heading off to do missionary work the last they saw him. No one's heard from him in nearly twenty years, and no one might've ever heard from him again except for the car in the creek. You see what I'm getting at?"

Gretchen felt as foggy as the walnut grove had appeared earlier. "No, I haven't a clue."

"What if Sam Winston is really and truly dead, and this Henry Little knew enough about you and the twins and what happened to the Winstons to take advantage of the situation?" the sheriff ranted. "Like you said, it's all there in the Walnut Ridge archives: Sam leaving on a youth mission for Africa, his going missing, Lily and Coop passing away and leaving the grove to you. Every bit of information's laid out like an encyclopedia, and all he had to do was wait for the right moment. So good old Henry Little comes out of hiding, ditches his Olds, and shows up on your farm. Now he's got you hooked on his amnesia story like worm bait to a hungry catfish, and he's reeling you in."

My word, if that didn't sound like the plot for a really bad movie, Gretchen wasn't sure what did.

"Good God," she sputtered, unsure if she'd ever seethed before, but she was seething right that minute. "You're certifiable," she told the sheriff. "I've never heard such insanity in my life! You think the man I've taken in is a missing preacher who's dodged the law for twenty years?" She paused to get a hold of herself, the pounding at her temples now a full-blown headache. "Stop this nonsense, Frank Tilby, do you hear me? Don't bother me anymore!"

The man in her house—the man who'd kissed her—was either Sam Winston or his reincarnation. Gretchen knew it in her core. She didn't say as much to the sheriff because she didn't care whether or not he believed her. What mattered was her own heart, and it was telling her Sam had come home.

How else could she explain the inexplicable, like the storm that had come out of nowhere, the buds on the dead walnut trees, the mole on the back of his neck, the turquoise beads, and his remark about dragonflies? None of *that* was in the town archives.

"But, Gretchen, listen to me—"

"No, you listen to me," she interrupted him. "Leave us alone, or I'll phone Millie myself and tell her to keep you on a shorter leash. Now let's say good-bye before this gets any nastier, shall we?"

"Gretchen Brink! You need to come to your senses, woman!" Tilby sputtered, turning quite blustery. "You're a woman of a certain age pining for something that doesn't exist! You always were a dreamer, wanting things you couldn't have. You couldn't even see when the right guy stood in front of you, and you blew it."

Blew it with him? she wondered, knowing he didn't mean her chance with Sam.

"Are you referring to yourself, Sheriff?" She could hardly keep from shouting. How preposterous could he get?

"At least I didn't run off to Africa and leave a pregnant woman behind to bear my child alone."

"No, you married a woman you didn't love because it was the easy way out," Gretchen replied, so agitated the receiver shook in her hand.

"Why don't you calm down and see things rationally—"

"And why don't you go to hell!"

She slammed down the handset and squeezed her eyes shut, pressing fingers to her forehead.

"Gretchen?"

Her heart in her throat, she swiveled around to see the man standing there. "How much did you hear?" she asked, wishing she'd never answered the phone. Wishing she'd told Tilby from the start to keep his damned nose out of her business.

"I heard enough," he said, his eyes a slate gray above his high cheekbones.

"I'm so sorry, but the sheriff can't seem to let this go."

"Maybe it's you he can't let go of," the man remarked and began walking toward her. "And every minute I stay here, I understand why more and more."

She bit her bottom lip, unable to look away from him, thinking how the sum of his parts measured up to Sam Winston all right: his height, his slim build, the structure of his face, his reluctant smile, his strong but gentle demeanor. Only when he touched her now, when he drew her into his arms and held her there, pressing his chin against her hair, Gretchen felt something she'd never felt with Sam before.

A physical connection. A true spark.

One that had taken forty years to ignite.

Choices

Some choices we live not only once but a
thousand times over, remembering them for the
rest of our lives.

—RICHARD BACH

TWENTY-TWO

July–August 1970

Sam Winston had barely seen Gretchen all summer, not since his high school graduation. She had been seated with his parents in the third row of the gymnasium, rising to her feet when he'd crossed the makeshift stage in cap and gown to receive his diploma. Her smile had glowed like a sunburst from amidst the dozens of other faces.

But that was back in early June, and it was already late July. He'd be taking off soon for a six-month humanitarian mission in Africa while Gretchen returned to school for her senior year. When he'd asked, she had come by the farm a while back to give him a haircut. But she hadn't been by since. Sam wouldn't doubt that she was wary of being around him, as he'd avoided her for months, sulking throughout the spring after her "can't we just be friends" remark had ripped his heart out.

By the time he'd managed to swallow his pride and accept whatever terms she placed on their relationship, Gretchen had gotten a full-time job as a waitress at Patty Pig's BBQ on the edge of town, where the rural route connected with the interstate highway. It kept her busy enough that she'd turned him down the last few times he'd tried to get together.

So he'd made a point to go to Patty Pig's just to see her, asking to be seated in her section, for all the good that did. The joint—oh, and it was a joint—had been noisy and crowded, an incessant string of "you done me wrong" country songs blaring from the jukebox, truck drivers loudly jawing, the smell of pork, cigarette smoke, and unwashed humanity thick in the air.

As he chewed a sloppy brisket sandwich, he watched her race back and forth between the tables in her bright yellow uniform, pale hair pulled off her sweat-damp face. Half her job, he decided, appeared to involve dancing away from strange men grabbing at her rear end.

"Can I see you later?" Sam had asked after she'd torn his check from her pad and slapped it down on the table. She'd looked so deflated, like she needed a little cheering up, and he wondered if Annika was responsible. Since her father had left, Gretchen always seemed to be doing too much. "Nothing big, I promise. Maybe we can go for a drive," he'd suggested.

"Later tonight?" she'd said, frowning, and tucked her pencil behind her ear. "I don't know, Sammy. We'll see," was the best she could give him.

Only, they didn't end up going for a drive, not that night or any night for weeks on end. Not until Sam got a phone call from Gretchen around dinnertime on a Monday evening, barely a week before he was set to depart for West Africa in mid-August.

"Can you meet me at the park?" she'd asked, such urgency in her voice that Sam worried before he even knew anything was wrong. "I need to talk to you alone."

"When?"

"Is now too soon? I have a shift in two hours."

"Now's good," he assured her.

He took the truck into Walnut Ridge, driving as fast as he safely could on the unpaved road, clouds of dust kicking up in his wake. When he reached the town square, he parked smack across from the sheriff's office. He half expected to run into Frank Tilby, who was in training as a deputy to his old man.

But Sam didn't bump into the sheriff's son on the sidewalk, or when he popped into the drugstore to buy two ice-cold bottles of Coke. Downtown Walnut Ridge seemed blissfully empty in the heat of high afternoon, in that lazy hour before dusk.

He marched across Main Street, passing the gazebo and the bandstand, heading over to the park proper where the local kids flew kites and played soccer. The green space was empty now save for a few stragglers not yet ready to abandon one of the remaining days of summer for home and supper.

Sam found Gretchen sitting on a bench, staring into space, her pretty face crumpled, looking for all the world like her life had just ended.

He slid onto the bench beside her and offered her a Coke. "You thirsty?"

She shook her head but took it anyway, tucking it between her thighs, bare below the ragged bottoms of her denim shorts. He could see a scrape over one kneecap, and it reminded him of the Saturdays they'd run loose on the farm, getting all sorts of cuts from climbing trees and pretending they were pirates, seeing who could scramble up the imaginary ropes to the bird's nest first. Gretchen often won, and she'd shout from the highest bough, "Land, ho!" Even with her hair tangled and face smudged with dirt, she'd beamed victoriously.

But she hardly appeared as carefree at the moment. Tears skidded down her face, plopping onto her blue tank top.

"What's wrong?" he asked, setting his soda on the grass so his hands were free. He touched her arm, not sure of what to do. "C'mon, you can tell me."

"I'm in trouble, deep trouble," she mumbled as more tears tumbled from her lashes. She had shadows below her eyes, blotches on her freckled cheeks. Her collarbone jutted noticeably above the scoop neck of her tank. She sure looked like she hadn't been sleeping much, or eating much for that matter. "I dug myself into a big hole, Sam, and I don't know how to get out."

If it had been anyone else, Sam might've instantly thought it was drugs or booze or petty theft. But he couldn't imagine Gretchen getting into anything heavy. No matter what her family had gone through, she'd always been the best kind of girl. She'd taken care of her blind sisters, had put up with a mother who rubbed all of Walnut Ridge the wrong way, had lost her father to divorce, and still managed to keep a smile on her face, most of the time anyway. But not now.

"What could you possibly have done?" he asked, dying to put his arm around her and comfort her, but afraid she'd take it the wrong way. He didn't want her to think he was coming on to her because she was feeling weak. "I'm sure it's not as bad as you think."

Her chin trembled as she nodded. "Oh, it's bad," she said, unable to meet his gaze. "I can't imagine what my mother will say when I get up the nerve to tell her. I wouldn't be surprised if she kicks me out." Gretchen exhaled noisily and fiddled with the neck of the Coke bottle, finally plucking the thing from between her thighs and depositing it on the bench. "I made a huge mistake, and I don't think there's any good way to fix it."

Sam still couldn't envision anything Gretchen would have done that could be so unforgivable. "Did you get fired? Did you steal something? Did you burn all of Annika's awful paintings?"

Glumly, she told him, "No, nothing like that."

So Sam asked the next thing that came to mind, the short hairs at the back of his neck prickling even as he said it. "Did that idiot Frank Tilby get you into trouble? Because if he did, I'll kick his butt."

He might be the sheriff's kid, but Tilby was no angel. Sam had seen him drunk as a skunk, out driving the back roads in his pickup with his buddies, hunting lights turned on, tossing beer cans out the windows. Had Gretchen been in the truck with him when he'd hit something or someone? Sam wasn't blind. He'd hung around some of the high school baseball games, watching Gretchen's eyes on Tilby. He knew they'd seen each other some, though he didn't like to think about it.

"If he's hurt you, Gretch—" Sam continued, balling his hands into fists.

"No!" She stared at him, wide-eyed. "I swear, Frank has nothing to do with this. I've hardly seen him all summer. All he does is play baseball, get wasted, and work for his dad."

Though he wasn't sure that he believed her—she could have been lying just to keep him from hunting Frank down and knocking out all his teeth—Sam gave her the benefit of the doubt. He leaned back against the bench, following her gaze and staring off into the distance. "If it's not Tilby, then what is it?" he said. "You'll feel better once you get it off your chest."

"I'm not so sure about that," she said and averted her eyes, staring at her lap again.

The sun had dipped below the line of trees, the sky less a blue than a mix of mottled pinks and purples. Hardly anyone remained except an older woman walking a dog that kept stopping to sniff every bush within leash length.

They sat there in silence for another ten minutes, the nightly chorus of crickets warming up their serenade. An owl did a soft *who-who* in the distance. Sam figured Lily was wondering where he was and why he was late for dinner, as he'd run out of the house without telling anyone where he was going. But Gretchen was more important than a scolding from his mother.

"I'm pregnant, Sam."

"What?" he said, not sure he'd heard right. She'd caught him half listening. "What'd you say?"

"I'm pregnant," Gretchen repeated, and still he couldn't believe it.

Sam peeled his arm off the back of the bench and turned to face her. Gretchen's head was down, avoiding him, which didn't help matters any as Sam found his own gaze drawn toward the spot beneath her ribbed tank top that covered her belly. She looked as slender as she always had. She must be wrong. She couldn't possibly be right.

"No," he whispered, mostly to himself. "You can't be."

"I missed my period," she told him, sniffing back her tears. "I went to a clinic over in Washington and took a blood test. There's no mistake, Sam. I'm going to have a baby."

"Maybe you need to take another test," he said, hardly able to focus. Both his brain and his heart clouded up, darkening like the evening sky. "Maybe the first one was wrong. I could take you back tomorrow and you could do it over again—"

"No." She tucked hay-colored hair behind her ears, her fingers trembling. "I don't need to retake anything." She dropped her hands to her thighs and began softly sobbing. "It wasn't wrong. I messed up and now I'm paying for it."

"How?" he asked, his breaths choppy, feeling as though his chest had been cut open wide. "How did it happen?"

"I was stupid is how. It was an accident," she said as she wiped futilely at her falling tears. "It was a crazy night at work, and I was so dead on my feet. Nothing's been going right for months and months, you know, not with Annika, not with"—*you*, Sam was sure she was going to say, but instead she finished with—"anyone. This guy who came into Patty's, he was so sweet to me. He was with friends, they said their car had broken down. He was so gracious, not at all like the normal crowd." Her freckled features screwed up, and she exhaled slowly. "When his pals took off, he hung around until I clocked out." She shrugged. "I left with him because he made me smile." She played with the frayed edge of her shorts. "I've hardly had any fun all summer, working so much, giving the money to Annika for bills. I can't even remember exactly how it all happened, but it did." She dropped her head into her hands, crying harder now. "It was just one of those things—"

Sam stared at her, unable to blink, barely able to breathe.

One of those things? Like, oops, I slipped and fell against the guy, and we made a baby. *God dammit. God dammit!*

At that point, Sam couldn't stand to listen further. Every word she'd already uttered was killing him, twisting his guts in the most painful way. He shut her out, closing his eyes, fingers curled around the edge of the bench until he felt splinters. He seethed inwardly and watched angry clouds rolling in. He fought to keep his heart from bursting out of his chest and creating a bloody mess.

Why, Gretchen, why?

How could she have done something like this? How could she have let this happen? Sam wasn't naïve; he knew she loved him but she wasn't *in love* with him, not the way he was with her. Still, he'd always imagined, had always hoped, that she would realize they were meant to be together. That someday, she would be his. They would marry, settle down, and have kids.

And now she was having some other man's baby?

He touched the beads at his throat, fingering the turquoise that had once been his grandfather's, wishing whatever magic they contained could make him forget everything he'd just heard. But he knew that wouldn't work. Gretchen's words had already been imprinted on his soul.

What do I do? he thought. *Grandfather, help me deal with this.*

The air whispered in his ear as the wind began to blow, rustling the leaves in the trees above them, ruffling the grass beneath his feet. It tugged at Gretchen's hair, whipping the pale curls about her face. She didn't even try to push them back, and Sam didn't do it for her either.

"Do you hate me?" she asked, her voice so small he was hardly aware she'd said anything at all until she touched his cheek, startling him, and he kicked over the bottle of Coke he'd set aside.

"I can understand if you do," she said and jumped to her feet. "I can understand if you never want to see me again. I let you down. I let everyone down."

Sam could hardly refute her. He couldn't think of a thing to say that would make her feel better. She could not have done anything that would have hurt him worse.

"It's okay, I understand. I'd hate me, too," she said, hugging her arms around her waist. "Well, okay, good-bye then, Sam. I hope you have a good trip." She turned her back to him, her head down.

And he realized that if he allowed her to walk away, she might never come back. That it would surely be the end of them.

"Gretchen!"

Sam couldn't let her go. If he left for Africa letting her believe he didn't love her anymore, that he'd rejected her completely, he could never forgive himself. In that split second, he understood what he had to do, however it pained him.

He hopped up and went after her, catching her by the wrist before she'd gone too far. "Wait," he begged, close to tears himself. "You can't leave me, not like this."

Gretchen stood stock-still, her hand limp in his grasp.

So Sam did the only thing he could, the only thing he knew

he could do and live with himself. "A while ago, I made you a promise that I wouldn't abandon you, and I meant it. If there's any way I can make things right, you let me know, and I'll do it."

Her damp eyes glistened in the dusk. "Sam?"

"Whatever you need, Gretch. Anything."

Her fingers slowly intertwined with his, and she squeezed his hand, smiling sadly before she released him.

"Thank you" was all she said.

She didn't take him up on his offer, not then. He didn't find out that she had until years and years later, long after he was already gone.

TWENTY-THREE

August–September 1970

Once Sam arrived in the coastal West African town and tossed his duffel bag into the back of a battered Jeep, already crammed full, he didn't have time to be homesick or even to dwell much on Gretchen. The drive out to the refugee camp near the interior border was one of the longest rides he'd ever taken, and not merely because the Jeep's driver had packed four grown men and one woman inside so that they were wedged shoulder to shoulder; but the heat was oppressive, the road even dustier than the rural route for Walnut Ridge, and they were stopped at numerous checkpoints manned by sweaty and angry-looking armed militants.

They left behind the waving palms of the port—and the director of the mission, who seemed inclined to stay within his air-conditioned office—until all Sam saw was desert surrounding them and then dots of white littering the landscape the closer they came to the border. He quickly realized all those dots were tents, thousands of them, maybe even a hundred thousand. And there were people everywhere, moving like trails of ants, many of them standing in lines, some waiting for water, some trying to locate missing family, and others seeking medical attention.

"Dear Lord," said the brown-skinned woman beside him, whose name was Colleen. Her eyes looked as big as saucers as she surveyed the sprawl of the refugee camp. "How are the five of us supposed to make a dent?"

"Or even a ding," a freckled and redheaded fellow named Brett groused from the front seat. He'd taken a semester away from college and looked like he was regretting it already.

Once the Jeep had jerked to a stop, they were all ordered out, told to grab their gear from the back, and given vague instructions about finding the proper tents. Before Sam could ask for more details, the driver hopped back into the Jeep and sped off.

"So where's the welcoming committee?" Colleen asked, glancing around; her backpack was so heavy that it caused her left shoulder to sink under its weight.

They were surrounded by faces black and white and every color in between. Sam even saw a few dogs and some goats.

"The youth ministry volunteers' tents?" he asked a few in passing. Some pointed them left and others right.

"Maybe we should just pick a direction and go," Colleen suggested.

"Yeah, but which?" Sam wondered aloud, searching for a sign of some sort, an arrow pointing the way, perhaps. But no such signs existed.

"Where's the rest of the group?" Colleen asked next and stood on the toes of her boots, looking for Brett and the other two from their shuttle.

"I haven't a clue," Sam told her, hanging on to the straps of his backpack and doing a slow circle around them, seeking

Brett's rust-red hair. But by the time he'd made a single turn within the noise and the smells and the confusion, he'd lost Colleen, too.

A bubble of panic seeped up from his gut, burning in his throat, and he thought about standing on the nearest truck and shouting for help.

"You must be fresh meat," a voice said from behind him before he did anything too rash. "You look confused."

"I'm just trying to find my way," he replied, and faced a woman who looked to be in her early twenties wearing a dirty white shirt and even dustier jeans. She stared him squarely in the eye.

"We're all trying to find our way," she quipped and gave him a crooked grin. "Just be careful of the clean-looking ones who say they're running things from their nice offices on the coast. Sods, the lot of them. They're the ones who know the least," she told him, adding with a shrug, "The rest of us have learned how to muddle our way through. It's either that or lose our minds."

"Got it," Sam said, appreciating her directness.

She wasn't pretty by any conventional means—tall, angular, hair as short as a boy's, a wide nose, and a noticeable gap between her teeth—but she had a take-charge air about her that he liked on the spot.

"Sam Winston," he introduced himself, letting go of a strap to extend his hand, "from Walnut Ridge, Missouri."

"Cate," she said simply, ignoring the gesture. "Follow me, Missouri, and I'll see if I can't get you settled so you can make yourself useful." She started walking, brushing past unsmiling men in tan military uniforms and women in bright-colored rags tugging children by the hand.

One such mother grabbed Sam's arm, begging him for something in a language he didn't understand.

Cate gently took the woman's arm, uttering a few words that made the dark head nod before she turned away. "It's heartbreaking," she said to Sam as they moved along, past another endless row of tents. "They've lost so much, and not just their possessions. Their fathers and brothers and husbands and sons. But you know what they say: war is hell. And, come to think of it, so is this place. Anyway, here's your new digs, Missouri."

Cate paused before a muddied canvas flap. "If you need anything, well"—she shot him that crooked grin again—"you'll figure it out yourself, or you can find me again."

"Thanks," Sam said as she gave a backhanded wave and disappeared into the swarm.

Feeling hot and not a little sick to his stomach, Sam ducked inside to find a dozen cots, most of them littered with someone else's detritus. He located the first empty bunk, topped with a coarse but neatly folded blanket and a pocket-sized Bible. He set his pack on the floor and slumped onto the makeshift bed, rubbing his head in his hands. As he pondered what the heck he was supposed to do next, two young men popped in.

"Are you with the new batch that just landed?" one asked, and Sam nodded. "Great! Come on with us, and we'll get you started canvassing."

Which, as Sam quickly learned, had nothing to do with art or political campaigns. Instead, it involved masses of paperwork, an endless list of refugees' names as they flooded into the aid camp. Sam was sent around with a fellow named Theo who spoke half a dozen languages, and it was Theo's job to pull information about family members from the displaced, translating to Sam, who did the best he could to jot everything down in some kind of order.

By nightfall, he was tired and hot and hungry. Dinner was rice and beans with bread and beer. As he lay down to try to get some sleep, he noticed that most of his tent-mates slowly disappeared. He wondered if he was missing some kind of prayer meeting or service, and he asked that of Theo the next morning.

"Are you kidding?" Theo said and laughed. "Give yourself a month of this, and you'll be desperate for someone warm. If you can't find a soul to connect with, you'll go bat-shit crazy around here."

But Sam hadn't volunteered for the mission to meet girls, and he didn't mind being alone. It didn't even bother him to feel lonely. He was rather used it, having never made very many friends, having never trusted anyone completely. Well, anyone except Gretchen.

Besides, after his first two weeks in the camp, with his ears constantly filled with the buzz of people crying and shouting and talking, often in languages he didn't know, he savored time by himself. He would take out the battered copy of Hemingway's *The Sun Also Rises* that he'd packed, slip Gretchen's photograph from between the pages, and gaze at her face, rubbing his thumb across the Kodachrome square, and he'd imagine he could feel the softness of her skin or the curl of her hair. She seemed so foreign to him now, someone from another world entirely. She reminded him of what he'd left behind, what was familiar. And he took comfort in that.

Sam's long days quickly fell into a pattern: up in the morning, bright and early, using hand-dug latrines that reeked of crap and buzzed with flies; swallowing down whatever food was offered, whether military MREs or rice and beans; distributing water to those who patiently waited in long lines; helping refugees search for missing family; doling out medicine or soap or whatever the hell they had to try to make life for the thousands of displaced humans even the slightest bit easier.

Having come from a place where he'd never wanted for much, Sam felt deeply affected by the desperation of the people at the camp. He knew he'd never grow accustomed to children with bloated bellies and dysentery and malnutrition.

Though he did what he could to ease their misery, it never felt like enough.

"Why is there so little water?" he asked Theo one afternoon after two months in the camp.

"Resources are finite, buddy, you know that. All we can do is dig more wells and truck in more jugs of the stuff." His friend removed his glasses to mop his wet forehead. "There used to be a lake just over the ridge there," he said, pointing toward a hump of earth that looked like a camel's back. "But it hasn't rained in these parts for ages so the thing's pretty much just a crater."

"That sucks."

"Yeah," Theo agreed, "it does."

The more Sam thought about it, the more he began pondering an idea, one that seemed crazy at first until he convinced himself it wasn't so crazy after all. If the stories his mother had told him about Hank Littlefoot making it rain were true, if this gift of conjuring up the weather had truly been passed down to Sam as well, why shouldn't he use it? Surely it would do no harm to try.

Sam had always been aware that he was different from everyone else. Even as a child, he'd felt a subtle stirring inside him that connected him to the sky and the earth in a way that wasn't typical. He had always been sensitive to changes in the air around him, and he'd realized early on that his emotions had a strange effect on the sun and the sky and the breeze. If he felt angry or sad or frustrated, the atmosphere seemed to get riled up as well, stirring up the wind and clouds, even the thunder and the rain.

Sam could only hope there was a chance he could summon up his deepest feelings and make something happen here. So he decided to give it a shot that very night. Maybe he'd fail, but no one would be the wiser.

At that point, Sam had been around the camp long enough to know how to move about without attracting unwanted attention. When the night was darkest and the camp quietest, he took a full canteen and slipped away from his tent, skirting the guard stations where the orange glow of cigarettes pierced the dark like fireflies. Once safely out of bounds, he hiked the mile or so through scrubby grasses and sandy soil to where the lake used to be. He wasn't sure what exactly to do once he got there, but he figured he'd come up with something.

Beneath the pale light of a quarter moon, the crater yawned before him, so vast he could only imagine how far its borders reached. Drawing in a deep breath, he stood at the precipice, peering into the empty basin below, noting the cracks veining the wall beneath where he stood, so many that it looked like a broken piece of pottery.

So where did he start?

Sam knew nothing about the rain-making ceremony. He had no mantra to chant, no movements or dance that could be guaranteed to influence the clouds. What he finally did was settle down on the dirt, his legs bent and crossed at the ankles. He put his left arm on his thigh and raised his right hand to touch the turquoise stones bound to the leather strap around his throat.

"Hi, Grandfather, it's me, Samuel Henry," he said aloud. "Any chance you can ask the sky to make it rain and start to fill this lake with water? I hate to see people sick and dying because there's not enough to drink."

Yep, that was pretty much it, he decided and closed his eyes, rubbing the beads and repeating, *Make it rain, make it rain, make it rain.*

The repetition of the phrase coupled with his exhaustion soon had him zoning out, slipping into a netherland between alertness and sleep. He wasn't aware of how much time had passed before he startled himself awake. He felt dizzy and dry; his lips were cracked and his throat was parched. He uncapped his canteen to take a swig of water. When he looked up at the sky, it swelled with stars, the moon as bright as before.

Damn.

It hadn't worked. He'd done nothing but miss much-needed rest.

Disappointed, he rose from the ground, wobbling on knees that weren't used to staying bent for so long. His muscles ached, and he stretched his arms to the heavens, whispering to the scant breeze, "I will not give up. I'll be back to try again."

He'd barely started back to camp when he felt the first drop on his face. Sure that he'd imagined it, he stopped and glanced up to see clouds scudding in and smothering the stars, blotting out the moon next. Around him, the dust began to dimple, a drizzle fast turning into a steady rain.

"Thank you, Grandfather!" he shouted to the heavens, hoping Hank could hear through the steady wash of water pounding the dry earth.

He ran the rest of the way back to camp, finding many of its inhabitants emerging from their tents, tipping faces to the sky and reaching out their hands, laughing and jabbering excitedly as if they'd never before seen rain.

On nearing his home away from home, he ran smack into Cate, who looked as much like a drowned rat as he.

"Can you believe this?" she exclaimed and grabbed him in an exuberant bear hug. "It's quite amazing! A miracle, really!"

Charged with energy, Sam impulsively pulled her tight to his chest and soundly kissed her. When she drew back, she grinned and took his hand, drawing him inside his tent as the rain pounded steadily against the canvas.

In the morning when they awakened, entangled on his bunk, the rain had ceased.

"That might be the last storm we see for six months," Cate said with disappointment as she pulled on her shoes before leaving.

But Sam knew the rain would come again.

He made himself wait another two weeks before going back to the crater. He had to take care, fearful of bringing too much water too fast and flooding the camp, and he couldn't risk that, not with hundreds more people still pouring in day after day.

On that second attempt, he did everything as he had the first time. He waited until the dead of night, settled on the ground near the edge of the crater. He rubbed the turquoise beads, called to his grandfather for help, and chanted the same mantra—*make it rain, make it rain, make it rain*—until he fell into that trancelike state, opening his eyes hours later to raindrops pelting his skin.

When he rose from the ground, he staggered, surprised at how weak and dizzy he felt. He could hardly stand upright, much less walk. Even worse, a confusion gripped him so that he wasn't sure where he'd come from or how to return. The rain erased his footprints on the dry earth, and it was only by luck that he made it back to his bunk by dawn, where he promptly passed out.

When he roused the next day, he found himself on a cot in the hospital tent, where one of the medics told him he must've caught a virus or gotten a parasite that sapped his strength. He gave Sam a shot of penicillin and told him to take it easy.

Only Sam didn't listen.

Two weeks after, he went back to the lake, which now held at least a foot of water, enough to cover the cracked floor. The moon seemed brighter this night, and Sam looked around him at the shadows, sensing eyes on him, although he saw no one around.

Carefully, he lowered himself to the earth and performed his ritual again, knowing he would do it as many times as he could until the lake had filled, despite the toll the last two rain-makings had taken on his body and his mind. He felt older and weary with an ache in his bones that lingered.

Make it rain, make it rain, make it rain.

He was lying on his side when he came to, and it took every bit of his strength to rise to his knees. Above him, the sky seemed angry, lashing out with rumbling thunder and lightning that charged the air. A silver bolt streaked from the heavens, hitting so near Sam that it knocked him flat, burning the palms of his hands. He was in such pain that he could barely get up and stagger a hundred yards before he fell to the ground again.

At some point, he heard voices around him, speaking rapidly in a tongue he didn't understand. Then he passed out so thoroughly that it was the next day before Theo found him and half carried, half dragged him back to camp.

"You look like hell, old man," Sam heard his friend say before he dropped him in his bunk.

Sam drifted in and out of consciousness for several days.

"You're not well, Missouri," Cate told him when he opened his eyes and found her seated at the foot of his cot. "Have you seen yourself lately?"

She held a shaving mirror to his face, and Sam hardly recognized his reflection. His hair had gone from near black to gray, as had the beard smothering his jaw and cheeks.

"You should get a full medical," Cate insisted, looking as worried as he'd ever seen her. "You might need a ticket out of here."

But Sam disagreed. He wasn't ready to leave, not yet.

It was three long weeks before he was remotely strong enough to go back to the lake, but, as soon as he could, he went. *One more time,* he told himself, and then he would quit. The crater was half filled, and surely a little more rain would be all it would take to provide for the camp for months to come.

Every step toward the lake made him wince, as did sitting down on the ground with nothing to lean on. Still, he gritted his teeth and got on with it. Then in the midst of his ritual, as he called upon his grandfather and began to chant, "Make it rain," he realized he was not alone. A cadre of guerrilla soldiers had surrounded him, and one pushed at his shoulder with the butt of a rifle, knocking Sam hard to the dirt.

"He's the one," a guttural voice announced. "He is the man who makes rain."

Even in his weakened state, Sam knew he was in trouble. He could only whisper his grandfather's name and beg him for help.

You must be strong until we find a way to get you home, he thought he heard a voice breathe in his ear; but it was muted by the scuffle of footsteps and clicking noises of guns being cocked as the shadowed figures began to talk.

"Get up!" The steel toe of a boot pressed against Sam's spine. "Get up now and come!"

But Sam was too exhausted to move. He felt half dead as it was, no longer the young man who had left Walnut Ridge full of vigor and hope, wanting only to do something good that would fill him up and erase the pain of a rejected heart.

"I said, get up!"

Rough hands grabbed at him, pulling and tugging, unmindful of his cries of pain, and the band of guerrillas dragged him off, capturing him as they would any spoils of war; taking away the life he had known, using him until they wrung him dry and there came a day when Sam Winston didn't even know who he was anymore.

The Truth

The truth is rarely pure and never simple.

—OSCAR WILDE

TWENTY-FOUR

April 2010

"There's a car coming," Bennie announced, scurrying into the parlor. "And it doesn't rattle like that bad muffler on the sheriff's cruiser."

Abby looked up from the photo album she'd spread open in her lap. She'd been sharing pictures from her past with the Man Who Might Be Sam—as her mom quietly referred to him, although Abby thought of him more as the man who could be her father. With each shot she pointed out, she described what she remembered of every birthday party and dance recital and school program he'd missed. Perhaps he was just being polite, but if he was disinterested, he didn't show it.

"Are you sure it isn't the sheriff?" Gretchen asked, getting up from the armchair where she'd been pretending to work on the weekly paper's crossword puzzle, though mostly she'd been peering across the room at Abby and the Man Who Might Be Sam.

"No, it's a small car," Bennie remarked, "with very squeaky brakes. Reminds me of the vehicle Nathan drove when he brought Abby down last Christmas—"

Before her aunt had even finished that sentence, Abby snapped the photo album closed, shoving it aside and jumping to her feet.

Nate had come? Was it possible?

She ran to the window, trying to see into the dark despite the light reflecting on the glass from within the room.

"Abby, were you aware that Nathan was driving down?" her mother asked.

But Abby could only reply with a shrug. If he was truly carrying out his threat to come to the farm, it was as much a surprise to her as anyone.

She cupped her hands over her eyes, blocking out enough of the reflected light to make out a familiar beat-up Honda Civic pulling up in front, the brakes squealing as it came to a full stop in front of the porch.

"Oh God, it is him," she said, finally forced to believe it. "He wasn't bluffing."

"Bluffing about what?" Gretchen asked.

"I think the boy's finally made up his mind," Trudy said over the click of her knitting needles.

"And it's about time, too," Bennie chimed in.

Despite how badly she wanted to play it cool, Abby couldn't do it. She'd never been good at fudging her emotions. She smoothed her rumpled shirt as she hurried to the front door and unlocked it, throwing it wide before Nate had even made it all the way up the front steps.

"You're here!" she gushed, stunned to see him in the flesh when she hadn't set eyes on him in weeks and they'd been barking at each other on the phone barely five hours earlier. She took a step out onto the welcome mat.

"I told you I'd come, didn't I?" he grumbled, but there was something close to self-satisfaction on his face, like he couldn't believe he'd done it either. "I drove so fast I'm surprised that old piece of crap didn't fall apart on the highway."

"You really meant it," Abby said, and her heart madly thumped.

"I had to see you." He paused, glancing uneasily toward the house as he came toward her, his hands buried in his pockets. "Is there somewhere we can talk?"

"You want to go inside?"

"Um, actually, I think I'd rather stay out here," he said, lowering his voice. Then he cleared his throat and stared over her shoulder. "Hello, ladies, Mrs. Brink." He jerked his chin in greeting.

"Hi, Nathan."

"Hello, dear boy, how are you?"

Abby turned to find that her mother and aunts had come up behind her. They crowded the doorway, gazing out wide-eyed at a clearly uncomfortable Nate. She gave them a stern look and whispered, "A little privacy would be great."

"But, sweetie, it's getting chilly out," Gretchen said, looking concerned, "and you're—"

"Fine," Abby insisted. "We'll just be a minute, okay?"

"Of course," her mom agreed and nudged her sisters away from the threshold.

Abby closed the door before the women could make a fuss

and drag poor Nathan in. He looked unsettled enough, shifting in his sneakers, all weary eyes and unshaven cheeks.

"You want to sit on the swing?" she asked, and he nodded gratefully.

Without a word, he followed her over. They settled down, and the swing swayed beneath their weight. Abby grabbed the chain beside her, holding on to keep steady. She braced herself, waiting for the question she knew was coming, namely whether or not she was knocked up. Only, to her surprise, that was not the first thing that came out of Nate's mouth.

"I did a lot of thinking in the car," he told her and set his hand near her thigh, barely touching her with his pinky. "Hell, I did a lot of thinking these past two weeks at Myron's. He's a good brother but, man, his place is a mess. You don't even want to know what I found under the sofa cushions."

"No, I don't," Abby said and began to gnaw on her lip, wondering what was coming next.

"It hurt a lot when you gave me that ultimatum." He shot her a sideways glance. "No guy wants to be rushed into making a decision."

"Six years is hardly rushing," she murmured, thinking they'd gone over this a hundred times and she was too tired to go over it a hundred more.

"I know, I know." He took a deep breath. "But the more we were apart, the more I realized you were right, about my being afraid. I kept telling myself that marriage was just a piece of paper, that it didn't matter, that loving you was enough." He paused and exhaled slowly. "Now I understand what you were getting at. Being engaged is like fulfilling a promise. It's proving that I have no doubts, that you're the only one for me. And you are, Abs," he said, the swing shuddering as he turned his whole body to face her. "I don't want anyone else. I don't even want to look. I've been miserable without you, and I'm tired of being apart when we've got so much to look forward to." He reached for her hands. His were so warm as they cradled hers. "I mean, we're going to have a baby, right?"

She bit her lip, suddenly wanting to cry.

"Hey, don't for a minute think my being here is just because of that," he said, sounding worried, like he'd said the wrong thing. "This is about us, you and me, and taking that next step, whether you're pregnant or not."

Abby perked up. "Are you sure about that?"

"Yes, I'm sure," he told her, and she really and truly believed him.

"Good, because we are," she said and took his hand, setting it on her belly. "Having a baby, I mean. You can't feel much yet, but she's in there."

"Holy crap," he let slip, his boyish face turning pale in the porch light. "There's no doubt?"

"Three pee sticks and a blood test don't lie."

"You're going to be a mom," he said and he stared at her middle, shaking his head the littlest bit as his own words sank in.

Abby felt a rush of tears, choking up as she told him, "I wasn't sure when I came here what I wanted, or whether I could do this without you. But something about this place made me realize how much I want this baby. I need her in my life. Things don't always happen like we plan, but they do happen for a reason. Maybe we needed to be apart to understand how much better we are together," she told him, brushing at her cheeks. "I want us to be a family. She needs to grow up knowing her father—"

"She," he interrupted, raising an eyebrow. "You keep saying 'she.'"

"Do I?" Abby glanced down at her belly. "I don't know why," she murmured, hardly willing to tell him it was part of a dream. "Just a feeling, I guess."

"I hope it is a girl, and she's just like you. Sensitive and strong and artistic."

"Oh, Nate." Abby sighed, feeling turned inside out but in the very best of ways.

"I love you, Abs." Nate leaned over to kiss her, softly, sweetly. "I want to be with you forever," he whispered.

They stayed that way for a long while, holding each other as the swing gently swayed, and Abby decided that getting Nate back was like lightning striking twice. She'd given him a chance to find his way back to her, and he had, kind of like the way the Man Who Might Be Sam had found her mother.

TWENTY-FIVE

There was no fog lying thickly over the walnut grove that next morning, just a serene blue sky and air so crisp you could taste it on your tongue, like a tart yellow lemon or cold apple cider.

Gretchen wasn't sure why the Man Who Might Be Sam had left her a note asking her to meet him at the walnut tree split by lightning, but she was game. Besides, Abby was still holed up with Nate, sleeping in after spending much of the night talking (so said Bennie, whose room was just next door, although she insisted she'd put in earplugs early on to give them plenty of privacy). Trudy and Bennie were busy as well, having rung up Walter Gibbons, the handyman. Both women sat on the front porch, awaiting his arrival. "Well, we need help cleaning up the yard, don't we?" Trudy had said with a sniff.

So Gretchen slipped on her gardening clogs in the mud-room and, when she stood, she patted her back jeans pocket to make sure what she'd put there earlier hadn't slipped out. Then she tucked her hair behind her ears and headed out, clomping down the back steps and through grass still littered with walnuts from the storm. As she strode past the barn, she could see the grove clearly, trees sprawling out in endless rows.

Even before she came within twenty feet of them, she could tell that Abby was wrong. There were no tiny green buds on the boughs. Instead, she glimpsed blossoms of the black walnut's strange, verdant flowers. The first time she'd observed them, she had remarked to a very young Sam that they looked like "Frankenstein's dripping fingers." Tiny leaves roamed the branches as well so the whole grove appeared bright and alive.

She had to pause and take it all in, it was such an amazing sight.

"How did you do it?" she whispered, sure that somehow the man who'd fallen from the sky—the man she believed was her Sam—had made this happen. Even if there were no facts to prove it, Gretchen knew in her gut that he was responsible for the storm that had brought him home as well. Wherever he'd been, whatever he'd done, it didn't matter. That he was back was all she cared about. That he would stay here with her was her only concern.

"Hey, this way!" she heard him calling, though she couldn't spot him yet.

She picked up her pace, her pulse throbbing in her veins as she rushed to find him. Then, suddenly, there he was, standing in the midst of the grove, right in front of the grizzled old walnut that was split in the center by lightning.

"I woke up this morning, and I remembered something," he said, his face flushed, his gray eyes growing brighter the nearer she came. "At first, I thought it might be a dream, but it was so clear in my mind, I knew it must be the truth." He turned away and gestured at the tree that rose above him. "I saw myself here. I saw my hand in front of me, holding a penknife, carving letters into the bark."

"What letters?" she said.

"Come." He reached out for her, and Gretchen slipped her fingers into his, allowing herself to be led around to the tree's other side.

"There," he said, such excitement in his voice it gave her chills. "Do you see it? Look closely as the bark has peeled, but it's still there, as real as I am."

Gretchen let him go and moved forward, searching the bark until she saw the crude heart gouged into the wood; within its jagged border, two initials: S + G.

Sam and Gretchen.

She turned and found him smiling—and such a smile it was! Hardly a thin line this time, his mouth curved warmly at the corners, and his cheeks were the pink of a child's. The welt had nearly vanished from his brow so that, for a moment, Gretchen saw Sam as he was years ago, not as she'd found him.

"You're really Sam," she said, and he laughed.

"Isn't that what you wanted?"

"Only my whole life," she said, trying hard not to cry. She reached into her back pocket. "Now it's my turn."

"Oh?"

"I have something for you." She handed back to him the turquoise necklace that he had found in the grove when he'd been out walking with Abby the previous morning. "What I didn't tell you yesterday was that this belonged to Hank Littlefoot and to his grandfather before him. It was once yours as well. You took it to Africa all those many years ago. The only way it could have ended up here is if you'd brought it back."

He squinted at the necklace in his scarred palm, and Gretchen was sure he saw it differently this time, not as a mere trinket but as something that defined him, something with true meaning.

When finally he glanced up again, he solemnly asked, "Could you help me put it on?"

"It would be my pleasure," she told him.

He kept fingering the stones as she knotted the leather thong at the back of his neck, not far above the teardrop mark at his nape.

"I don't know what the future will bring, or what your memories will show you when they finally return," she said, her voice trembling. "But I will tell you what I believe, and it's the God's honest truth. Whatever kept you away couldn't hold you forever. This is where you belong. It's your home, Sam, and it will always be here for you, no matter what."

"Home," he echoed and looked around them, at the blossoming walnut trees, at the pale sky above, bright with sunshine. "I could live with that."

Gretchen smiled. "Good."

They walked back to the house, arm in arm, heading inside to find the quiet of the morning broken by the ringing phone.

Gretchen wanted to ignore it but Sam nudged her. "It could be important."

It took all Gretchen's will, though, to stay on the line beyond the point of hearing, "It's Frank Tilby . . . don't hang up!" Then the sheriff began talking so fast she had no choice but to listen. "We found the remains of a man washed down Fork

Creek from where the '74 Cutlass was wrecked," he said. "ID in his wallet says he's Henry Stewart Little." He noisily exhaled. "You were right," he muttered, "and I was wrong."

"Of course, you were wrong, Sheriff," Gretchen told him, glancing over at Sam. "I knew it in my heart all along."

EPILOGUE

Gretchen waved, watching Abigail disappear down the drive in Nate's dented Honda, and she hoped she'd done the right thing, letting Abby leave thinking that Sam was her father. Abby had loved Sam Winston before she'd ever met him, and Gretchen believed that Sam loved Abby as well.

And still she was about to do something that could ruin everything.

"I took advantage of you," she said, sitting down on the swing beside the man she loved with all her heart. Her palms were slick with sweat, and she rubbed them on her denim-clad thighs. "I lied to everyone we love and told them you were Abby's father, and you weren't even around to protest."

"Why would I want to protest?" Sam said and leaned his head against hers. "Abby's a great girl. Any man would be lucky to have a daughter like that."

"But—"

"Gretchen, stop." He cut her off. "Haven't you figured out by now that some things are worth remembering and other things do best to stay buried? Besides"—he shrugged—"in the end, we all got what we wished for, right? Let's leave the past in the past."

His arm slid around her shoulders, and Gretchen pursed her

lips, not sure of what to make of this. If she had been more like Annika, she would not have let anything stop her from telling the truth to the world, even after all this time. But Gretchen wasn't her mother, who had driven everyone she loved away from her because she cared more about being unflinchingly honest than unconditionally kind.

What was the likelihood that Abby would ever find out besides? The man who'd fathered her was long gone, had never stuck around Walnut Ridge for more than that one night. And if Abby ever caught a glimpse of him, she'd never notice if she shared his mouth or his eyes. What Abby had was Sam's heart.

And *that* was more important.

Introduction

When my wonderful editor, Lucia Macro, asked if I'd be interested in writing about my experience with breast cancer, I leaped at the chance. Since my diagnosis in December of 2006 at age forty-two, I've openly talked about my "boobal trauma," often speaking to women's groups and at fund-raising events for nonprofits that support research, diagnosis, prevention, and the well-being of survivors. I figure that the more we know and share, the better off we all are . . . and the more we realize we're not in this alone. My experience made me part of a big Pink Army, and whenever I'm around fellow survivors, I feel such a rush of energy and positivity. There is nothing like pressing past what frightens us most to make us appreciate the simple things. We suddenly reevaluate everything we thought was necessary, realize who and what is important, and rid our time of people and things that drag us down. It's no wonder survivors are so upbeat. We don't take anything for granted, least of all our health. We don't take crap anymore either. That's one side effect I wish I could bottle and sell!

But the tale of "me, my boob, and I" goes beyond my diagnosis. The journey to discovering my true self—my better self—started a few years before that. The big turning point for me came when I hit forty, an age when our society seems to think a woman's shelf life has met its expiration date. So many advertisements tell us that to be viable beyond our thirties we must turn into middle-aged Barbies, Botoxing away our lines (and expressions!) and Spanxing away unsightly bulges. Why the heck we'd want to aspire to fakeness boggles my brain! I say, forty is when we should kick convention in the ass. It's the perfect time to enjoy life full throttle and accept the skin we're in, wrinkles and all.

In the past seven years since crossing the big 4-0, I've experienced so much more than I had in all the years before: more meaningful friendships, deeper love, greater self-acceptance, and true fulfillment in my career. This "second act" has been eye-opening, transformative, and glorious in so many ways. So I can't help but wish the same for every woman out there. I want to spread the word that getting older can be the most amazing time in our lives. We don't need to relive our youth. We just need to hold on to that childlike sense of wonder, being ever curious about the world around us and eager to laugh, with our hearts wide open.

What I hope my story conveys is precisely what I look forward to telling my daughter someday: It is never too late to find happiness. You are never too old to do what you want to do or be who you want to be. Life is a ladder, each rung a step toward our best selves and our greatest accomplishments. Surprises await us as we climb, some good and some bad, but each teaching us a bit about ourselves that we needed to learn, showing us a part of the world we'd never seen before, and opening our souls so that every emotion we feel is all the more intense.

Here's to love, whenever we find it; to celebrating success, big and small; and to slogging through the crap so we can come out the other side stronger . . . and remain "in the pink" for the rest of our lives.

Susan McBride

June 14, 2012

BOOKS
and
BOYS . . .

ONE

"PLEASE, DON'T LET MY DAUGHTER
TURN INTO A CRAZY CAT LADY."

Turning forty didn't faze me.

Reaching twenty and leaving my teens behind felt far more unsettling. Even thirty seemed more pivotal, since that's the age when we're supposed to get our act together, be invested, own property, and leave singlehood behind for suburbia, procreation, and minivans.

Still, I wasn't at all sad at bidding adieu to my thirties. They'd been a great learning curve, a chance to see some major goals accomplished; namely, getting published and beginning my professional writing career after more than a decade filled with hard work and rejection. Being able to support myself doing something I love was a gift, and I treasured it all the more because it had not come without great sacrifice. In the years I'd spent working to get my foot in the door, I'd endured lots of rejection from the publishing world and plenty of digs from less than true believers inside and outside my family, like The Jerk at my grandmother's funeral who strongly suggested I "hang it up." (Somehow, I refrained from punching him in the nose.)

My outside jobs had kept my bills paid, and I had saved enough to buy a condo that I filled with furniture and doodads I'd been collecting in anticipation of finally jumping into the wonderful world of thirty-year mortgages. Finally, at forty, I felt settled, like a bird who'd built a really cool nest, and it didn't bother me that I hadn't met Mr. Right to share it with.

Heck, I hadn't even met Mr. Maybe. But I had good friends and a good life. I was downright content and didn't feel incomplete in any sense. Not until I got a kick in the pants in the form of a less than stellar physical exam. My cholesterol was too high (who knew that Snickers wasn't a vegetable?), and I had palpitations due to anxiety. My maternal grandfather had died after multiple heart attacks, and it unnerved me to think that I could be heading down that path.

My internist at the time suggested I find some way to better deal with stress. "Why don't you start drinking?" she suggested (she was totally serious). Since I'm not fond of alcohol, I went cold turkey on junk food, eating lots of fruits and vegetables and no red meat, and I began to work out with a vengeance. Within six weeks, I'd toned up, dropped several sizes, gained strength and stamina, and lowered my total cholesterol from the mid-200s to 187. An added benefit: my heart rate quit accelerating like a Lamborghini on crack whenever I found myself worrying (which was often enough—I'm a natural-born type A).

Fueled by renewed energy and a surge of confidence, I set up a shoot for a new author photo, meeting with a renowned photographer in St. Louis who initially deemed me "too skinny" and advised I "eat some steak" to prepare for the appointment. (Definitely the first time in my life I'd been called "too skinny" by anyone.) The makeup artist flipped out my "anchorwoman hair" in a very cool, messy style that I ended up adopting postshoot. Not only did I get some great photos out of that session (which I'll be using until I'm ninety-three and pushing a walker), but I felt reborn, like the new, improved me!

That photo session occurred in July of 2005, four months shy of my forty-first birthday; yet I felt younger than ever, both inside and out. Inspired by the positive changes in my health and body—and the forward trajectory of my writing career, sparked by surprisingly good sales of *Blue Blood* and the release of my second series mystery, *The Good Girl's Guide to Murder*—I had a newfound desire to step out of my comfort zone. I would carve out precious time to try new restaurants, see exhibits at local museums, and expand my social circle as well as my horizons.

That included a conscious decision to be more open about the men I met and not shut anyone down just because they didn't look a particular way or wore funny shoes (my mom likes to remind me of a brilliant guy I dumped in high school because of his fondness for desert boots). To be honest, I'd spent a lot of time in my adult life avoiding the dating scene, preferring to be alone—say, reading a good book—rather than waste my time with some random dude just for the sake of going out. Not being much of a drinker, I was never big on the bar or club scene.

But as forty-one came and went, and I was still single— albeit happily—I figured it wouldn't hurt to change my list of "must haves" regarding men, which hadn't altered much since high school. I needed to look less at the physical package and more at what was inside. My criteria basically came down to this:

- Does he make me laugh?
- Do we have plenty to talk about?
- Does he keep me on my toes?
- Does he smell good?
- Does he eat with utensils?
- Does he drive his own car and not live with his mother?

These new criteria certainly opened up a brave, new dating world.

It inspired me to say yes more often than no, and my social life blossomed. Still, I didn't seem to meet anyone who floated my boat. Perhaps I was meant to be a modern-day Amelia Earhart, albeit flying without a copilot (and minus the "disappearing from the face of the earth" part).

My boyfriendless state concerned my family far more than it did me, as one of my male cousins approached me privately during the weekend of my brother's wedding and asked, "Are you a lesbian? Because if you are, that's okay."

I told him that, while I wasn't a lesbian, I appreciated that he was so open-minded.

"I just can't find the right guy," I confessed, thinking surely I couldn't be the only single woman over forty on the planet who hadn't yet met her Prince Charming.

Call me Pollyanna, but I didn't dwell on my state of singlehood often. My days were filled with writing the books I loved, my weekends were often spent traveling, and my friends

and family filled any space between. Yet no matter how I ex-
pressed my satisfaction with my life, my mother feared that I
was destined to become a crazy cat lady (though I only had two
cats!), shuffling around in bathrobe and slippers, cleaning lit-
ter boxes in between book deadlines.

I think it made her even more nervous that I wasn't afraid
of being alone for the rest of my life. My philosophy: if that
was how it worked out, that was how it worked out. It wasn't
like I was going to mail-order a groom from Russia or Thai-
land. I didn't feel like I was missing out, even when I got cards
and e-mails from friends with photos of their spouses and
children. Not everyone is meant to go the marriage-with-two-
point-five-kids route.

Surely I wasn't the only female who didn't obsess over wed-
dings or buy bridal magazines and pore through them, picking
out wedding dresses well before finding my mate and falling
madly in love.

Perhaps I was just being practical, having read a study that
insisted a woman over forty had a better chance of being killed
by a terrorist than she did of getting hitched. Or else I was too
set in my ways, content with doing things on my own terms,
never having to compromise (not a bad thing!).

Yes, there were times when I pondered how lovely it would
be to have a committed hand to hold and adoring eyes to gaze
at over candlelight, a best friend slash lover who understood
me like no one else.

"So you'd get married if you found the right man?" my mom
would ask now and then, just to reassure herself.

"I would certainly consider it," I'd say. "So long as I was

really in love and we could live in a duplex so I could lock myself inside my half when I needed privacy."

"I'm sure that would be just fine," she'd reply and pat my hand, a hopeful—or was it delusional?—smile on her face.

I realized quickly enough that Mom's deep-seated need to marry me off was bound tightly to her desire to have a grand-child. Though my younger brother was newly married, he and his bride seemed in no hurry to pop out the rug rats. So I think my mother was putting all my eggs in *her* basket.

What happened next is something straight out of a TV sitcom: my enterprising mom took it upon herself to send an e-mail to *St. Louis Magazine,* at the time searching for a new crop of "top singles" for their November 2005 issue. If I had the e-mail right now, I'd share it, but, unfortunately, I don't. All I know is that she said something akin to "Please, find a man for my daughter so she doesn't end up a crazy cat lady."

The magazine took the bait and sent me a questionnaire as they narrowed down likely candidates. It wasn't but a few months later that I learned I was one of ten women selected (only two of us over forty). They chose ten men as well (one over forty). Reminding myself of my promise to broaden my dating horizons—and the fact that I had a third mystery coming out, *The Lone Star Lonely Hearts Club,* appropriately enough—I figured, "What have I got to lose?" And I jumped in wholeheartedly.

At the September photo shoot with the other nineteen singles, I met a handful who would become friends through-out the process. One of them, Jeremy Nolle, was a software applications engineer. Not only was he smart, but he was very good-looking (I hadn't realized they made computer geeks that appeared to have leaped off the pages of *GQ*!). He was also twentysomething, too young for me. But there were no rules against having younger male friends, right?

The party to debut the 2005 "Top Singles" issue on November 3, 2005, was held at the Contemporary Art Museum in downtown St. Louis. Somehow, I managed to find Jeremy amidst the three hundred or so people in attendance. I wanted to set him up with my older sister, who happened to be (um, still happens to be!) a serial dater of younger men. I was chatting with Jeremy when several of his coworkers showed up. One was tall and slim with dark hair, a shy smile, and warm brown eyes. "This is Ed," Jeremy said, and we aimlessly babbled over the very loud music.

Though I had no idea at the time, meeting Ed that night would change my life.

About the author

About the book

Read on

Insights,
Interviews
& More...

Meet Susan McBride

Suzy Gorman

SUSAN MCBRIDE is the author of *Little Black Dress*, a Literary Guild bestseller and a Target Recommended Read. She has also written *The Cougar Club*, named a Target Bookmarked Breakout Title and one of *More* Magazine's "Books We're Buzzing About." Foreign editions of *Cougar* have been published in France, Croatia, and Turkey. Susan lives in St. Louis, Missouri, with her husband, Ed, and their daughter, Emily. You can visit her website at http://susanmcbride .com. ❧

Discussion Questions for *The Truth About Love and Lightning*

1. What do you think is worse: telling lies, like Gretchen, or being so blunt it's hurtful, like Annika? Have you ever told a lie to spare someone's feelings?
2. How is Abigail's situation similar to her mother's situation nearly forty years before? How does Gretchen's raising her as a single parent affect the choices Abby makes?
3. Why do all the Brink women jump to the conclusion that the stranger who "fell from the sky" is Sam Winston?
4. Have you ever had someone from your past—a lost love, perhaps—appear from out of the blue? How did it affect you?
5. How does the loss of one sense cause other senses to sharpen? Do you think Bennie and Trudy see themselves as anything other than normal, since clearly Gretchen finds their heightened senses extraordinary?
6. Are there really magic men (or women), like Hank Littlefoot, who can make it rain or otherwise influence our surroundings? Do you believe in the supernatural?
7. What is it about the walnut farm that keeps drawing its inhabitants home? Is it something paranormal or more of an emotional pull?
8. What is the significance of the weather throughout the story, particularly the "walnut rain"? ▶

Discussion Questions for *The Truth About Love and Lightning* (continued)

9. Have you ever realized you truly loved someone only after it's too late, as is the case with Gretchen and Sam? Do you believe in soul mates?
10. Was Gretchen wrong to not tell Abby the truth in the end? ∾

Have You Read?
More by Susan McBride

LITTLE BLACK DRESS

Two sisters whose lives seemed forever intertwined are torn apart when a magical little black dress gives each one a glimpse of an unavoidable future.

Antonia Ashton has worked hard to build a thriving career and a committed relationship, but she realizes her life has gone off track. Forced to return home to Blue Hills when her mother, Evie, suffers a massive stroke, Toni finds the old Victorian where she grew up as crammed full of secrets as it is with clutter. Now she must put her mother's house in order—and uncover long-buried truths about Evie and her aunt, Anna, who vanished fifty years earlier on the eve of her wedding. By shedding light on the past, Toni illuminates her own mistakes and learns the most unexpected things about love, magic, and a little black dress with the power to break hearts . . . and mend them.

THE COUGAR CLUB

Meet three women who aren't about to run and hide just because the world says they should be on the shelf and out of circulation.

Kat: Her life seems perfect until she loses her high-powered advertising job *and* catches her live-in lover in a compromising position—with his *computer!*

Carla: This sexy TV news anchor is in danger of being replaced by a

twentysomething blond bimbo. Wasn't it just yesterday that she was the up-and-coming star?

Elise: A married dermatologist, Elise thinks her plastic surgeon husband is playing doctor with someone else.

Kat firmly believes that aging gracefully isn't about giving up; it's about living life with your engine on overdrive. So this unofficial "Cougar Club" quickly learns three things about survival of the fittest in today's youth-obsessed society: true friendship never dies, the only way to live is real, and you're never too old to follow your heart.

TOO PRETTY TO DIE

They call them "pretty parties," and they're the latest rage among Dallas debutantes—get-togethers with light refreshments, heavy gossip, and Dr. Sonja Madhavi and her magic Botox needles. Former socialite Andy Kendricks normally wouldn't be caught dead at such an event, but she's attending as a favor to her friend Janet, a society reporter in search of a juicy story. And boy does she find one when aging beauty queen Miranda DuBois bursts into the room—drunk, disorderly, and packing a pistol.

Miranda's wrinkles have seen better days, and she blames it all on Dr. Madhavi. Luckily, Andy calms her down and gets her home to bed . . . where she's found dead the next morning. The police suspect suicide, but Andy knows that no former pageant girl would give up that easily. She's determined to find Miranda's killer herself, but she'll have to be careful. After

6

all, Botox can make you look younger, but it can't bring you back from the grave.

NIGHT OF THE LIVING DEB

Renegade rich girl Andy Kendricks isn't the belle of *any* Dallas ball—and that's just the way the debutante dropout likes it! She's got a good life and a great man: her defense attorney boyfriend, Brian Malone. Brian's such a straight arrow that he had to be dragged kicking and screaming to a close friend's bachelor party at a sleazy local "gentleman's club."

So why is the groom-to-be saying that Brian left the bacchanal arm in arm with "the hottest body in the Lone Star State"? And what was that hot body doing stone-cold dead in the trunk of Brian's car? And where *is* Brian anyway? The cops are looking for Andy's allegedly unfaithful/possibly homicidal beau, who hasn't been seen since the party. But Andy can't believe her upstanding lover is a murdering fool, and she's determined to prove it—though she might end up with a lot more broken than just her heart.

THE LONE STAR LONELY HEARTS CLUB

Wealthy Texas widows need loving too . . . which is why Bebe Kent joined a dating service for "discriminating" seniors soon after relocating to the swanky Belle Meade retirement community. Unfortunately, Bebe didn't live long enough to meet "Mr. Right." And though doctors declared her death totally natural, extravagant blue-blooded Dallas socialite Cissy Blevins Kendricks believes her old friend's demise was hastened—and she's ready to check herself into Belle Meade incognito to prove it.

Cissy's rebellious, sometime-sleuthing daughter, Andrea, wants no part of her mother's glittering social whirl—and she's anything but pleased to have Cissy muscle her way into Andy's milieu. She has no choice, however, but to join her mom in search of the truth—especially when more well-heeled widows start turning up dead . . .

BLUE BLOOD

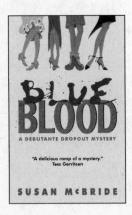

To the dismay of her high-society mother, Cissy, Dallas heiress Andy Kendricks wants no part of the Junior League life—opting instead for a job as a website designer and a passel of unpedigreed pals. Now her good friend Molly O'Brien is in bad trouble, accused of killing her boss at the local restaurant "Jugs." Though no proper deb would ever set foot in such a sleazy dive, Andy's soon slipping into skintight hot pants and a stuffed triple-D bra to gain employment there and somehow help clear Molly's name. But Andy's undercover lark is soon bringing her into too-close contact with all manner of dangerous adversaries—including a shady TV preacher, a fanatical Mothers Against Porn activist . . . and a killer who is none too keen on meddling rich girls.

Don't miss the next book by your favorite author. Sign up now for AuthorTracker by visiting www.AuthorTracker.com.